PAMELA HEARON

In EmmyLou's Hands

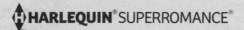

HARLEQUIN® SUPERROMANCE®

Recycling programs
for this product may
not exist in your area.

ISBN-13: 978-0-373-60962-8

In EmmyLou's Hands

www.Harlequin.com

Printed in U.S.A.

"Here I sit, not an arm's length away, all but begging you to kiss me, and you want to argue about it."

"I'm not arguing about it. I just can't imagine that you're being sincere." Sol pinched the bridge of his nose and squeezed his eyes. "I don't want to be toyed with, EmmyLou."

He threw the truck into Drive and pulled back onto the road, fuming. The heat and their silence made the air in the truck hard to breathe. He turned onto her lane, then brought the truck to a stop in her driveway and cut the engine. Without a word, he got out, determined to walk her to the door so she couldn't throw not being a gentleman in his face.

But she was already out before he closed his door. She came around and met him at the front. "You're right. I do toy with guys sometimes. It's called flirting." She stepped against him and slid her arms around his waist. And then her lips were pressing his, warm and inviting.

The jolt he felt was strong enough to shake the dust off his libido. Without a thought or a consideration, he held her to him and answered her mouth with the fervor it demanded.

Being toyed with might not be so bad...

Dear Reader,

When I first introduced EmmyLou Creighton as Maggie Russell's best friend in *My Way Back to You*, the question started showing up, time after time: When will EmmyLou get her own story?

For those of you who've met her, it might seem strange that a character as flamboyant and "out there" as EmmyLou would be reticent about sharing anything. But we all have our public side and our private side, and EmmyLou is no different. It took some time to earn her trust to the point that she was willing to open up because EmmyLou isn't just another pretty face—she has a deeper side...a crippling secret that many who read this will readily identify with.

Of course, EmmyLou's hero had to be her equal in every way, which included her depth and level of intrigue. Sol Beecher—once Taylor's Grove's most eligible bachelor but now its most mysterious recluse—was the perfect one to coax Emmy's secrets out of her and perhaps even share his own.

Have I caught your attention? I hope so! And I hope you enjoy EmmyLou and Sol's story—*In EmmyLou's Hands*.

Until next time,

Pamela

Pamela Hearon grew up in Paducah, Kentucky, a place that infuses its inhabitants with Southern values and hospitality. Here she finds inspiration for her quirky characters, her stories' backdrops and her narrative voice. Pamela was a 2013 RITA® Award finalist and a MAGGIE® Award finalist for her first Harlequin Superromance story, *Out of the Depths*. *The Summer Place* was a 2014 National Readers' Choice Award finalist. Visit Pamela at pamelahearon.com, and on Facebook and Twitter.

Books by Pamela Hearon

HARLEQUIN SUPERROMANCE

Out of the Depths
The Summer Place

Taylor's Grove, Kentucky

Moonlight in Paris
His Kind of Perfection
My Way Back to You

Visit the Author Profile page
at Harlequin.com for more titles.

To Camden, Taj and Quincy.

If you read this many, many years from now,
perhaps you'll smile and feel that you know
Gigi a little better.

Acknowledgments

It takes so many people to bring a book from its
inception to the printed page, and I'd like to take
this time to say thank you to a few.

Thank you to my editor, Karen Reid, for teaching
me so much about romance writing. I've worked
with you on six books now. Each has been
pure pleasure.

Thank you to my agent, Jennifer Weltz of
The Jean V. Naggar Literary Agency.
You are quite simply The Best.

Thank you to my critique partners at
WriteRomance—Maggie Van Well,
Angela Campbell and Sandra Jones.

Thank you to my family for your encouragement,
your understanding of my time commitments
and your love.

And thank you to my husband, Dick,
whose hands forever hold my heart.

CHAPTER ONE

"MY FAMILY HAS a beach house in Gulf Shores, Alabama."

No sooner were the words out of EmmyLou Creighton's mouth than she knew she'd spoken too soon. Of course, that was nothing new—her mouth had a tendency to stay several strides ahead of her brain most of the time. Grabbing her phone in one hand, she held up a finger on the other to put the conversation with her two friends on hold while she texted her mom.

Beach house taken June 23-30?

No, came the reply.

Pencil me in.

Seriously?

I'll explain later.

She tossed her phone down and drummed

the table with her long fingernails to signal that speech could once again commence.

Bree Barlow and Audrey Dublin looked at each other and shrugged, oblivious to the amazing feat EmmyLou had just accomplished.

"Don't you see?" She directed her comment toward Audrey. "You can use a week at the beach house as the grand prize."

Audrey's gray eyes, which had been pinched with worry two minutes ago, widened. "For the raffle? Oh, Emmy! You can do it just like that?" She snapped her fingers.

Emmy laughed and snapped hers in answer. "Just like that."

Even Bree, who was enjoying her first girls' night out since the birth of her second child, came out of her exhausted lethargy to gasp her approval. "That would be such a fabulous prize! Taylor's Grove has *never* had anything like that."

"Taylor's Grove, Kentucky, never had anything like me."

"Are you sure about this? I mean, a text and it's done?"

Emmy laughed at the skepticism in Audrey's voice. "It's done, sugar. Trust me. Everybody in the family gets a week in the summer if we want it, but we have to claim the week, which I just did. We also get weeks during the rest of the year if it's not rented, but it almost always is."

Their server showed up with another tray of drinks. "Guy at the bar sent these over."

"Again?" Bree groaned at the third bottle of sparkling water set in front of her. "Would you please tell him to save his money and just send *her* a beer?" She indicated Emmy with a nod, and then wagged a finger between her and Audrey. "I'm nursing and she's a newlywed, so we're off the market."

The server grinned. "Different guy. But I'll tell the next one." She replaced the empties in front of Audrey and Emmy with full bottles.

Emmy's glance drifted down the bar until she found the young man looking expectantly their way. "Kind of cute, but way too young. Twenty-five, maybe. Still wet behind the ears." She raised her beer bottle with a nod of gratitude but broke eye contact immediately.

Having done this for far more years than she liked to acknowledge, Emmy was the go-to expert on all the subtleties of pickups. At thirty-five, although everyone guessed her to be eight to ten years younger, she could fill a book about turnoffs, turn-ons, tune-ins, tune-outs and tone-downs.

Years of experience, however, had brought her no Mr. Right—no one to settle down with and have the family she wanted so badly. She hadn't lost hope, even though her close friends were now happily married with kids.

"I'd think you would like younger guys, Emmy." Audrey took a sip of her rum and Coke. "More stamina."

"Jackrabbits." Emmy shivered in mock disdain. "My preferences lean toward the ones who are... slower, you know? Not like those giant tortoises that take *forever*. Have you ever seen those shows on the National Geographic Channel? About the huge ones that live on the Galápagos Islands? My God, you *know* she just wants to turn around to him and say, 'Will you get on with it?'" She placed her hands on the table and pushed slowly out of her chair, opening her mouth and dragging out a grunt before plopping back in her chair and repeating the action.

Bree and Audrey giggled at her imitation.

"I'm looking for one of those cute turtles that plods along all efficient-like at a nice steady pace but starts to scurry when he hits the beach. And once he plunges in, he just paddles along with that smooth stroke until the tide goes down." She fluttered her eyelids and gave a dreamy smile. "Mmm!"

Her friends exchanged knowing glances and nodded in agreement. "Mmm!"

"Hey, wait a minute. What's wrong with this picture?" Emmy slapped the table with her palm.

"Here I am, offering my family's beach house to raise funds for a school I never attended in a town I've only lived in for a couple of years, but said town's not taking care of my needs in return. Y'all snatched up the last two good turtles Taylor's Grove may ever hatch."

"True, we got the best ones," Audrey agreed. She shook a finger in Emmy's direction. "But Sol Beecher's still available…and he's your closest neighbor."

The name caused Emmy's teeth to clench. "Yeah. Thank God that translates as a quarter mile away." She snorted. "Try raffling off *that* snapping turtle and see how much you get for him. I wouldn't give a plugged nickel for a night with him." She doubted the present company was aware she'd *had* a night with Taylor's Grove's most eligible bachelor fourteen years ago, shortly after she and her friend Maggie Wells had started the hair salon in Paducah, Kentucky—just outside of Taylor's Grove.

Maggie, a Taylor's Grove native, had introduced Emmy to her friend—handsome and oh-so-sexy Sol Beecher. Three dates in, they'd ended up in bed, and he'd never called again. She could still feel the sting if she thought about it…which she didn't.

But Audrey's and Bree's husbands, Mark and Kale, were Sol's best friends. And Kale and his dad had just purchased the local marina from Sol at a hefty price if word on the street was correct. Emmy could sense a lecture coming on from Bree about her teasing of Sol.

Bree squinted as if trying to remember something difficult to recall. "He's different than he used to be in high school. He was Mr. Popular then. Outgoing…fun. Of course, he chased anything that wore a skirt."

"Until it came off…um… I'll bet." Emmy covered her slip of the tongue.

"Something happened in Afghanistan." Audrey stared into her drink as if the answer could be found there. "He came home with that limp—"

"Caused by the weight of that chip on his shoulder," EmmyLou interjected.

Audrey leaned back and crossed her arms, tilting her head and turning a studious eye Emmy's direction. "I've never heard you come down on anybody the way you do him. What's he done to you?"

Emmy had said too much, so she pulled out her humor to cover, like always. "I'm just wondering how long I'd have to bang that shell with these hammers—" she put a hand on the outside of each breast and pushed, making her generous cleavage mound up even closer to her chin "—before it would finally crack."

"*You're* cracked." Audrey's giggle was a bit

too loud, and Bree laughed around a yawn, both signals it was time to go home.

But Emmy couldn't let the subject of Sol Beecher go without a last dig. "Now that Mr. Beecher's come into a right good sum of money, it'll be interesting to see how much he'll pony up for good ol' Taylor's Grove Elementary."

She raised her beer in the air, loudly da-dumming her way through a college football fight song she'd picked up somewhere.

"IT'S SMALL COMPARED to your grandparents' old place, Sol. I mean…tiny. After living in that big, rambling house, wouldn't you feel cooped up in a space like this?" Regina Dallas wrinkled her nose as she glanced around the modest two bed room she'd put at the end of the list of properties to show him today.

Sol leaned on the kitchen counter and gazed out the window into the backyard, pretending to ponder her question. What he really did was get the weight off his leg so he could answer without gritting his teeth. "It's more like what I'm look-ing for, although I can't convince you of that."

He'd allowed the friend of the family, a real estate agent, to drag his ass in and out of houses for the past three days and was frustrated with her choices. Anybody else he would've fired for not listening to him after the first two showings.

Behind him, Regina gave a motherly sigh. "I just don't understand why you'd want to downsize at your age. One of these days, you'll get married…have kids…"

Sol ignored how her words made him feel like he'd been kicked in the chest by a mule.

"And then you'll wish you'd taken the money from the marina and fixed up the old home place."

The fact that she was thinking about him personally and not the money she would make in a business transaction softened his response. He didn't growl back that a wife and kids weren't in his future. Instead, he shrugged. "Maybe. But for now, downsizing to something more manageable seems the smartest move." He still faced the window, but he was certain her eyes had dropped to his *bad leg*.

Everybody's did.

Managing *anything* very long with this damn *bad leg* was a struggle, but keeping the secret all these years that it was a prosthesis was even harder.

The pity he saw in people's eyes *now* made him want to spit. Being thought of as an amputee would have been more than he was able to bear.

He swiveled around to face her using the spin technique he'd perfected. "Washer and dryer hookups?"

"Basement."

He nodded like that was no big deal rather than acknowledging it as a definite no. Stairs were a problem with both hands free—impossible with a laundry basket. He'd been forced to turn the formal dining room in his current house into a makeshift bedroom. Oh, he was definitely capable of getting up the steps to bed. But the thought of trying to get out in the event of a fire would have kept him awake.

"This leads to the garage." Regina headed toward the door at the west end of the kitchen, and Sol followed. When they stepped through the opening, the sight of the small garage almost made him smile with relief. He'd found his reason to decline this house without admitting that the basement laundry was the real problem.

"I need at least a two-car garage for the car and boat. Preferably a three. I'd like to garage the truck, too."

Regina rolled her eyes and made a noise he recognized as annoyance. "One bedroom, one bath, a three-car garage on several acres. You're asking for something that doesn't exist. At least not around Taylor's Grove."

"Just keep looking, okay?" He hit the button that raised the overhead door. "Give me a call when you find something." He made his exit, leaving lockup duties to Regina.

Since selling the marina, he didn't have a

whole lot pressing on him these days. Finding a job would be a necessity come fall—mentally if not financially. Sitting around doing nothing wasn't an idea he relished. But he was treating himself to this one summer off. He'd never had one, even as a kid. Summers were a time to work from sunup to sundown when you owned a marina.

The next four months were his. He would fish Kentucky Lake and swim in the warm water after dark when nobody could see him. He knew that was dangerous, but he didn't give a rat's ass. Hell, he might live even more dangerously and give up these damn blue jeans for a pair of shorts every now and then. Sit in the backyard in the sunshine. Get a little bit of a tan on his pasty white leg... and the pasty white stump alongside it.

Maybe a tan would help him remember the bronzed kid with the great physique who had girls hanging all over him...help him remember a time when he wasn't a pitiful freak.

"Get off the damn pity pot," he admonished himself in his rearview mirror as he arrived in Taylor's Grove. "Some never made it back at all."

The circular park at the center of town was the local gathering spot. Today a small crowd had gathered in a knot around what looked to be a lemonade stand.

Sol would've preferred to drive by without

having to interact, but his friend Mark Dublin's wife, Audrey, and her daughter, Tess, were working the stand. They spotted him, flagging him down with friendly waves.

Guilt got the best of him. He groaned an "Oh hell" under his breath as he parked.

Nell Bradley met him at the curb as she headed to her car. She insisted on a hug, as always. And Johnny Bob Luther stopped him to share a joke that he'd heard maybe thirty times before from the old man. He laughed in appreciation of Johnny Bob's skillful telling rather than the punch line. And then there was IvaDawn Carrol's inquiry about how his parents were enjoying life in Florida. Even though they'd been there for five years now, IvaDawn always made it sound as if they'd just moved. Audrey's mother, Helen, sat on the bench in the gazebo—silently nodding to the voices in her head that her early-onset Alzheimer's provided.

By the time he got to the lemonade stand, the crowd had moved away. And surprisingly, it turned out not to be a lemonade stand at all.

"We're selling raffle tickets," Tess informed him. "Ten dollars apiece."

Sol gave a low whistle. "What happened to three for five dollars?" That had been the going price for as far back as he could remember.

Audrey flashed him an apologetic smile.

"We've got a grand prize this year that's a real bargain for ten dollars."

"Better than Patti's pie a week for a year?" The owner of the diner across the street was notorious for her decadently delicious pies.

"A week at a beach house in Gulf Shores!" Tess fist-pumped the air with cheerleader enthusiasm and an infectious grin that showed off her new missing tooth.

"Man!" Sol was indeed shocked at the extravagant prize. "That put somebody back a chunk." A zing of guilt flashed through him. He'd just gotten that huge amount of money from Kale in the sale of the marina, and he hadn't yet given a dime of it to the school.

"The house belongs to EmmyLou Creighton's family. Emmy's donating her week to us."

EmmyLou Creighton. The sexy-as-hell-and-didn't-she-know-it bombshell who'd hit the local scene, what…maybe fifteen years ago? He'd gone out with her a few times when they were younger. Back then he'd been too full of himself to stay with anyone for very long. And now? If he thought about it too hard, he might think that EmmyLou intimidated the hell out of him with her grab-the-world-by-the-tail attitude.

The only thing he was up to grabbing most nights was the whiskey decanter.

"How are sales?" he asked.

Audrey gave a relieved sigh. "Really good. Better than we'd hoped for."

"Tell you what, Tess." He took his wallet out and handed the little girl a fifty. "Put my name on five of those suckers."

Tess grabbed the pen and counted out five tickets. "How do you spell Sol?"

He winked at the little girl, who was the spitting image of her mom at that age. "S-O-L."

Tess went right to work on her project.

Sol leaned closer to Audrey and lowered his voice. "And I'll tell you what I'd like to do. When all the sales are finished, I want to match whatever you make. I'd like to have everybody in Taylor's Grove's name on at least one ticket. Can you do that?"

"You bet we can! Wow! Thank you so much, Sol!"

Audrey gave him a huge hug. The first time a good-looking woman had hugged him with happiness instead of sympathy in eight years.

It felt damn good.

"MATCH? AS IN give dollar-for-dollar everything you make?" Emmy grabbed the can of hair spray from her workstation at the salon and added the final touches to Audrey's newly straightened locks. "Girl, you've got the most gorgeous natural color I've ever seen. You need to let me go wild with the teasing someday. And then you could put on a crop top and short shorts and look just like one of those models in the Guess ads. Mark would get an erection so hard he'd pole vault over the bed."

Her friend's face turned as red as her hair, and she did a quick glance around to see if anybody else heard. The quietest of her friends, Audrey was easy to shock, so of course Emmy tried every chance she got. "You've got weird thought processes, Emmy," Audrey observed. "We were discussing Sol's raffle contribution. How you went from that to Mark's erection—" she whispered the last two words "—is beyond me."

"You want me to explain?" Emmy made eye contact with Audrey in the mirror. "It just occurred to me that Sol's doing this nice thing, which seems totally out of character for someone who goes around with a sneer on his face ninety-nine percent of the time." Audrey opened her mouth, probably to take up for him, but Emmy wouldn't hear it. "Don't give me all that *but he's crippled* crap. Everybody's got stuff they have to deal with, and yeah, he took a bullet or something and I hate that for him, but he doesn't have to act like the whole world's his enemy." She used the end of the comb to lift the hair at Audrey's crown to form a perfect bump. "Soooo, I was thinking that he's got a hard-on for the world, but it's totally different from the hard-on Mark would have for you if you dressed up like one of those models in the Guess ads."

Audrey dropped her head back and winked. "God, you are such a freak. But I love you anyway."

"What's not to love?" Emmy propped her hands on her hips and thrust her chest out, eyeing herself in the mirror. She worked hard at staying fit and doing everything humanly possible to fight the years. But it was Saturday, and while Audrey was going home to a husband who loved her, EmmyLou Creighton would be spending the night alone.

With a show of the innate closeness the two of them had developed, her dog Bentley came to her then and nudged her hand with his nose. He'd gotten too big to pick up, but she squatted and gave him a tight hug as Audrey stood up and stretched.

"It's hard to believe Bentley and Bandit came from the same litter." Audrey scratched Bentley behind the ears.

"What's hard to believe is that anybody would've dropped off a precious mama dog like Cher and her puppies. Some people are just too ornery for words." Emmy kissed Bentley several times around the eyes. "I think Cher showed herself to you on purpose, knowing you'd take her in and find good homes for her babies. Probably even knew you'd keep one, they were so stinking cute. I know I was a goner for Bentley as soon as I saw him and those big puppy eyes. That's why he's so big. Nobody can resist him, so everybody feeds him." He licked her nose, which made her laugh. She wasn't going home alone tonight after all. She'd be in the company of Bentley, who adored her. "Sol Beecher's one of those people who are too ornery for words, too. The man needs a dog to get his mind off himself."

Audrey laughed and shook her head as she laid her payment on Emmy's workstation. "And the conversation has come full circle back to Sol."

"So he's gonna match the funds, huh?" He was doing a good deed, but it made her peevish just the same. Everything about the man made her feel that way.

"That's what he said." Audrey nodded. "I even called him later in the week to see if he wanted to change his mind. I mean, this could turn out to be pretty expensive for him. But he insisted that he wants to match dollar-for-dollar."

An idea popped into Emmy's mind, no doubt borne on peevish wings—a way she could raise more money for the school and aggravate the hell out of Sol Beecher in the process.

"Give me a stack of those raffle tickets, Audrey." She smiled innocently at her friend. "I'll bet I can sell jillions of them here at the salon."

EVERY SEAT WAS filled in Taylor's Grove Elementary's gymnasium/cafeteria on raffle drawing night. The cacophony rivaled that of a basketball game, and the crowd of bodies had heated the temperature at least fifteen degrees since Sol had arrived—reluctant, but here nevertheless.

Audrey's plan to thank him publicly for his donation made him as uncomfortable as wearing a wool suit in July. In fact, he'd initially refused to attend when she first brought it up. But then they'd sent in the *big guns* in the form of little Tess, whose pleading gray eyes had been his undoing. So here he was, having given up his seat to Miss Beulah May Johnson, with his leg aching so badly he had to smile through clenched teeth, speaking to people and pretending to be enjoying himself when all he wanted to do was get the hell out of there and go home where he could gnash his teeth in private.

His checkbook was hollering louder than his stump, though. This event was about to set him back twenty-three hundred twenty dollars. When he'd told Audrey he'd match whatever they made, he'd expected the usual thousand or so, maybe less since they were charging ten dollars a ticket. He'd never have guessed Taylor's Grove residents would give up tens so readily. Apparently a week at the beach was a hotter commodity than he'd realized. The kids had even set up tables around the squares in nearby towns and sold the hell out of tickets in places where Taylor's Grove Elementary was considered a rival.

The donation was for a worthy cause—as many new computers as the money would buy—so it was hard for him to be too disturbed about the high amount.

What did disturb him, though, was the wicked grin EmmyLou Creighton shot his way just now as she entered. It was as though her eyes had sought him out of the crowd when she walked into the gym even though she wasn't usually prone to smile at him at all. Her high heels announced her approach to Audrey, who looked surprised but thrilled to see her. Actually, every man in the place looked thrilled to see her in the tight lime-green skirt that pulled the eye straight to her ass no matter how hard you tried to look away.

The temperature in the gym rose another twenty degrees...

An astonished look swept over Audrey's face when Emmy handed her an envelope, and then both women glanced his way. Audrey's look was wide-eyed and apologetic, while EmmyLou's smile oozed with smug.

Oh shit. The price has just gone up.

A trickle of sweat found the crease along the center of his spine, which he straightened as Audrey headed his way. His gaze locked with Emmy's and stayed there. "I don't care how much it is," he whispered when Audrey got close. "I'll match it."

"But, Sol, it's—"

"Dollar-for-dollar, Audrey. I gave my word." He broke eye contact with Emmy and caught Audrey's smile. The gleam in her eye elevated him to hero status—a place he hadn't been in a long time. It sent a flicker of warmth through him. Of course, he didn't dare look Emmy's way again. The brunette had bested him and she knew it—and looking at her was what she expected *every* man to do.

But for the first time in a long time, desire flushed through him. Not a desire to get laid. A desire to get even.

The sassy siren needed to be taught that she couldn't get her way about everything.

In his peripheral vision, he saw Emmy clicking her way toward him, hips swaying with more action than a tow sack full of cats in heat. His chest tightened with a breath that caught on an inhale. Thankfully she was merely taking the seat that Arlo James had offered.

It was at the end of the row where Sol stood,

close enough that he caught the scent of her perfume once his breathing resumed. It was nice... light. Not at all the scent he would've imagined a woman like EmmyLou Creighton wearing. He would've pegged her as the kind whose perfume invaded your nose before she invaded your space and then hung around long after she was gone. And—

Why in the hell was he dwelling on the woman's damn perfume? Wouldn't she have loved that?

He swiveled to lean his back against the wall, shifting his weight to his artificial leg.

Emmy cast a sidelong look his direction that started at his knee and moved up slowly to his face. "You want to sit?"

"Naw." The scowl he gave her came naturally, stemming from part pain, part anger and part embarrassment that a woman was offering him her damn seat. "I'm good." He crossed his arms over his chest and pushed away from the wall. "But you keep traipsing around in those heels and someday you'll limp worse than I do."

She arched one cool eyebrow. "I'll only limp worse than you do if one of them breaks off."

Sol could swear he felt a vacuum as the people within earshot sucked in a simultaneous breath.

Nobody spoke to him like that. Nobody ever mentioned his leg. They treated it like the crazy cousin confined to the attic in years past. Everybody knew it was there, but no one was willing to bring it up. People kept their eyes averted, but he could feel the looks.

This woman had balls, although how she could hide them under that tight skirt was beyond him. He snorted a half laugh at the thought...just as Audrey approached the microphone.

Thank God this would all be over soon.

EMMY HAD NEVER been to one of these raffle nights and hadn't realized it would go on for... *forever*, if the numbness of her butt was any indication.

She really needed to get up, and stubborn-ass Sol Beecher standing next to her obviously needed to sit. She heard his painful grunts every time his weight shifted. But she'd offered once, and he'd come back with one of his smart-ass answers uttered through that ever-present scowl. She wouldn't offer again.

The man had *major* attitude problems. What had she ever seen in him? Besides the sculpted chest and broad shoulders that filled out those T-shirts he was so fond of wearing. And he did have gorgeous brown eyes that caught you by surprise because his hair was a golden, sun-streaked blond.

But that hair! She shivered in disgust. What

used to be cute, sexy, surfer dude shaggy was now just flat-out unkempt and screamed *I don't give a rat's ass*. Oh, it was clean—she'd give him that. But just once she'd like to go at it with a pair of her shears.

The thought of running her fingers through his fresh, just-cut hair brought on the familiar sensation that curled low in her belly.

Seriously...sad sack Sol? Oh, please... She rolled her eyes at her overactive imagination.

But her butt tingled to life as the eighth graders started their skit.

Whatever it takes to get through this, she decided.

Ten nice prizes had been donated to the raffle from Taylor's Grove businesses, so the committee had decided to space out the drawings by letting each class perform some kind of act. Emmy had loved the kindergartners' rendition of "Old MacDonald" complete with animal costumes, and the first graders' skit about the animals of the Serengeti had been cute *and* informative. But somewhere around the fourth grade's recitation of Lincoln's Gettysburg Address, her attention in the kids had waned and turned to the man standing beside her.

"And we finally get to the reason most of y'all are here." Audrey's voice boomed over the microphone, and a chuckle passed through the crowd.

"But before we draw the ticket for the grand prize, there are a couple of people we need to recognize for their generous donations of both time and money. EmmyLou and Sol, would y'all come over here and stand by me?"

EmmyLou stood and smoothed her skirt as Sol stepped in front of her and crooked his elbow, offering his arm to her. She took his arm graciously, trying to ignore the masculine feel of him beneath her fingers. His gait was odd, his hip bumping hers as they walked, and she was much too aware of his tightening bicep every time he bumped her that told her he was straining hard to keep from limping.

She drew a relieved breath when they reached the center of the room, grateful that they hadn't been called up on the stage, and then realizing that Audrey had chosen not to be onstage for Sol's sake.

Audrey held her hand out, and Emmy felt herself being traded from Sol to her friend.

"EmmyLou Creighton hasn't lived in Taylor's Grove all her life," Audrey said, "but she acts as if she has. Not only has she provided us with the biggest grand prize we've ever had but also took it upon herself to sell the largest number of tickets." Audrey's voice quivered with excitement. "Thanks to EmmyLou, we added three hundred eighty-seven more tickets to the drawing—" Audrey paused and gave a laugh "—which you may or may not want to thank her for." A responding laugh moved through the audience. "But that translates to an additional three thousand eight hundred seventy dollars for the school!"

The audience surged to their feet in a standing ovation, and Emmy's heart, which should have swelled with pride, instead flew into a panicked rhythm as Audrey pulled her into a hug.

After all these years, she'd thought the stage fright was gone. But here it was—the invisible fist that reached from her tonsils to her breastbone, the grip that crushed her airways until she was sure she would die.

She tried to breathe through the panic like always, but it seldom worked. Oh God…the hug was over…the applause was dying down…people were lowering back into their seats…and the freaking microphone was being held to her mouth.

She had to say *something*.

The crowd grew quiet. Everyone was waiting…listening for her voice.

"I…uh…" *Crap!* Her mind went blank. She couldn't remember the words she was supposed to say. Nothing behind her eyes—her brain was just a big blank wall with nothing written on it. She shrugged and forced a smile. *Tell the truth.*

"I...um..." Her voice vibrated with fear. "I just did it...um...to aggravate Sol."

A roar of laughter met her admission, and some people rose to their feet as she strutted back to her seat, confident now that she was done speaking and feeling like she'd dodged a bullet.

When the crowd was again seated and quiet, Audrey continued. "It's no surprise that the man of the hour is none other than our own Sol Beecher, whose generosity to Taylor's Grove is unprecedented. He not only requested that every person in our community have a ticket in the drawing—"

"Yay, Sol!" A man's voice boomed through the auditorium, followed by a round of applause in agreement.

"—but also allowed his name to go on a measly five tickets even though he agreed to match the total sales dollar-for-dollar. And in case you missed it, I offered him an out on that when Emmy showed up with her surprising last-minute addition. He refused."

An astonished gasp came from the woman behind Emmy, and she felt the flicker of guilt in her stomach. She extinguished it quickly by reminding herself that she'd already confessed her sin in front of God and this whole crowd.

"And so, by doubling the amount collected from raffle ticket sales, we now have a new total of—" Audrey nodded to a kid in the band, who broke into a drum roll "—twelve thousand three hundred eighty dollars!"

Another roar went through the crowd, which was once more on its feet. The standing ovation went on and on, lasting even longer than the Gettysburg Address, by Emmy's estimation.

Sol looked positively miserable, and for once Emmy empathized with him…until Audrey handed him the microphone, and his deep, clear voice rang through the auditorium with not a single bobble.

"Taylor's Grove has always been there for me, and I'm grateful. Of course, I didn't realize I was…" Emmy again saw the handsome twenty-something he'd once been shining through the gruff camouflage as he glanced at Audrey's paper and grinned sheepishly. "Six thousand one hundred ninety dollars' worth of grateful." The audience laughed, and he waited for them to quiet. "But I love this town and all of y'all— except EmmyLou Creighton."

Another wave of laughter and another standing ovation as he limped back to the wall beside her, never looking her way.

Emmy's shoulders drew back as her spine stiffened in anger at the rebuff.

But an easy smile covered her wrath…and the knowledge that the jerk's admission was exactly as truthful as her own.

CHAPTER TWO

June 22

EMMYLOU GRABBED TWO towels as she stepped out of the shower, wrapping her wet hair with one, drying herself with the other, briskly. She should have been dabbing her skin gently rather than scrubbing it like a potato, but she was much too jittery. As she turned, her eyes dropped to the reflection in the full-length mirror of the skin on her thigh just below her butt cheek.

Oh Lord...is that the beginning of cellulite?

"No...no," she whimpered. "Cellulite isn't allowed. Not today."

But sure enough, on closer inspection, there were indeed a couple of small dimples. Why, oh, why hadn't she been proactive and gone ahead and splurged on that miracle cream while QVC had it on sale? "Now it'll cost me an arm and a leg," she huffed.

The mention of a leg brought her back to the reason she was jittery...

Sol Beecher would be here soon.

"Over six hundred tickets in that drawing." She slapped the towel over the bar, spreading it out to dry. "The man has five and one of *them* gets picked as the winner. What are the odds?" She snorted at her reflection. "Why, those odds would be six hundred to five, I believe." She tried to do the math in her head, but it got jumbled, so she gave up, satisfied to be in the neighborhood of correct. "Something close to one hundred something to one."

Today Sol was picking up the keys to the beach house. She'd been planning what she'd wear for the event for two weeks and had finally decided on her gold bikini. She would be lounging by the pool—totally oblivious that this was the day they'd arranged. When he arrived, she wouldn't have her cover-up available. In her own backyard? Of course not. She would invite him into the house, so he'd have to follow her—and no doubt check her out thoroughly—and he would be the sorriest man alive that he'd ever allowed her to slip away.

But now? Now his vision would fill with the sight of cellulite—two dimples of it, one for each eye. A much easier math problem than the other one.

What it added up to was that she was back to square one about what to wear.

She rushed to her closet, jerking hangers,

searching for the *new* perfect outfit to show off her…assets. And make him sorry.

Geez, he could get her riled.

Since her first date at the age of fifteen, she'd *never* lost a guy she wanted. That wasn't to say no one had ever broken up with her. Lots of them had. No, that was an exaggeration. A *few* of them had. But those breakups came at times when she was ready to call it quits.

Sol Beecher was the only one who ever walked away leaving *her* still wanting *him*.

Still she hadn't completely admitted defeat, even after all these years.

Someday he would get through the self-absorbed funk he walked around in. He would *see* her…*want* her. And when that happened, she'd kick his bad leg out from under him and let him fall on his metaphorical ass.

The lime-green skirt had previously failed to catch his attention, and the gold bikini was out.

Wonder Woman costume? Nah, too obvious.

The chime alerted her that a vehicle had pulled into her driveway. She sprinted to the bedroom window and let out a groan at the sight of Sol's black truck. "Early? Noooo!" She snatched her watch from the vanity and examined it. Sure enough, the stem was pulled out. She'd thought it was ten-ten, when in reality it was ten fifty-five.

Sol Beecher was only five minutes early.

Bentley woke from his nap in the middle of her bed. He jumped down and headed to the door as she threw the towel from her hair and ran back into the closet, grabbing the first top and bottom her hands touched. No time to dry her hair…or even run a comb through it. No time for makeup. The shorts were old jeans she'd cut off—ragged and frayed at the edges—while the T-shirt was one a friend had brought her. Bright purple, it sported a picture of Chewbacca on the front with MILWOOKIE above him in green block letters.

The sound of the doorbell mixed with Bentley's bark of greeting.

Emmy rammed her toes into some flip-flops and her fingers through her hair on her way to the door. Bentley loved being out in the yard, but he didn't have on the collar that went with the underground fence. So she grabbed the collar he was wearing as she turned the doorknob. Excited by the company, Bentley jumped back, causing her to jerk the door open with a *swoosh*.

Sol's brown eyes widened in surprise…and then squinted. "EmmyLou?"

Go ahead, buster. Rub it in.

"Yeah." Embarrassment made her insides cringe, but she refused to let him see her discomfort. "Just got out of the shower." Bentley danced with excitement, hopping up and down like a deranged kangaroo. "Come in, would you? He's going to rip my arm out of its socket."

"I'm a little early. I figured I'd just stop by on my way into town." Sol stepped inside and closed the door. "But I see I should've called first. This is obviously a bad time."

The way his eyes raked over her went through her like a tack into corkboard. "Not a problem," she snapped, releasing her hold on Bentley.

The dog made straight for the man's bad leg… and began humping it.

"Oh good Lord!" Emmy scrambled to disengage the two, but Sol lost his balance and stumbled back against the door, luckily catching himself. "Oh crap, I'm sorry. Really. I'm so sorry." She was overdoing the apology. "Get down, Bentley. I've never seen him like this."

"Would you just get me the damn key?" Sol forced the words out. "Please."

She pulled Bentley along and closed him up in her bedroom, then hurried to the kitchen to grab the key and the list of rules for the use of the beach house. She paused there to catch her breath and give her brain time to come up with something humorous to alleviate the awkward moment.

She and Sol didn't get along, but that didn't make it okay to humiliate him.

Aggravate? Yeah. Humiliate? No.

She looked down the rules, stopping as number six caught her eye…and gave her an idea. A true EmmyLou-ism.

She sauntered back to the living room, handing him the key when she got within arm's reach. "That's the key." She then held out the paper and he took it, his eyes scanning it. "Just a list of rules for the house," she explained. "Common sense mostly. Don't put cans down the garbage disposal. Don't start a campfire in the living room. Don't pick the lock on the family's private suite."

He met her gaze, his eyes hooded.

"That's where we keep our private stuff." She lifted an eyebrow. "Wouldn't want you knowing my secrets…or going through my drawers."

Most people would've laughed. Not Sol Beecher.

He shook his head as he opened the front door. "No worries, then. Been there. Done that."

He must have sensed she was about to kick his ass, because he moved outside faster than she would've thought him capable of.

She slammed the door behind him.

Damn him! If humiliation was what he was about, she could be all over him like ugly on an ape.

This game was on.

NOW, THIS IS LIVING.

Sol dug his toes deeper into the sand and took

another sip of his bourbon, reminding himself that he'd almost allowed his anger to get the best of him yesterday and let this opportunity pass him by.

He was glad he hadn't, even if he'd had to endure EmmyLou's obviously planned slight. Or perhaps, *unplanned* was the better way of thinking about it.

She would've been dressed to the nines with her makeup and hair done for any other adult male on the planet. But not him. She had to prove just how low he rated on her scale of men. If he was a gambler, he'd wager that, apart from family, he was one of the few men who'd ever seen her without makeup.

Of course, the joke was on her. With her dark brown hair and smooth olive complexion, she was more beautiful *without* all that makeup, but you'd never convince her of that. She was one of those women who wanted you to believe she got out of bed with everything in place.

As a matter of fact, the one night they spent together, she *did* sleep with her makeup on…and got up early the next morning to fix herself up before he woke.

Crazy-ass woman.

He shouldn't let her get under his skin, and he shouldn't have made that parting comment. But the woman had a way about her that made him want to… He took another sip of bourbon, letting its slow burn uncover the truth. Made him want to…

Don't go there. Ms. EmmyLou Perfect may have prettied up for you years ago, but now she doesn't even view you as a man.

It was difficult for anybody else to see him that way, he guessed, when he could hardly see it himself. The man he'd used to be, the cocksure man about town who'd played the field like an all-star…that guy got blown away, along with his lower leg, his hopes and his dreams, by a rocket-propelled grenade.

But he wouldn't dwell on that this week.

The beach house was a perfect combination of comfortable family home and convenient guesthouse just steps away from the Gulf of Mexico with only a stretch of sugary white sand in between. According to the fire escape diagram on the kitchen wall, there were two suites downstairs and two up, though he couldn't confirm that since he'd elected not to attempt the stairs yet. The nice, wide balcony on the second level would be the perfect place to catch the sunset, though. So sometime over the next week he'd make the climb.

Difficult, but worth it.

EmmyLou's laughing brown eyes flashed into his mind again. As she'd warned, the family suite was locked. One of those boxes hung on the door handle—the kind with the combination that opened a compartment that held a key. The locked door piqued his curiosity, especially because it was directly across from the suite he'd claimed. But he doubted the room contained any deep family secrets.

The way EmmyLou's mouth ran, no secret could remain safe with her for very long.

The beach had been crowded when he arrived this evening, but it was deserted now. The gentle, phosphorescent waves lapping at the sand called to him. He detached his prosthesis and grabbed the despicable but necessary crutches.

Walking in the sand was tricky, but there was no one around to mark his awkward, slow progress. He understood how those newly hatched baby sea turtles must feel—drawn innately to the water...determined to make it or die trying.

The sand cooled the closer he got to the lacy edge of foam, so the first touch of water across his foot surprised him. It was warm and so inviting. He wished to hell he had a prosthesis suitable for use in salt water.

But he didn't, and wishes were about as helpful as tits on a boar.

He eased out another couple of steps until the water hit his calf at the midpoint, letting the peacefulness seep through his—

"Damnation!" A branding iron seared the skin on his leg. His gaze dropped to the water, where the moonlight caught the opalescent glow of the army of jellyfish. They had him surrounded! Knowing it was a mistake didn't keep his brain from encouraging him to run, so he sprinted... but only for one step. And then he fell. One of the little sons of a bitch washed into the leg of his cargo shorts on the next wave and proceeded to sting him on the stump. Another came to the first one's defense and attacked the top of his foot.

Sol scrambled for the sand—the baby sea turtle with his gears in Reverse—somehow managing to keep a grip on his crutches while trying to keep the sand out of his artificial knee socket by holding the half leg out at a ninety-degree angle. With dry sand beneath him, he was safe. He stopped on all threes and caught his breath, wondering if anybody had seen his absurd antics. If they had, they must have pegged him for deranged. In his present position, he looked a lot like a dog trying to take a piss.

A laugh rolled out of him, released from a storage hold he hadn't opened much lately, while the icy hot tendrils still irritated the places where they'd made contact. Rolling over onto his back, he lay there until his laughter subsided and he closed his eyes and breathed in the salty air, feeling...alive.

Happy to be here.

He should call EmmyLou and thank her. The thought spurred him to action.

Maneuvering onto his knee, he used the crutches to get back to a standing position and moved at a much smoother pace across the sand this time. As soon as he reached the deck, he grabbed his prosthesis and walloped his butt a good lick.

The best thing about having an artificial leg was being able to kick yourself in the ass when ridiculous ideas popped into your brain.

"OH JOE WAYNE...oh Joe Wayne...oh Joe Wayne."

The woman beneath him sounded like a CD with some lint that caused it to stick, and Joe Wayne Fuller found it mighty distracting. Maybe if he changed things up a bit...rolled over to his side...

The room whirled as he eased to the left, but Ramona's sturdy thigh shoved him back into place. Her legs locked tighter around him, and she began to buck harder, drumming his ass with her heels. "Oh, yes, baby. Just like that. Give me more of that."

"You like this?" he panted, trying to stay focused and not think about how much his head was spinning and how much pain her heels was inflicting. He'd have bruises, for sure...and a helluva hangover. "You like—ow! Sunshine, you got to—oof!…take it easier. You're making me lose—"

"No! Don't stop!" Her teeth sank into his shoulder.

"Shitfire! No more biting. You promised." A week with Ramona had left his neck and shoulders looking like he'd been to a damn vampire convention.

"Sorry," she whispered. "Just don't stop. Don't stop." The last word came out on a snarl that sounded like a rabid dog.

He hoped to hell when this was over, he didn't have to put her down like they did Old Yeller.

"Oh Joe Wayne…oh Joe Wayne…"

Speaking of "yeller"…

"Don't stop. Don't stop. Don't stop."

Joe Wayne squeezed his eyes shut, reminding himself to keep Ramona far away from the Wild Turkey tomorrow night…if there was a tomorrow night…if he lived through this beating.

"Don't stop. Don't. Stop! Stop!" Ramona sucked in a gulp of air and hurled him off of her and the bed.

"What the hell?"

A car door slammed.

"My husband!"

"Husband?" Joe Wayne scrambled to his feet. "You never told me you—"

"Oh, shut up and leave." She was out of the

bed now with a wild look in her eye, and Joe Wayne's gut told him this wasn't a good time to argue. Ramona snatched clothes from the floor and shoved them into his arms as she pushed him toward the bathroom.

The front door opened slightly, wood cracking as it slammed against the chain lock, followed by a man's roar. "Ramona! Get your ass out of bed and let me in!"

"Your only chance to make it out alive is through that window," she whispered and then let out a yell. "I'm coming, baby!"

Joe Wayne pushed it open and sized up the opening...a mighty *small* chance, by his way of thinking.

"Don't stop to dress." The warning in her tone sent prickles up his spine.

"What about Patsy?" He threw the clothes out the window and climbed onto the toilet to hoist a leg through. *Ow!* He ground his teeth to keep from crying out as his private parts scraped across the rough wood. "I can't leave without my bike."

"Get it tomorrow." Ramona gave him a helpful push, sending him tumbling to the ground, then closed the window behind him. A second later, the window opened again, and his boots thumped him in the head.

Joe Wayne grabbed the clothes and boots, gripping them to his chest, and took off behind the neighbors' houses, his heart chugging for all it was worth. He ran like a jackrabbit under the cover of darkness until his lungs felt like they was gonna bust. When he couldn't take a breath without a hot poker stabbing his side, he finally gave up and stopped to dress. Leaning on the side of a garage, taking in huge gulps of air, he rammed one leg into his jeans and then the other and jerked hard.

The waistband stopped its upward movement at the top of his thighs, pinning his legs together and not letting them move. "Shitfire!" He gritted his teeth as his right hip connected with the ground.

Jerking the jeans off, he examined them. Not his. Ramona's. And even though she was a curvy woman, there was no way his ass was gonna fit into her jeans. A snatch of color caught his eye. Her orange thong hung on his foot.

Dread filled his gut as he grabbed the T-shirt. Yep. Just as he'd 'spected. Hers, too—the black V-neck with pink sparkling letters that proclaimed A Hard Man on the front and Is Good to Find across the back.

He took a deep breath, running his hands through his hair. No keys. They were in his jeans, which he hoped to hell she'd somehow managed to hide. He couldn't even get into the compartment on his bike where he kept his stuff. His only hope was to get to the beach house.

He stood and pulled the T-shirt over his head. It was tight, and the shoulder and sleeve seams groaned under the pressure. It was also just a couple of inches shy of keeping him from getting arrested for indecent exposure if he happened to be seen, which he didn't plan on.

He'd been pondering ways to get some publicity shining on his almost nonexistent career, but being arrested roaming the streets, half-drunk and half-dressed, in women's clothes wasn't the image he was going for.

A hefty punch of self-loathing hit his gut as he slipped on the thong.

But thank God for his boots.

He glanced down, shuddering at the sight—just another weirdo roaming the streets in the middle of the night.

He remembered that EmmyLou had booked renters into the beach house for the week.

He hoped to hell they had a sense of humor.

CHAPTER THREE

THE SHOWER IN Sol's bathroom was difficult though not impossible to navigate as long as he held on to the hand bar. But the water wasn't helping the jellyfish stings. If anything, it made them worse. The intense stings had morphed into an intense itch.

Sol had searched the kitchen cabinets for meat tenderizer—wasn't that supposed to be the go-to miracle cure?—but found none. He'd remembered hearing somewhere that urine would ease the sting, also, but he wasn't that desperate.

He turned off the water and dried inside the shower, then got out and reattached his prosthesis. The itch was annoying enough that sleep would be an absent friend, which really didn't matter because he could spend the entire day tomorrow in bed if he wanted. So instead of slipping into pajamas, he pulled on a clean pair of cargo shorts. After so many years in long pants, he'd forgotten how cool, loose and unfettering shorts could be.

Without meat tenderizer, bourbon was sure to

be the next best thing for his stings, provided it was applied internally. He went to the bar in the large common room and found a new bottle because he'd finished the dab that was left in the old one.

The first sip went down smoothly. The second caught in his throat when a sound caused him to flinch. A cough sent the bourbon several places where it shouldn't have been—onto the bar, down his bare front and, most irritating, up his nose. It burned up into his sinuses making his eyes tear. Great! Between the jellyfish and the bourbon, he was literally burning and itching from head to toe, inside and out. And the fact that someone was knocking on his back door…at two-thirty in the morning…did not bode well for this situation improving.

But he chose to ignore the knock. Probably just some drunk anyway.

Coughs continued to wrack his system until the liquid cleared from the passages it wasn't meant to come into contact with.

Whoever was at the sliding glass door must have heard, because the knocking grew more persistent.

"Hey!" A male voice. "I need help."

The word *help* called Sol to action. He grabbed his phone in case he needed to call 911…or the police…and hustled toward the hallway.

The kitchen light gave him a fairly good view of a man standing at the door that led to the deck on the beach. The guy needed help all right—but not the kind Sol could give.

Some kind of crazy-ass, scantily clad cross-dressing dude.

But he broke into a smile when he saw Sol. "Hey, man! Oh, thank God." He dropped his head back in a relieved gesture. Then he straightened and pressed his forearms and face against the glass. The gesture pulled his T-shirt up, revealing an orange lace thong that basically covered nothing.

The man wasn't bloody. He stood upright. He obviously wasn't hurt. And he didn't seem to be in a hurry to get away from anybody.

"Go on." Sol yelled from several feet away. "Get out of here." He started to turn.

"Wait!" The nutcase pounded the door with his palms. "No, man! Hey! Don't go!"

Sol moved closer, but only to flip the light switch on the wall. The deck light remained on, putting the visitor in a spotlight. Someplace he was used to being, no doubt.

"Look, I'm Joe Wayne Fuller. My family owns this house."

Sol pulled up straight, pausing to study him a moment.

"My sister, EmmyLou Fuller, arranged your

stay. Ain't that right?" The guy's head bobbed up and down, answering his own question.

EmmyLou Fuller? Sol had never heard her use that last name, but the name EmmyLou was too distinct not to refer to her. If this joker was her brother, she'd probably put him up to this.

The woman had already proven she'd go to great lengths to try to best Sol Beecher.

"Call her. She'll tell you I ain't dangerous or nothing. I just got into a *situation*." He crunched his fingers in the air, forming imaginary quotation marks around the word. "I…uh… I lost my clothes, and, oh hell, man. Just call EmmyLou. She'll vouch for me."

"I'm not calling her. It's two-thirty in the morning." Sol put his hands on his hips and stood his ground.

Joe Wayne—if that was really his name—pressed his forehead against his arm and took a deep breath. "Well, would you at least get me some clothes from the family suite? I can't go nowhere else like this."

So he knew about the family suite.

Sol blew out an angry breath and jerked his phone up to find EmmyLou's number.

A CALL AT two-thirty was not a rare occurrence in Emmy's world.

Her two younger brothers, both single, were

forever calling her when they came in after a night of drinking and carousing. And even the two older ones, both married, called after spats with their wives or when they needed help understanding the female gender.

But a call from Sol Beecher at this time of night hadn't occurred in fourteen years. She blinked at his name on the caller ID, and her heart did a strange triple beat. But then she remembered he was at the beach house—he was probably calling to complain about something that didn't suit him.

She fumbled with the button and pressed the phone to her ear. "If you've stopped up the plumbing, you'll have to wait until morning. Just think of the beach as your private litter box for the night."

"Yeah, well, the plumbing's held up so far. But the litter box is going to come in mighty handy for your brother, who's standing on the deck."

Emmy shot straight up in the bed. "My brother? Which one?"

"Says his name is Joe Wayne Fuller."

The edge of a groan seeped out. "Oh good Lord."

"He's wearing a black woman's T-shirt—"

Oooo, that could be good news. "Is she with him?" She hadn't realized she'd fisted the sheet in her hand until it relaxed.

"Who?"

"The black woman, because it's probably my friend Shirley, and—"

"A black woman isn't *with* him." *There he goes getting snippy.* "He's wearing a woman's black T-shirt, an orange thong and cowboy boots…nothing else. And he's beating on the door to the deck, saying I need to let him in to get some clothes."

Emmy plopped back into her pillow, pressing a finger and thumb against her eyes. "Let me talk to him."

"I'm not opening this door." She could visualize Sol shaking that stubborn, shaggy head of his. "He looks crazy."

"Is he drunk?"

Sol's voice grew louder. "Are you drunk?"

"Not no more. But I wished to hell I was," came the reply, slightly muffled, but she'd recognize that drawl anywhere.

"Listen, tell her me and this friend was having a little fun." Emmy strained to hear her brother's story. "But her husband came home and I hauled ass out of there and I got the wrong clothes and no money and I had to sneak all the way across town in the dark half-nekkid and I need some damn clothes!"

A loud *smack* told her he'd hit the glass door.

"So there you have it." Sol again. "Straight from the crazy-ass's mouth."

"You could use a few lessons in anatomy." She'd left herself wide open for another one of those *been there, done that* quips, so she hurried on. "Look...would you mind letting him in long enough to grab some clothes? And maybe loan him a few dollars? I'll pay you back when you get home." God, she hated asking him for a favor. But when it came to her brothers, she'd grovel if she had to. Besides, she owed Joey. He was the one she'd let down the most. Well, him and Mama. Always Mama. "Joey's harmless. Even when he's drunk, he's a lovable drunk."

She heard the door slide open and drew an easier breath.

"Thanks, man." Joey's voice kicked up a notch. "Thanks, EmmyLou. Love you."

"Okay. He's in," Sol growled, and the sexy sound caused a flutter in her belly. "You can go back to sleep."

"Sol...um... I'm sorry about this." Emmy chewed her bottom lip. "But...thanks. I owe you."

"Yes, you do." He didn't sound like he was kidding. "Hey, by the way, do you know if there's any meat tenderizer in the house?"

Emmy's brain stuttered at the abrupt change in topic. *Sheesh!* People said *she* had strange thought processes! "I...don't...know. But if you buy your steaks at Campbell's Meat Market—it's only a couple blocks away—you won't need tenderizer."

"Oh man!" Emmy heard the shock in Joey's voice. "What happened to y—"

"Okay, EmmyLou. Thanks. G'night."

The phone went dead, and for a brief moment, emptiness surrounded her bed before the familiar voice chided her. *Why would you buy such a big house? You're probably never going to get married now. All your friends married a long time ago.*

"Boys are so much easier than girls. If you ever get pregnant, pray for a boy. Of course, it's getting too late for you to have any children now."

"Shut up, Mama."

Emmy folded the pillow around her head as if that would silence the voice.

"Your brother's down there with no money and probably no place to stay except with one of his no-account friends. He needs help, missy, and you more than anyone else owe him..."

Emmy threw the pillow on the floor and climbed out of bed. It was a nine-hour drive to Gulf Shores. Probably more like ten with stops to gas up and stretch.

"We're not gonna stay, but we'll need a few things."

Bentley drew a long sigh as she pulled the overnight bag from her closet.

"...YOUR LEG?" JOE WAYNE finished his sentence, wishing he hadn't as he watched the guy's face turn the color of a pomegranate.

"Shark bit it off while I was surfing." He leaned down and scratched a red welt on his foot.

"No shit? Hot damn!" Joe Wayne had always admired surfers. They looked so cool, riding waves like bull riders of the sea. He'd never been able to keep his balance on one of the suckers. Probably because the only time the urge hit him to try was after he'd had a few. "You still surf? You one of those guys they show on TV who suck it up and go ahead and do everything they did before?"

"Nope. Shark might be wanting dessert." The houseguest pounded his fist on the cuff above his prosthesis before performing an about face and heading toward the front of the house. "Get some clothes on, will you? You look like a damn fool."

Joe Wayne followed him toward the front as far as the family suite. Then he let the guy go on ahead to the living area...or, more probably, the bar, where he'd surely been when Joe Wayne showed up. Joe Wayne was ready for another drink or two himself, but getting rid of this string between his legs was the first priority. How did women stand the things?

He punched the code in, fumbling the keys out

of the container. When it opened, he let himself into the large set of rooms, sighing at the mess he and Ramona had left when they'd vacated and moved to her house. His intentions had been to come back and clean it up. But he hadn't found the time yet to work it into his schedule. Not that his schedule was full—he had zero gigs this week—but cleaning house wasn't his thing.

A pile of his dirty clothes still lay in the bottom of the closet where he'd left them. Dirty had never smelled so good. He slipped out of his boots—damn, his feet were tired—and into a pair of his jeans and his own T-shirt. And thank God he'd left his guitar here…a precaution after Ramona had picked it up one night and threatened to smash it across his head if he didn't fix her another drink. Damn mean woman when she was drunk. But then, he'd never seen her totally sober, either.

All the way to the beach house, he'd pondered how he could retrieve Patsy and the rest of his stuff without getting his ass whipped.

No stroke of genius had hit him yet. Maybe what's-his-name would have an idea.

He shuffled down the hall and found his new best friend with a whiskey—no, that was clearly a bottle of Four Roses, so make that a bourbon. "You get into Dad's private stash? He'll skin us both."

The stranger shook his head. "Brought this myself." His tone said he wasn't sharing, either.

Joe Wayne considered going back to the room for the keys. One of them unlocked the liquor cabinet. But he'd left some beer in the fridge, and right then, a cold one sounded okay. "Dad drinks Four Roses, too. Says anybody who drinks it must be a Southern gentleman."

No response, but the former surfer shifted his weight onto his artificial leg and rubbed the top of his good foot against it.

Joe Wayne attempted to pry him into conversation again. "What's your name, anyway?"

The stranger squinted like he was figuring on whether or not to give out that information before he finally answered. "Sol. Sol Beecher."

"Joe Wayne Fuller." Joe Wayne held his hand out.

Sol cocked a half grin before shaking. "Yeah. We've already met."

Joe Wayne rounded the bar to get to the refrigerator. "So you're a friend of EmmyLou's?" He grabbed a beer and popped the top, guzzling half of it in one gulp.

Sol snorted. "I wouldn't say that. I won a raffle. A week here at the house was the prize."

"You know her, though? EmmyLou?"

"Yeah. I know her."

Not much of a conversationalist, this Sol

Beecher. But he finally broke the silence. "You her half-brother? Or…has she been married?

Joe Wayne finished the beer. "Nope." He grabbed another.

"Her last name is Creighton. Yours is Fuller."

Joe Wayne took only a sip this time. "Creighton's her middle name. Fuller's her real last name. She started using Creighton 'cause she didn't want people to…" Shit! Running his mouth off— giving up his sister's secrets to someone he didn't even know. "Oh hell, just ignore me. I'm drunk."

Sol looked him squarely in the eye. "And you'll need to be hitting the road soon."

"Yeah, about that. Seeing as how you seem to be here all by your lonesome…" Joe Wayne glanced around but saw no evidence of anyone else. "You're here by yourself, right?"

"Right." Sol set the glass on the bar harder than necessary. "And I like it that way." He leaned down and scratched the top of his foot again.

"You're doing a powerful lot of scratching." Joe Wayne steered the subject away from his sleeping place for the night. Figured he'd approach it again later. "You get wasp stung or something?"

"Jellyfish. Three places. They're not stinging anymore, but the itching's driving me crazy."

Joe Wayne gave a sympathetic shake of his head. "You showered before you treated 'em. Don't ever do that—makes 'em worse."

"Yeah. Thanks for that." Sol gritted his teeth and hit the bar with the end of his fist. "Got me on the cheek of the ass, too."

Joe Wayne's laugh earned him an angry glare. "I went through the kitchen looking for meat tenderizer—"

"That ain't what you need. You need—" Joe Wayne stopped. "Tell you what. You agree I can stay here tonight and I'll tell you how to get rid of the itch. It's three o'clock now. A few more hours can't be so bad, can it? You're gonna sleep through them anyway." He gave Sol a huge grin. "Unless that damn itching keeps you up all night."

A look came into Sol's eyes that Joe Wayne recognized. Defeat. "All right," Sol snapped. "Just tell me what to do."

"I'll do better than that. Wait here and I'll get you the cure."

Joe Wayne went to the kitchen and retrieved one of the giant bottles of vinegar they kept under the sink just for jellyfish stings. He trotted back up the hall and presented the bottle to Sol. "Get in the shower and pour this on the spots full strength. Let it stay on for a few minutes and then soak in a hot tub for twenty minutes. Itching'll be gone."

Sol grabbed the bottle of vinegar and his refilled glass of bourbon. "Thanks. I'll see you in the morning."

Joe Wayne waited until the door to the downstairs guest suite closed. Then he got a glass out of the cabinet. "Twenty-five minutes alone with a bottle of Four Roses?" He poured a hefty couple of shots into his glass. "Don't mind if I do."

CHAPTER FOUR

SOL BANGED ON the door of the family suite. "Joe Wayne!" He bellowed the name. "Time for you to get up. Rise and shine."

"Go 'way," came the muffled grumble.

Sol had slept with the windows open, lulled into deep relaxation by the sound of the waves, and hadn't woken until after eleven. He could never live here because he'd become a beach bum, for sure. Obviously, that's what had happened to his uninvited guest.

He opened the door and barged in. "That's my line. Time for you to get up and get out of here."

Joe Wayne lay sprawled on his back in the same position Sol had left him when he half carried him in here, much too inebriated to make the journey from the bar on his own.

The young man covered his eyes with his hand. "Turn off the damn light!"

"That's the sun. It's after one o'clock." Sol moved to the window and jerked the curtains wider, filling the room with sunshine.

Joe Wayne groaned. "Shark took your heart, too, didn't it?"

The unexpected intrusion into Sol's week had been an aggravation, but getting out of the shower last night to find his bottle of Four Roses half-gone was unforgivable. He opened the window to allow fresh air in—and the body odor out. "Get your ass out of bed. Now. And take a shower. You smell like a sewer."

A gecko crawled onto the screen and Sol paused to watch it, relieved to hear movement behind him that indicated Joe Wayne was finally sitting up.

Sol turned from the window and started toward the door, clapping Joe Wayne on the back as he passed him. "Lunch is almost ready." The plan was to feed him and send him on his way... as quickly as possible.

Last night in the dark, Sol had missed the photographs that covered the wall to the right of the private suite's door. He stopped now to look, his eyes drawn to a grouping of EmmyLou at different ages, decked out in over-the-top frills—sashes crossing her torso, declaring her Fairest of the Fair.

A beauty queen. No wonder she's so self-absorbed.

He guessed her to be around sixteen in the

last one. Beautiful—but not as beautiful as she'd looked when he'd picked up the key at her house.

The memory of that humiliation propelled him out of the room with a quick call over his shoulder. "Fifteen minutes."

A disgusted sigh followed by a shuffling sound told him Joe Wayne was on the move at last.

Sol returned to the kitchen, where he had the beginnings of a couple of Monte Cristo sandwiches lying on the cutting board. He heated the butter in the skillet as he whisked the eggs and milk together, then dipped the sandwiches and let them brown slowly.

He'd just flipped them to the other side—smiling at the perfection of the golden color—when Joe Wayne made his appearance...obviously clean, but still wearing the same damn dirty clothes.

Sol wrinkled his nose. "Don't you have something else you can put on?"

Joe Wayne ran a hand through his wet hair and tucked it behind his ears. "Nope. Everything in there—" he threw a thumb over his shoulder "—is dirty. All my clean stuff's in the compartment of my motorcycle."

Shock rolled through Sol. "You left your motorcycle behind?"

Joe Wayne rubbed the back of his neck. "Had to. It was a near-death experience. I was hoping—" he drifted toward the sliding glass door, looking out on the beach "—that maybe you and me could figure out some way to get it back."

Sol lifted the sandwich with the spatula to check its progress as he shook his head. "Sorry. You're on your own."

"Come on, man." The sound was as close to a man-whine as Sol had ever heard. "Ramona's husband'll kill me if I get anywhere near that house. He's probably already done something horrible to Patsy—that's my cycle."

"And what makes you think anyone else would be safe?"

"I thought…" Joe Wayne shrugged, cutting his eyes in Sol's direction and downward. "Maybe he wouldn't do nothing to a guy with a fake leg."

"Use the cripple to garner some pity, huh?" Sol tossed the plastic bowl into the sink, sloshing the remainder of its egg-and-milk contents up the sides.

"If gardenin' pity'll get Patsy back…hell yeah."

"Hell no." Sol found the plates in the cabinet and took two down. "Get us each a bottle of water." He used the spatula to point at his companion. "Only water."

EmmyLou's brother did as he was told, slinking to the refrigerator like a whipped puppy, as Sol plated the sandwiches and cut each one in half, adding a dollop of strawberry jam for dipping.

"Let's eat on the deck," he suggested. "I can't stand it in here with…" He paused. "This fresh air and sunshine is too nice to miss."

Joe Wayne followed him out, and they settled into the chairs at the table. His companion wolfed a fourth of his sandwich down without saying a word, but grunting often with approval.

"What do you call this? Some kind of fancy French toast?" Strawberry jam oozed out the side of Joe Wayne's mouth.

"Use your napkin." Sol scooted one across the table. "And it's a Monte Cristo."

Joe Wayne snorted with his mouth full, sending crumbs onto his plate and the surrounding area. "Like those funny British movie guys? Dad used to love their stuff. Thought they were hilarious."

"That's Monty Python. This is Monte Cristo—as in the Count of…"

Joe Wayne shrugged. "Never heard of him."

Sol took another bite to block the sarcasm poised on his lips.

"Gonna be hard for me to leave—" Joe Wayne shook his head and gave a regretful sigh "—till I get Patsy back. But once I do, her and me'll hit the road quicker'n a frog on a june bug."

"Forget it. You're on your own."

Joe Wayne took another giant bite. "Have it your way. But seeing as how you and I are going to be hanging out together for a while longer, why don't you tell me what really happened to your leg?"

"I don't talk about my leg," Sol responded.

"Well, maybe you should. Might make you less of a turd."

"HELLO?"

That was not Joe Wayne's voice on the other end of her brother's cell phone.

"Sol?" Emmy crossed her fingers and hoped not as she tossed her luggage onto the hotel bed.

"Who is this?" The threatening edge sharpened, going beyond the aggravation of Sol's normal tone with her. This was…mean.

"It's EmmyLou," she said.

"Well, when you get ahold of your friend, tell him…"

Oh good Lord. This wasn't Sol, either.

"…that if he ever comes sniffing around my wife again—"

The husband!

Emmy ended the call.

The guy still had Joey's phone. Not a good sign. Where was her brother?

Her thumb scrolled through her recent calls and pressed the number from early that morning.

"Hello, EmmyLou." Definitely Sol. Her toes

curled at the sound no matter how hard she tried to stop them.

"Hi, Sol. I was trying to reach Joey, and—"

"Hey, sis."

So Joey was still alive. That neither the husband nor Sol had killed him after last night's fiasco was a pleasant surprise. Her brother might not have fared so well if she'd been the one staying at the beach house. But if he thought that friendly tone would get him out of a lecture, he had another think coming.

"Don't you 'hey, sis' me. Acting like everything's all hunky-dory after making an ass of yourself in front of my friend last night. What in the cornbread hell did you think you were doing? And with a married woman? Shame on you, Joe Wayne Fuller."

"So y'all *are* friends. The way Sol acts, I wasn't sure. 'Course, it was a little weird that he had your phone number so readily available last night. And here you are, calling him again."

"Don't go trying to shift the attention away from your stupid-assedness. Just tell me you got out of Sol's way as soon as you grabbed some clothes last night, and right now you're there simply because you stopped by to apologize."

The dead silence on the other end crawled up her spine and confirmed what she already knew.

"Joey, please tell me you did not…"

"I was too drunk to go anywhere last night. I passed out on the bed."

"But you left first thing this morning, right?" Bentley whined in exasperation, eager for his walk.

"Noooot exactly."

"You are *not* still staying there!" She took out her frustration on the luggage zipper, jerking open the compartment holding the dog's gear, and took his water bowl to the bathroom sink to fill it.

"I got nowhere to go and no way to get there 'cept on foot. Patsy's in Ramona's yard, and I'm sure that pit bull husband of hers is laying in wait to bite me in the ass. Sol refuses to help me get her back—"

"Oh good Lord, do not drag Sol into this. I drove all night to get down here, and I'm checked into a hotel. Give me a few minutes to walk Bentley, and I'll be by to pick you up. We'll go get Patsy."

"Forget that bullshit. You shouldn't've come, 'cause you're not going over there with me."

"Oh hell no!" Sol's voice, in its typical aggravated mode. "Give me that phone." There was a shuffling sound of the phone being passed, and then Sol's growl came over the line. "EmmyLou, this is Sol. Are you in Gulf Shores?"

"Yes, I am." She lifted her chin defiantly to

the reflection in the bathroom mirror. "I came to help Joey."

"That's completely uncalled for." He was all Mr. Take Control. And while her head wanted to tell him to mind his own business, everything below her neckline tingled appreciatively. But his sigh was pure aggravation, reminding her who she was speaking with. "All I need is another Fuller down here..." Emmy stiffened at his use of her real last name. What had Joey told him? "...needing me to take care of her during my relaxing time at the beach."

The last phrase was drenched in sarcasm, and she couldn't let the cut-down pass without a comeback. "As I recall, taking care of *my needs* wasn't one of your strong suits, Mr. Beecher." A total lie—Sol had been fabulous in bed. But he'd never called her back, so he'd get no accolades.

"Aw shit." Oh good Lord, Sol had handed the phone back to Joey. "See, I knew something had went on between you two. Don't tell me no more, 'cause I don't want to have to lay him out. I might need his help."

Emmy's reflection rolled its eyes. "No need to protect my honor, Joey. I'll be there to pick you up in a few minutes. Just do me a favor, and please don't tell Sol my history. I'm EmmyLou Creighton to everybody in Taylor's Grove. I'd like to keep it that way."

"Your secrets are safe with me, sis."

EmmyLou dropped into the desk chair with a groan, defeated. Joey could be totally clueless sometimes, bless his heart.

She was so screwed.

"AND ON THAT, I'm going to hang up. I'll be there in thirty minutes."

Joe Wayne recognized his sister's tone—the one that meant she had no confidence in what he'd told her, which was laughable considering it was her lack of confidence in herself that had spoiled everything. They could be making millions by now... He took a deep breath and let it go.

"See you in a few," he answered. "Love you."

"Love you, too."

"She'll be here in a half hour." He handed Sol the phone and turned his attention back to his sandwich. Or that's what he pretended to do. In reality, he studied the man sitting across from him.

So something had happened between Sol and EmmyLou. Something neither of them wanted to admit to. Well, the guy was a bit of a strange bird—but likable in spite of that hard-ass bullshit he put on. Like right then. He was sitting there, chewing his sandwich all slow, staring out at the Gulf like the sight had his total concentration. But Joe Wayne had seen his reaction when he heard EmmyLou was here. Something deep-rooted surfaced for an instant...something akin to fear. And he perked up when the topic of her secret hit his ears, although he played it cool like he hadn't really taken it in.

"Rocket-propelled grenade blew it off in Afghanistan." Sol's voice was low and even, like he was talking about that pelican he could see standing at the water's edge.

But the impact of the statement caused Joe Wayne's throat to close around the bite he'd just taken. He chugged half the bottle of water to wash it down. "I'm sorry, man."

Sol closed his eyes as if the words hurt him, and Joe Wayne saw the muscle in his jaw twitch as he opened them again. "You don't need to be sorry. You had nothing to do with it. I hate it when people are sorry."

"I mean I'm sorry for your loss," Joe Wayne explained.

"It's a leg. Save your mourning for people."

Joe Wayne understood his point, but he figured the best way of showing it was to not say anything.

He must've figured right, because Sol went on. "Nobody in Taylor's Grove knows I lost my leg. They think I caught a bullet and just have a bad limp."

"That's a helluva thing to keep quiet about."

"Can't stand for people to be sorry for me—the way you were just now. I stayed in Texas the first year and went to physical therapy to get used to the prosthesis. After that, it was easy to wear long pants and keep it hidden. And I don't ever talk about it."

"Which is why you didn't want EmmyLou coming down here."

Sol looked at him directly, and the side of his mouth rose in a partial smile. "Your sister's mouth is in constant motion."

Joe Wayne laughed. "A common Fuller family trait."

"So I've gathered." Sol gave a disgruntled sigh. "And now that she's coming over here, I'll have to get back into my jeans."

"How long's it been…since you lost it?"

"Eight years. During my second tour of duty."

Joe Wayne held his water bottle up in a salute. "I appreciate your sacrifice, man."

Sol shook his head. "Half a leg's a small a thing compared to what others gave."

Joe Wayne drank to him anyway and then took another bite with the understanding that the subject was closed. He liked this guy. He had an honorable air about him. "What happened between you and EmmyLou?"

"None of your business," came the answering growl.

Yep, honorable…with a heaping helping of ornery on the side.

CHAPTER FIVE

PARKING UP THE street in a black pickup truck with a pair of binoculars trained on Ramona's house was not the smartest reconnaissance plan Sol had ever been part of, but the Fullers had collectively vetoed his suggestion to get the police involved. So the next best option seemed to be to watch the house for Ramona's husband or both of them to leave and to hope for an unlocked door or window, which Joe Wayne seemed to think was likely.

Looking around the run-down neighborhood, Sol couldn't imagine such a scenario. This was a far cry from neat and tidy Taylor's Grove and his own house, which he'd bet had never been locked since the day his grandparents moved in. But it confirmed that his decision to follow Joe Wayne and EmmyLou had been the right move, despite her protests that she didn't need his protection.

Damn stubborn woman.

Joe Wayne came into view, slinking around the side of the house, head darting back and forth, guilty as sin and looking every inch the part. He sprinted to the edge of the driveway and up the street toward EmmyLou's car. Sol hurried from the truck to hear his report.

"She's in the backyard."

A break—finally! "Did you arrange to get your keys?"

Joe Wayne shook his head. "Not Ramona. Patsy. She's around back. And I seen the legs of my jeans laying out by the garbage, too. My guess is Ramona made herself a pair of shorts to get rid of the evidence." He caught his breath on a wistful sigh. "I heard her husband tell her they was out of baloney and somebody was gonna have to go get some. Maybe it'll be him. And maybe it'll be soon."

The temperature was creeping up to the point of being uncomfortable, and Sol was itching to get back to the beach house and the breeze off the Gulf…and the prospect of solitude once EmmyLou and her brother were out of his hair.

"I have an idea." EmmyLou's breathless exclamation raised his body temperature—and his disgruntled attitude—even more. "Let's call your phone, and when they answer, we'll pretend you're an undercover CIA agent." The brown of her eyes deepened with excitement, sending Sol's memory soaring back to the night they spent together, which, in turn, reminded him how far he'd dropped on her scale of desirability. "We'll say there's a bomb planted on the cycle and they need to move it to the road with the keys and the phone, and we'll come by and pick it up."

Sol mustered his most condescending snort. "That may be the most ludicrous idea I've ever heard."

"That so?" If the convertible top had been up on EmmyLou's car, she might've ripped it in her hasty exit from the driver's seat. "I don't hear you coming up with anything better. I drove all night to get here, and I'm going to have to do it again tonight to get home for work tomorrow. I'm ready to go back to my hotel room and get some sleep, but instead, we're standing around, roasting in this heat all afternoon, waiting for an event that might not happen." She slammed the door and leaned back on it, crossing her arms in a pose that was somehow beguiling in its belligerence.

"If you'd stayed home, you wouldn't be having to deal with this." Sol shifted his eyes to Joe Wayne. "Look, I'll just go to the door, and when she answers, I'll ask for the keys and your phone."

The male half of the Fullers squinted a wary eye. "What if *he* answers?"

Sol shrugged. "I'll ask to speak to Ramona."

"And he'll throttle you on the spot." Joe Wayne's shrug mocked his own. "No questions asked."

EmmyLou didn't say anything, only glared at Sol as she stomped around to the trunk of her car and got out a bag, slinging it across her shoulder.

"What's in there?" he asked.

"Hair tools and makeup. I'll tell Ramona she's won a makeover. When I get her alone, I'll tell her who I am and get the keys and the phone."

Joe Wayne's face broke into a pleased grin. "That just might work."

"No!" Sol exclaimed. Didn't the woman have any sense of danger? "You're not going in there."

"Watch me."

She walked fast. Sol had to break into his awkward jog to catch up with her. When he did, she turned a scowl in his direction. "And what do you think you're doing?"

"I'm not letting you go in there alone. I'm your assistant. Perry."

"My assistant is Demitri." Her scowl morphed into a smirk. "And he'd *never* let his hair look like that."

"Today he does." Sol couldn't recall if he'd combed his hair this morning…or yesterday. It was one of those things that didn't seem too important anymore.

The conversation stopped as they stepped onto the front stoop. EmmyLou rapped on the door as Sol let out a sharp breath.

THE WOMAN WHO answered the door had obviously been a real looker at one time, but her features had settled into a premature hardness that aged her maybe a decade, if Emmy was any judge… and she usually was. The husband hovered a few feet in the background, looking even meaner than he'd sounded over the phone.

"Hi there." Emmy gave a warm smile and extended her hand. "Ramona?"

The woman didn't return the smile or take her hand. Instead she scanned Emmy from head to toe and back. "Who's asking?"

"I'm Chloe Cramer from the Beauty Bar Salon, and this is my assistant, Demitri. Ramona's name was drawn as the winner of a surprise makeover from our salon. Is she here?"

"A makeover? No shit?" Ramona's smile softened her face and gave a glimmer of the pretty girl she used to be. "I'm Ramona. Come on in."

Emmy shot Sol a triumphant grin. This was going to work. She stepped inside with him close at her elbow. Lifting her chin confidently, she covered the distance to the giant man in the Save The Squirrels, Eat More Possum T-shirt, whose tattoo-covered arm muscles bulged as he crossed them over his broad chest. "And you must be the lucky guy in this pretty woman's life."

"Naw, I'm her husband," he snarled.

Emmy wasn't sure if he'd meant that as a joke,

but she kept her smile fixed. She hadn't realized Ramona had moved to stand beside her, and she gave a startled jump when the woman's hand squeezed her arm.

"Are you going to do it here? Right now? I never won nothing before. This is the best thing that ever happened to me!" The woman actually squealed with delight.

"I...uh. Well, actually, we usually try to do it when the husband isn't home, so the final look is a surprise for him, as well." Emmy's mouth was moving so fast, she just let it go and prayed what she said sounded plausible. "If we can move somewhere more private and work out the details, we'll figure out a better time for us to come back."

"How long you need?" The husband threw a menacing look Sol's direction that caused Emmy to shudder. "I don't like leaving my wife with a strange man in the house any longer than I have to."

Augh! She should've anticipated that Sol's hotness would be a liability. "Oh, you don't have to worry about Demitri. Does he, love?" She forced a giggle and patted Sol's chest before turning back to the brute. "He's head-over-heels in love with his husband, and they make absolutely the most adorable couple you've ever laid eyes on."

The man's eyes narrowed, making the grin he

turned on Sol more threatening. "Yeah. I figured as much." His eyes darted to Emmy. "So, how long you need?"

"An hour," she said.

"And a half," Sol added, his voice sounding an octave lower than usual. "We don't want to have to rush."

"I'm going for a beer." The husband brushed past them, deliberately bumping hard into Sol, who stumbled against Emmy but quickly righted himself.

"Pick up some baloney while you're out," Ramona called before the door slammed, and then the questions bubbled out of her. "Are you gonna do color? And cut it? I've been thinking about going shorter. And will you do makeup, too?"

Emmy waited until she heard the vehicle start up outside, then held up her hand for Ramona to stop. "Ramona, I'm sorry. I'm actually Joe Wayne Fuller's sister, and I'm here to get his phone and the keys to his motorcycle."

Ramona pulled back, her face hardening into the old crone again. "You mean there ain't no makeover? You lied about all this just to get the stuff from me?"

"Well, yeah." Emmy shot a *help me* look at Sol, but he just smiled and crossed his arms over his chest. "I hate to do it, but we couldn't think of any other way to get to you without making your husband suspicious."

Ramona jerked her phone out of her back pocket. "I oughta call him back here right now and let him whip both your asses. Get out of here before I decide to do just that."

"But Joey needs his phone and his keys." If the woman had any affection for her brother, maybe this technique would work.

Ramona stomped her foot. "And I need a damn makeover."

"Come on." Sol pulled Emmy's arm, but she stood firm.

"No." She shook her head with a sigh, accepting what she had to do. "I *am* really a stylist with my own salon, so if a makeover is what it's going to take, you'll get a makeover." She unzipped the bag and pulled out the box of color she'd picked up for a client yesterday. "The only color I have in my bag is Red Hot Red."

"That'll suit me just fine…probably." Ramona grinned. "Make me happy, and you'll get what you came for."

SOL BREATHED IN a gulp of the afternoon heat, thankful to be leaving the place with all of his teeth intact. It had been touch and go for a while, but Emmy's plan had worked.

She held up the keys and phone, flashing them

in the sunlight. Joey let out a whoop and came running from the cover of the bushes.

"You did it!" He grabbed his sister in a tight hug. "Thank you. Thank you!"

"You know I'm here for you, sugar." She swatted his backside. "Now go get Patsy. Husband's due back any minute."

"Whooeee, yeah! I'm coming for you, Patsy! Daddy's here." Joe Wayne darted around the corner of the house as Sol and Emmy headed back toward their cars at the end of the street.

She cast Sol a sidelong glance. "Gonna admit you were wrong? My idea turned out to be a winner."

"I admit I was wrong." Sol stopped and, covering his heart with his hand, gave a slight bow. "You're a wizard. That woman looked like a different person by the time you got finished."

EmmyLou raised her hands in front of her and flashed him a wicked smile. "Some people say I've got magic in these hands."

His groin clenched with need at her comment, but before he could respond verbally, Joe Wayne tore out of Ramona's backyard on Patsy, giving a war whoop and a thumbs-up as he passed.

Sol decided to let Emmy's last comment go unchallenged and changed the subject. "So, did this flash of genius really come to you here? Do you always travel with your tools?" He pointed to the bag slung over her shoulder.

"I keep this one in my trunk because I go to homeless shelters and nursing homes pretty often. Sometimes the school there in town."

Her kindness touched him, but the warm glow immediately turned to an irritated flare as he realized he seemed to be the only person in the world not on the receiving end of it. She was always bent on knocking him down, no matter the situation. "Playing me as a gay guy to those people was a bit unfair, don't you think?"

Her laugh held no remorse. "He believed it, didn't he?" They reached her car and popped the trunk, slinging her bag into it. "And now I'll be on my way."

Looking closely at her face, Sol could see the tired lines around her eyes. "You're not heading home right now, are you? You're in no shape to drive."

"Nope. I'm going back to the hotel and sleeping until midnight. That's a full eight hours, so I'll be fine." She pointed to the car parked too close behind her. "Will you watch me out?"

Sol directed her back slowly until she had room to pull forward onto the street. As she gave him a wave of thanks and goodbye, he ignored the fleeting feeling of regret that she wasn't staying a little longer.

He stalked back to his truck and unlocked his door just as a pickup pulled alongside his.

Ramona's husband.

"Hey, Demitri."

Sol's neck hairs rose with apprehension at the menacing tone. He jerked the driver's door open but couldn't get in quick enough.

For such a big guy, Ramona's husband moved fast. He ran around his vehicle, and his fist connected with Sol's nose before Sol could pivot out of the way.

Crunch!

Pain and a multitude of colored lights exploded behind Sol's eyes. He lost his balance and staggered backward, coming up against the side of his truck. The metallic taste of blood coated his tongue, and the hand that he raised to his face soon dripped with red.

"We don't like your kind around here. Go away and stay away, you hear?" He didn't wait for an answer. Climbing back in his truck, he roared up the street.

Clenching his teeth shot pain through Sol's cheekbone that drilled into the sinus cavity straight into the damn-this-is-excruciating center of his brain. He found a sweaty handkerchief in his back pocket and used it to catch the blood that poured from his nose like someone had turned on a faucet. Without a doubt, it was broken. He typed *Hospital* into his GPS and waited while the routing loaded.

"Thank you, EmmyLou Creighton." He ground the words out through the pain.

The woman's name had become synonymous with torture in his private lexicon. He would get even with her if it was the last thing he did.

And between her shenanigans and her brother's, it very well might be.

NO MATTER THE story behind it, Sol had taken the punch meant for him, Joe Wayne learned when he stopped back by the beach house late that afternoon. He couldn't let that pass without showing his gratitude. And so, despite Sol's pretend anger and mock protestation, Joe Wayne had decided to stay an additional night at the beach house. He'd fixed a nice dinner from the provisions Sol had on hand—steak on the grill, baked potatoes, salad, and fresh fruit for dessert. He'd opened Dad's wine cabinet and served one of the best reds in the house. And now, as they sat on the deck, he strummed his guitar and serenaded his new friend, who sported a swollen nose and two black eyes on his behalf. In between songs he filled their glasses—the good crystal stuff, not what they left out for renters—with Dad's cherished Four Roses.

Yessirree, Sol Beecher was a helluva man. He

walked taller on one leg than most men did on two. Fact was, he was exactly the kind of man Dad had always wanted EmmyLou to end up with. Too bad there was so much bad blood between them.

"That's the night… I remember…best of all." He strummed the final chord of the song and let it drift away on the warm night breeze from the Gulf.

Sol rested on a chaise with his head tilted back. His friend gave a grunt of approval, which Joe Wayne had already learned was about as complimentary as the stubborn mule got. "You ever think of trying to go professional?" Sol asked. "Being from Nashville, don't you know people who know people?"

Joe Wayne took a sip of the bourbon to ease the tension that popped up in his jaw at the question. "I *am* a professional. Small-town bars and honky-tonks, mostly. No major gigs in a helluva long time," he admitted. "But I make enough to eat on and to buy enough gas to move on to the next place."

"You live out of motels?" Sol lifted his head and eyed him directly, looking like a raccoon with something on his mind.

"Not usually enough money for a motel room." Joe Wayne shook his head, but he couldn't hold back the grin. "There's always a woman wanting to take the star home with her and take care of his needs."

"Sounds like a lonely life."

"Something else we have in common." Joe Wayne strummed another chord, fleshing out a new song with a few plucks and the emotion weighing on his heart. "Lonely men…lonely women…settlin' down…on Lonely Street. Not an end…not a beginnin'…just a hope…someday they'll meet."

"Never heard that one," Sol said.

"Just made it up." Joe Wayne fingered the tune playing in his head. It would probably be gone by morning. Alcohol was an effective eraser. He brought the song to a close.

Sol clapped a couple of times—high praise from Mr. Surly. "Ever play in front of a big crowd?"

That one took a swig to answer. "Ever heard of the Grand Ole Opry?"

Sol nodded and then hissed in pain and took another gulp.

"Eighteen years ago, me and EmmyLou shared that sacred circle."

His companion sat up real quick-like and drew a sharp breath between clenched teeth. "You and EmmyLou performed at the Grand Ole Opry?"

"In the circle." Joe Wayne couldn't hide the pride even if he wanted to…which he didn't. "Ever hear of The Fullers?"

He watched recognition dawn in his companion's eyes. "Hell, yeah. I had some of their CDs."

"*Our* CDs." He tapped his chest with his finger. "Me and EmmyLou's."

Sol was all Mr. Interested now. He straddled the chair—maneuvering his artificial leg almost as well as his real one—and cradled his bourbon between his hands. "What happened?"

"Well, ya see, I was good, but EmmyLou was the draw." Joe Wayne's jaw was flapping loose as a goose now, his mind running through rationalizations that would justify giving up his sister's story. "Hell, you saw the pictures of her in there on the wall. Beauty queen with the voice of an angel." Sol would understand her better if he knew. And besides, EmmyLou… EmmyLou and Mama…had blown everything way out of proportion. What happened wasn't *that* big a deal—hardly a deal at all, actually.

He tried to wash away the bitterness on his tongue with another sip. Nope, still there. He gulped, and the bourbon surrounded his anger, making it palatable and much easier to swallow. And it slowed him down. "But this ain't my story to tell. Ask EmmyLou." A few strums on the guitar, and the tension released in his arms and neck, his back and his hands. "What was that song I had going a minute ago?"

"Lonely men…lonely women," his companion sang in a voice that wasn't half-bad, but not half-good, either.

Joe Wayne's fingers took off on a different tangent, the first tune lost in the marine fog in his brain. "Not half-bad...not half-good...life's weird math just don't add up. Not half-sad...not half-happy... 'less I'm sipping from a cup. Bourbon helps to fill the spaces...helps my mind to wander free. One good slurp and I'm expoundin'... on life's geometry."

CHAPTER SIX

THE NINE-HOUR DRIVE back to Taylor's Grove was as uneventful as Sol's week had been once Joe Wayne left. No traffic jams. Very little construction. Bright sunshine the entire way. Even the diner he'd stopped at in northern Alabama had food that rivaled the one at home.

Yet, with all the rightness surrounding him, his world was a half bubble off plumb. Because of EmmyLou Creighton Fuller.

He couldn't get the damn woman out of his mind.

True to his word, Joe Wayne left after the Patsy caper, though not for a couple of days. But when he did, he locked up the family suite and all its secrets therein.

That door—and the woman it had come to symbolize—was sealed off, which frustrated the living hell out of Sol.

So she had secrets. Hell, everybody had secrets. He sported one of the biggest ones around. Over and over—when he was drunk—Joe Wayne had reminded him that he'd lost his leg in an honorable endeavor. *"Nuthin' to be ashamed of."*

He wasn't ashamed. He simply didn't want all that hero attention.

But the next time Joe Wayne and his sister got together…if there was any drinking involved—and, of course, with Joe Wayne there would be—the information would undoubtedly be divulged. Probably in the form of a ballad. Oh, yeah, Joe Wayne had sworn that the Patsy fiasco made them blood brothers of a sort, and implied that the status gave Sol an exemption from being discussed. But the saying "Liquor is quicker" seemed to have been invented with Joe Wayne in mind.

And how long would EmmyLou's mouth be able to hang on to such a juicy bit of news?

Only until the next time it opened…which was never a long wait.

The answer lay in finding a way to keep the woman quiet, and the closer he got to home, the more urgent the need became.

He turned off the radio in his truck, needing the silence to concentrate.

The secret behind the private suite's door would've given him leverage. Each time he passed it, he paused to look over the structure and assess its weakness, fiddling with the real estate agent box, trying every random combination that came into his head. None worked.

The greatest frustration came from the assurance that the harder he tried not to think about the mystery of EmmyLou, the more obsessed he became. She was the human equivalent of the real estate agent box, and all he needed was the right combination.

One entire rainy afternoon even found him searching the term *EmmyLou Fuller* on his phone. What little information the query turned up was fifteen years old or more. She and Joe Wayne had a couple of big hits on the country music charts. She'd participated in beauty contests from the time she was five until she was seventeen but never went on to any of the big ones like Miss Tennessee.

Her life involved no huge scandal as far as he could tell. She hadn't been kicked out of pageants for drinking or having sex with the judges.

One day she simply slipped from public view and was forgotten. So why the name change?

He supposed he could hold what little he knew about her over her head—a preemptive strategy to have in place when Joe Wayne put his real sister before his fake blood brother. But letting her know that he *had* something on her before it even came up seemed like overreaction.

Or maybe he should just level with her. *I don't*

want people to know about my fake leg just like you don't want people to know about your fake name. Deal?

And he could watch himself slide from half man to no man at all in her perspective in a matter of seconds. Or worse, she'd start being kind to him and giving him that pitying look.

Oh hell no.

Despite the fact that it aggravated him, the one thing he *liked* about EmmyLou Creighton was how she didn't cut him any slack because of his bum leg. Except the day her dog had humped it— she'd seemed sympathetic then. He'd hated that.

The Cadiz exit appeared, and Sol left I-24 to make the rest of the trip on two-lane roads. As he approached the stop sign at the bottom of the ramp, he glanced at the rearview mirror.

What he saw wasn't so much his own reflection with two bluish-green bruises circling his eyes and a piece of adhesive tape holding his nose in place. Instead, it was the answer he'd been searching for.

He grinned at the painful sight.

"JOE WAYNE WENT on and on about your friend he met at the beach house. Sol?"

Her mom's mention of Joey and Sol in the same sentence brought a flush to Emmy's face. The thought of her brother's hijinks was bad enough, but adding Sol Beecher to the images made her want to crawl in a hole…or seek a new identity. Again.

"Sol's not really a friend," she corrected her mother, sensing the turn this conversation was about to make. "Just a guy from Taylor's Grove."

"Well, Joe Wayne told us he's not married, and he's around forty." *Yes, indeed. Thar she blows!* "I never dreamed that Podunk town you moved to might have an eligible bachelor near your age. You shouldn't let this opportunity pass you by. Lord knows, you've let *that* happen too often— and I'm not just talking in the marriage department."

The long-familiar tightness in her gut, which always accompanied a visit or phone call from her mom, twisted into an ache. "This isn't an opportunity, Mama."

"Nothing ever *is* with you. That's exactly the kind of failure talk that got you where you are. Nowhere."

EmmyLou bit back the retort on the tip of her tongue. Mama never heard when she talked about her successful salon or how much she loved living in her beautiful home on the outskirts of the friendly village. If it didn't somehow bring direct attention to Mama, it was considered a failure. Emmy had learned the rules of engagement long ago.

A blessed beep sounded in her ear. "Hey, I've got another call, so I'll have to let you go. Tell Dad I love him. Bye."

"Think about what I said." Her mom rushed and got in the last word…as always.

Emmy tapped the button without checking the caller ID. "Hello?"

"Hey, EmmyLou. It's Sol."

Out of the frying pan, into the fire. Heat surged through her at the sound of the wolf-like growl. She gritted her teeth. "Hi there. You back? And all in one piece?"

A long pause brought the hairs on the back of her neck to attention. "You talked to your brother."

"Yeah. I'm sorry about your nose—"

"Oh. That. Yeah, it doesn't help my looks any." She heard him draw a long breath. "So if you're home, I'll bring the key by."

"I am. Out by the pool," she lied, but it wouldn't be a lie for long. She headed for her closet. "Just pull on around to the end of the drive, and you won't even have to get out." She had it all planned. He'd get an eyeful as she walked from the pool to his truck, and Bentley wouldn't have a chance to hump his bad leg again.

"Be there in a minute," came the gruff reply.

All she had to do was slip into her gold bikini and run to dive into the pool. She'd known Sol would be dropping by sometime today, so she'd done her waterproof makeup first thing after her shower. Her hair was pulled back into a cute, calculated bun that would keep its shape when wet.

On the way to the pool, she called Bentley, who came running from somewhere upstairs, as she grabbed the thermal glass of iced tea from the fridge and the magazines from the island.

She arranged everything around the chaise and then dove from the diving board to gain that sun-kissed glisten. Bentley jumped in from the side and dog-paddled to the steps. He shook himself and sprawled out on the warm concrete while she settled into the chaise and thumbed leisurely through the magazine. By the time she heard Sol's truck in her driveway, she was confident she and her canine companion looked as though they'd been out there all day.

Her timing was a tad off. As she rose from her chair, Sol was getting out of his truck, so he missed the beginning of her entrance. And with him standing outside his truck, she wouldn't get to lean over toward his driver's side window. *Oh well.* She started her slow, seductive walk.

Bentley darted past her, barking a happy greeting to the visitor.

Oh good Lord! Not the hump again! She broke into a sprint to catch him before he reached Sol, but she was too slow.

This time Sol was prepared, though. He knelt down and turned his entire attention to the cheerful pup, giving scratches behind the ears. He bent his head back, eyes closed, keeping out of range of Bentley's slurpy kisses—and missed Emmy's approach entirely.

She caught Bentley's collar, got him calmed while Sol rose awkwardly and pretended not to notice the stagger as he fought for his balance.

So it wasn't until both of them stilled that she saw his face. "Oh my God!" She covered her mouth to keep from crying out again at the sight. Sol's deep-set eyes were ringed with multicolored bruises that arched down into his cheekbones. His swollen nose was taped, but the part that peeked from under the bandage was bruised a darker hue than his eyes. "You look awful."

"Should've seen me Tuesday." He grinned—or, at least, the corners of his mouth stretched apart to show his teeth. It was not a good look on his normally handsome face.

"Quit smiling," she shuddered. "Your face is so swollen, when you smile it makes you look like a goat." Bentley jerked her arm, having turned his attention toward a squirrel. She let him go, and he took off across the yard toward a giant maple.

"You let him run loose?" The genuine worry in Sol's voice for her dog softened her, but the warm fuzzy was gone an instant later when he added the admonishment, "You shouldn't do that. He'll run out on the road and get killed."

"He never goes anywhere near the road." She swept her arm toward the front of her property, then brought it back to rest on her hip, striking a subtle pose. "The underground fence runs smack through the middle of the front yard since he has all this area in the back." She swung around to face him, but his eyes remained on the distant fields that were part of his own property. "And most of the time he has on the collar that goes with the fence. Today he doesn't because we're swimming." Her gesture toward her bikini went unnoticed. Hell's bells, what did it take to get this guy's attention? "But he doesn't seem to know the difference. He's learned to stay inside the fence boundary even when he doesn't have the collar on. I'm gonna try the same technique on the next guy I date."

A snort! At least it was something.

"Well, if he turns out to be somebody you care about, keep that boundary far away from Joe Wayne. Trouble follows your brother around like a dog at heel."

It was EmmyLou's turn to snort. She nodded her agreement, and their eyes tangled for a moment. She'd forgotten how drop-dead gorgeous his light brown eyes were—sort of a creamy caramel that made her mouth water. She closed the space between them by lowering her voice to a more intimate level and touched her fingertips to his arm. He visibly straightened. "I'm so sorry about your nose and all Joe Wayne put you through," she said.

Sol leaned toward her ever so slightly. "I thought you might feel that way. So…" He dug in his pocket and pulled out the key, dropping it into her hand. "Here's your key." He took a folded piece of paper from his shirt pocket and handed it to her. "And my bill."

"Your *bill*?" What the Sam Hill was he trying to pull? She opened the paper to find an itemized list of numbers.

Sol gripped his hips and gave his head a sorrowful shake. "I paid six thousand dollars for a chance to win a week in your house. That should've given me seven nights to do what I wanted. Instead, I had to play nursemaid to your brother and only ended up with three nights to myself." He pointed to the top figure. "I extrapolated—" *what the hell did that mean?* "—by dividing the original six thousand one hundred ninety by seven. That comes to eight hundred eighty-four dollars a day—I didn't bother with the cents—times four, which comes to three thousand five hundred thirty-six dollars." He slid his finger down the list, ignoring Emmy's glare. *The nerve!* "Joe Wayne ate the groceries I bought and drank an entire bottle of Four Roses bourbon that belonged to me. He also drank the one belonging to your dad, by the way. Then, of course, there was the little incident of my broken nose…"

"That was *your* fault!" Emmy punched a finger toward his face, making him flinch. "You should've just gotten in your truck and driven away."

Sol gave her a smile—nothing worse than a condescending goat. "The guy moved faster than my leg would allow. And it was *you* who made up that cockamamie story about me and my husband."

"It was the only thing I could think of on short notice."

"I figured," he said quietly and then leaned toward her, his face hovering just a couple of inches above hers. "That's why I lowered that charge to a thousand." He straightened, and the air she didn't realize she'd been holding stuttered back into her lungs. "Which makes the grand total—" he pointed to the last figure on the paper "—four thousand eight hundred twenty-three dollars."

She wadded the paper in her fist and thrust it into his face. "I'm not paying this."

He shrugged. "Suit yourself." He opened the door to his truck, but before he got in, he turned back toward her. "The people who ran that school raffle will be awfully upset when they hear what a joke their grand prize turned out to be. Your generous donation will be the laughingstock of Marshall County. And you with it."

EmmyLou threw down the paper and stomped all over it while he backed out of her drive, waiting until he was out of sight before she picked it up and smoothed it out for another look.

Absurd! She wasn't paying this. It wouldn't stand up in a court of law, would it?

A horrifying image flashed across her brain— the salon, boarded up and closed with For Sale scrawled in red across plywood covering the windows.

She stomped over to her phone and snatched it up, punching Joey's number.

IT TOOK JOE WAYNE a few seconds to figure out where he was. The fog from last night's drunk still clogged his head. He'd left the beach house how long ago? Thursday. Rode straight to… Gadsden. Knox's house. His brother and new girlfriend… Rocky? Roxy?…headed to Talladega on Friday. He'd been here by himself two nights. That made today Sunday…probably. With his eyes still closed to the light pounding nails into his brain, he fumbled for his phone, relieved to find the uncomfortable lump under his right rib cage.

A quick peek at the display assured him that today was indeed Sunday.

Whew! Still in good shape. One more night here and then on to Mama and Dad's guest house in Nashville.

A couple of calls yesterday landed him three nights of gigs in northwestern Tennessee, but they didn't start until Thursday.

The Break-'Em-Up Bar on the outskirts of Clarksville was always packed with military types from nearby Fort Campbell, Kentucky. It had a reputation as a brawling place—hence the name—and the last time Joe Wayne played there, a fight had broken out between some of the locals and some of the transplants. Joe Wayne had continued singing until a beer bottle missed his head by a half inch. The tips were good, the beer was free and the management paid him in cash. And to top it off, he'd left with the woman who'd thrown the bottle. She admitted, with the sexiest little giggle, that she'd just been trying to get his attention.

Lee Anne? Raye Anne? Something Anne.

Maybe she'd be there again. If not, he'd get a cheap motel room.

The phone vibrated in his hand. Thank God he'd had the wherewithal to turn off the damn ringer last night.

"'Lo?"

"Joey, Sol just left here, and guess what he gave me?" EmmyLou was talking real loud, and Joe Wayne laid the phone on his pillow. He recognized her tone. It meant you really didn't have to answer even if she asked a question.

"A bill! Yeah...you heard me right. He presented me with a freaking bill because he said you stayed with him at the beach house for *four nights*! Four nights? Are you kidding me? He made a six-thousand-dollar donation to the school and won that prize, and now he's implying that we reneged on the prize because he didn't get to relax and so he's charging four nights back to us. Then he goes on to say that you ate his food and you drank his liquor...and he's blaming me for his broken nose. So...what do you have to say for yourself?"

Joe Wayne rolled over to face the phone. "Sol's a good guy."

"Sol's an idiot!" she fumed. "If he thinks I'm paying this bill, he's crazy. But if he pushes it— and he's ornery enough to do so—I don't have four thousand dollars lying around. You're gonna have to pay the biggest part of it."

Joe Wayne didn't feel any of the urgency he heard in his sister's voice. Sol Beecher was peevish, but he wasn't mean. This just sounded like the kind of stunt he'd pull to get under Emmy-

Lou's skin…and it was working. "I don't have no money, sis. You can't get blood from a turnip."

"What if he sues me or something? You don't know how vindictive he can be."

"What do you mean?"

"He wants revenge…because I sold all those raffle tickets and ran the total way up after he'd promised to match it."

Joe Wayne grinned at his sister's antics. "Sounds like you're the one who's vin-dick-ted. I mean, you also told Ramona's husband he was gay, which got his nose broke."

"Auf!" The sound she made when she was pissed. "I was trying to help *you.*"

"And I love you for it. But you and Sol are gonna have to work this out between y'all."

"I am *not* getting stuck with your debts…"

And I'm not getting stuck with your lies… I'll just be on my way…sorry that I couldn't stay… but I'm not getting stuck in your sighs.

Words…tune…it all came rushing into his head at once. "Gotta go, sis." He ended the call and hit the video button, singing the verse and the chorus into the phone while recording it. Sol's idea…a good one.

He laid the phone on the nightstand and threw his arm over his head. It was a little after three o'clock. Another hour of shut-eye. Then he'd get up and see if he could stretch those lyrics into a whole song.

And he'd think more on the other idea that just came to him, too.

A visit to EmmyLou just might be the destination of choice after Clarksville.

CHAPTER SEVEN

EMMY'S DAY STARTED EARLY, and every minute from waking until now had been filled—with exercise, customers, errands, taking Bentley to the doggie park and grocery shopping.

She'd earned this reward, so she eased down into the full-body lounge area of the hot tub, careful to keep the icy beer in her hand above the water as the heat encased her. "Mmm, this feels soooo good."

Bentley poked his nose into her hair in response and sniffed, which made him sneeze. Then he trotted off and plopped down near the back steps, letting out a long sigh. Apparently he was as tired as she was. His soft snore soon drifted her way.

The beer numbed the neurons in her brain enough to slow down the snapping of the synapses that occurred each time she thought about Sol Beecher and his damn bill. And she'd thought of little else over the past few days. Though her work time passed smoothly, his smirk met her mind's eye every unguarded moment. She'd gritted her teeth until her jaws ached, and now she dropped her head back and adjusted the inflation of the pillow until it cradled her neck perfectly. She turned the jets to high and tried to alternate her focus between humming and deep breathing.

One set of pulsing liquid fingers moved up her spine and then back down into the small of her back while another swirled around her calves and thighs. A hard, masculine form doing delicious things to her body would've been preferable, but even the tiniest inkling of such thoughts drove Sol into her mind with the force of a Mack truck.

She finally gave in and allowed her mind to wander to memories of her one time with Sol, and as she did, the tension drained away until only a jellylike substance remained where her tight muscles had been. Where had she gone wrong with him? She'd played the vixen part just like she always had with every man she'd been with. And he'd been enamored...until the morning after, when he'd become one of those jerks she'd heard about who couldn't wait for you to wake up and get out. Love 'em and let 'em go—that was Sol Beecher in a nutshell.

At least it had been until his last tour of duty in Afghanistan. He'd come back with that bad limp and a worse attitude, and he hadn't been out with a woman in eight years. Taylor's Grove kept close tabs on its own, and if he'd had a date, the town would have known. He certainly hadn't gotten *it* shot off like some people speculated, either. She'd deliberately brushed against him in crowds—enough to know that his well-endowed man parts were alive and kicking.

She figured he'd gotten his heart broken by a woman over there. Maybe the femme fatale pushed him out the door with a "See ya" that implied the word *sucker*. That pleasant image of Sol being brought to his knees relaxed her even more. She gave in to the blessed drowsiness and closed her eyes.

She wasn't sure how long she was out—the moon's position overhead said it couldn't have been much more than a few minutes—but her body came to full attention as soon as her eyes popped open. Something wasn't right. She switched off the jets and listened. Cicadas singing. Crickets chirping. Bullfrogs croaking. All normal summer sounds.

With something missing.

She shot to a standing position, naked and dripping in the center of the hot tub as she turned a full three hundred sixty degrees. "Bentley!" she screamed.

But he was gone.

THE WATER OF Kentucky Lake was warmer than the Gulf had been, though nowhere near as clear.

Sol relaxed on his back, drifting around the cove with little thought to danger. No damn jellyfish to watch out for…just the occasional water moccasin. But he'd grown up on this cove and knew to avoid the east end, where the tangle of dead willow and underbrush created a haven for snakes and turtles and offered some of the best crappie fishing on the lake if you were in a boat…which he wasn't.

The air mattress had been a second thought, but a good one. As strong as his arms were, his stamina wasn't what it used to be. But last week at the beach had awakened a craving in him to be back in the water. Not on it. *In* it. Sure, swimming alone at night was dangerous, but nothing like the shark-infested waters of Taylor's Grove gossip, so he'd take his chances.

Last week had awakened a lot of things.

For eight years, he'd been focused on one thing only—his leg. Learning to walk on it. Accepting life with it. Adjusting to working at the marina with it. Keeping it hidden. He'd forgotten there was a world out there with adventures and experiences. Hell. Hard as it was to admit, the whole motorcycle and broken nose chaos had been kind of…not fun, exactly…but exciting. For a while, his focus had shifted from himself to other people and their problems. He'd been a part of the body rather than the prosthetic leg of humanity.

And he'd decided that come fall, he would look for a job that would surround him with people. Maybe he could be a hunting and fishing guide. Nobody knew this area of western Kentucky like he did.

And one more thing had been awakened, much as he tried to ignore it. His desire—*need*—for a woman. But having a woman meant giving up his secret. And giving up his secret meant pity.

And by some ironic twist of fate, the woman he couldn't get out of his mind was the same woman who wouldn't have given him the time of day if he'd had a clock embedded in his forehead.

EmmyLou Creighton Fuller. *Damn, she was cute when she was mad.* The look on her face when she figured out he'd given her a bill? Priceless.

He chuckled, and a responding sound broke the stillness of the night. A bark?

He paddled around to face the shoreline where, sure enough, a dog pranced up and down, tail wagging.

EmmyLou's dog.

"Buckley?" *No, it's some country music singer's name.* "Brooks?" *That isn't right, either.*

The dog gave a happy bark and plunged in, swimming toward him as fast as its dog paddle would carry it.

"Shoo!" Sol sat up and waved his hands toward the shore. "Beat it. Go home."

The dog ignored him—EmmyLou's influence, no doubt.

She'd said Sunday that he wore a collar connected to her underground fence. The bright moonlight showed no collar.

It didn't take but a few seconds to put together the scenario. With no collar, the dog had escaped, and his mama would be frantically searching. If EmmyLou was headed this way, Sol had to get out of here fast.

He rolled to his stomach. The dog was almost even with him as he started paddling toward shore. "C'mon, boy. Let's go back," he coaxed, and the dog gave a whimper as Sol passed him headed in the opposite direction.

The animal's labored breathing was a worry. Sol had never heard of a dog drowning, but it surely could happen. He stopped and waited for the dog to make an about-face. "Come here," he grumbled as he maneuvered to a sitting position. His companion moved up beside him, and Sol reached over and hoisted the exhausted heap of fur onto the air mattress. The dog's sigh was pure appreciation. He swiped Sol's inner thigh with his tongue.

Sol pressed his torso firmly against the dog to get his arms far enough into the water to paddle.

The racing heart of the tired animal eased his aggravation some, even when his overpowering right leg kept making their progression toward shore more of a zigzag than a straight line.

With his breathing finally back to normal, the dog sat up and turned to lick Sol's face. The air mattress hissed—punctured by a toenail—and the next moment they were both in the water swimming again. Thankfully they weren't too far from shore, but Sol still felt the burn of exertion—a damn good burn.

EmmyLou's dog beat him to the sand and met him with kisses as Sol crawled from the water onto the towel he'd spread out and left dry shorts on, all the while making plans as to how to get the animal home.

The back of his pickup would be the best option. As if the smart-ass dog heard and understood his thoughts, it immediately rushed and jumped into the cab of the truck through the door Sol had left open after he removed his prosthesis and donned the crutches.

"Damn it, dog!" he called over his shoulder. "Get your wet ass out of my truck."

He woofed back his friendly but proud refusal.

It took some doing, but Sol finally managed to shimmy out of the wet swimsuit—not an easy feat while remaining seated but nigh to impossible balancing on one leg. He dried off and maneuvered back into his shorts, making plans all the while. The shorts would require him to stay in his truck when he got to EmmyLou's. In fact, he'd call her and have her meet him in the driveway.

Pulling his phone from the pocket of his shorts, he thumbed the number that, ironically, showed the greatest number of recent calls to his phone.

"Hello?" The word was breathy, anxious, and Sol cringed at his body's reaction to the sound.

"EmmyLou. It's Sol. I have your dog."

"Oh thank God!" Was she crying? "I just started looking for him! I fell asleep in the hot tub." That information shot straight to Sol's already-under-attack groin. "And when I woke up, he was gone. I ran right into the house to put some clothes on."

Whoa! Full-blown erection! Sol hissed, pulling in his breath through his teeth.

"I figured he might be headed your direction." She was still blabbering, oblivious to the effect she was having on a man whose sexual need ranked eleven on a ten-point scale. "So I've struck out through that field on the east side of your property."

"Actually, we're down by the lake."

She gave a strangled cry. "Oh no! Is he okay?"

"He's fine. I have my truck, so I'll bring him home. Just meet me in your driveway."

"Okay. Thank you so much. I don't know wh—oh, wait. I hear him. Bentley?"

Sol craned his neck to look back at his truck. Sure enough, the damn animal was gone. Good riddance. The next bark came in stereo—one ear catching the sound in the air and the other through the phone.

"Bentley! Over here, precious!" EmmyLou called again as Sol held the phone away from his ear. "He's close by. I'll get him home. Thanks, Sol."

The phone went dead.

Sol nodded and slipped his phone back into his pocket. Shifting his weight onto his knee, he grabbed the crutches and pulled himself to a standing position. He moved carefully around the uneven ground, gathering his wet things and throwing them across his shoulder. Then he started to the cab, already fuming about the mess he would find there.

He pushed the door completely open and flipped on the interior light.

His breath exploded from his lungs.

"Oh hell no!"

His prosthesis. He'd left it right there on the seat.

The damn dog must've pulled it out when he ran off. But a quick look around didn't show it lying anywhere near the driver's side of the truck.

He went around the truck once, then widened the area illuminated by the moonlight. No sign of it anywhere.

"Damn! Damn! Damn!" Pounding his fist on the roof of the truck punctuated his words but did nothing to lessen his frustration.

Reaching inside the truck bed, he jerked the huge flashlight from its holder and flipped it on, scanning the area and locating what might have been a vague line of compressed weeds. He followed the trail where it disappeared into a line of thick foliage consisting largely of wild rose. Thorny wild rose.

The prosthesis would most likely have gotten caught in the brambles, and the dog would've given up on his ten-thousand-dollar throwing stick.

He imagined for a moment EmmyLou's cute, angry face if he handed her *that* bill.

Which, of course, he never would.

No, instead he'd have to dig around in his closet to find the old prosthesis—the one he hated wearing because it was heavier and didn't fit well anymore. He'd have to come out here tomorrow once the sun came up, lugging the tools he would need to cut through that mess, and he'd have to sit on his ass to get the job done. But he'd find that prosthesis one way or another.

He picked his way carefully back to the truck, climbed in and started the motor.

He was about to shift the truck into gear when a sharp rap on the window stole his breath. He jerked his head toward the sound to find Emmy-Lou leaning against his door.

Damn it. Thank me later.

He let the window down and gave a deep sigh. "Hi, EmmyLou."

"Hey there, Mr. Beecher." She held up his pros-thesis, the sneaker still attached. "Lose something?"

CHAPTER EIGHT

FOR JUST AN INSTANT, Sol glared at her like she was some of the pond scum he'd scraped from the bottom of his boat. Then his eyebrows drew in and one corner of his mouth turned up. "Well, no. Why would you think that belonged to me?"

Oh brother. Playing coy, was he? Well, she was the master at that game. No way would she let him know how hard her heart was beating at the shock of this discovery or the shame that was eating her alive at that moment because of all the ugly, unsympathetic comments she'd made about his bum leg.

No sirree, in her hand she held the leverage to make him drop his stupid bill, and she intended to use it, guilt be damned.

"Well, for starters, it's common knowledge that your left leg is your bad one…" Bentley jumped at his new toy, and she held it up out of his reach. Although it was lighter than she would have expected, it was heavy enough to cover the tremble in her arm. "…and I'll be damned if this doesn't just happen to be a lefty. Second, you admitted

Bentley was with you, and then he shows up with this. And last." She pointed to the sneaker covering the foot. "That neon-green sneaker looks exactly like the pair you had on at my house Sunday. So quit this playacting and admit it's yours, 'cause otherwise you haven't got a leg to stand on."

His lips—gorgeous, kissable, full lips—twitched in a near-smile before puckering to blow out a slow breath. "Okay. You've got me." He switched off the ignition and pushed opened the truck door. Bentley answered the invitation by leaping into his lap, planting a paw right in the middle of his crotch. "Oof!" Sol pushed her pet onto the passenger seat, then swung his own legs—make that leg—out of the truck.

Emmy's throat closed at the sight—a tip of white knee with nothing below it protruded below the hem of the shorts. The other lightly tanned calf beside the empty space was well-developed with the bulging muscles of a weightlifter.

"Now you know." He stood up, one arm gripping the top of the door and the other braced against the roof of the truck. She momentarily forgot the non-leg as her eyes traveled to the cargo shorts slung low on his hips. He wasn't wearing a shirt, and the chiseled planes of his tanned stomach pulled her eyes up to the handsome pectorals and sculpted shoulders, and then past the unkempt hair to the eyes that flashed with defiance in the moonlight. Damn if her dry mouth didn't suddenly moisten.

She cocked a brow and lifted her chin in her own fake show of defiance. "Now I know."

His smooth jawline tightened. "You gonna give it to me? Because begging on bended knee isn't something I'm good at."

Over the initial shock and with her wits more about her now, she stepped back, crossing her arm, with the fake leg gathered against her chest. "No. I'm not just handing it over to you."

"Have it your way." He dropped back into the seat, swerving around and slamming the door at the same time. "Insurance will buy me another. Keep that as a souvenir."

Augh! His cool attitude got under her skin faster than a mosquito bite. She took two steps to the window. "Bentley, come!"

Thankfully the dog chose this once to be obedient. He loped back across Sol's lap to stick his head and front paws out the window, drawing grunts and some cursing from Sol along the way.

Emmy stepped back a few steps and patted her thigh. "Come on."

With a bark that showed his enthusiasm for this game, Bentley pushed the rest of the way through the window, landing at her feet, eagerly waiting for the large sneaker-stick to be thrown.

Sol didn't glance their way. He started his truck.

This wasn't going at all like she'd imagined. "Good luck keeping this a secret until your insurance comes through."

He shrugged. "Got another one at home. It doesn't fit as well, but it'll do in a pinch."

"Ooooo!" She stomped back to the truck. "For Heaven's sakes, Sol. I don't want your leg. What would I do with it?" She rested her elbow on the side mirror so he couldn't pull away and gave a dramatic shrug. "Might make an interesting croquet mallet, though." She swung it along the ground, causing Bentley to get so excited he spun in a circle. "Or a boat paddle." She pantomimed rowing with it a couple of strokes. "Maybe a lamp with the right shade."

"I want to go home, EmmyLou." His tone was one he'd use with an errant child. "Say what you want to say and then step away from my truck."

"Say please," she taunted.

He threw the truck into gear and inched forward, causing her to lose her balance. She grabbed at the open window, her fingers brushing his hard bicep. His back stiffened, and she saw his fingers flex tighter around the steering wheel. So he wasn't impervious to her. But neither was she to him, as the pleasant tingle zipping through her body reminded her.

"Oh, all right." She moved her hand away to

avoid the distraction and refocused on her mission. She had no desire to go tromping back across that field again in these short shorts, even with the cowboy boots she'd had the foresight to put on. And she still wanted to talk him into swapping his leg for her bill. Obtaining a new prosthesis surely wouldn't be preferable to making a deal. "Take us back to my house?" she suggested. Being out there on a moonlit beach surrounded by summer sounds and a guy who jump-started everything except her ego was sending her mind places it had no business going. "We'll finish these negotiations there."

"No negotiating. Either give me my prosthesis or don't."

She noticed that he didn't call it his leg, and that somehow seemed significant. Once again she stepped back, propping the item on her shoulder like a soldier at attention with a rifle.

"Get in," he growled.

"Should I put Bentley in the back?"

"He can't do any more damage than he's already done. Probably less if he gets in on the other side," he added dryly.

"C'mon, Bentley." Emmy ran to the passenger's side and opened the door before Sol could change his mind. Bentley jumped in ahead of her, greeting Sol with gleeful licks to his face.

She reached down to push away whatever the

metal was that she was sitting on. Her stomach tightened in recognition. Crutches. The kind with round bands that slipped over the forearms. No wonder his torso was so well-formed. Walking with those contraptions had to be a workout, though she'd never seen him use them.

She felt his eyes on her, and she met them, keeping her emotions hidden, she hoped. His look dared her to show pity.

"Pitch those in the back," he ordered, and she obeyed.

Bentley chased the new sticks to the backseat.

Sol snorted and shook his head as EmmyLou drew a long breath that quivered violently in her chest.

SOL HADN'T SUFFERED humiliation too many times in his life, but this experience was sure to stand out as the mother of them all.

There he was, in his truck, half-clothed, with the most gorgeous woman he'd ever known— scantily attired in short shorts, cowboy boots, and a body-hugging tank top with no bra. And instead of trying to figure out how he might get her into his bed, he was wondering how he would get his prosthesis out of her damn clutches!

God, how time changed things.

She said they'd negotiate. How in the hell could

he negotiate when she had him off-balance…in every sense of the word?

She turned to the backseat to check on Bentley, and Sol's peripheral vision caught her cleavage in that low, round-neck top.

Oh man! His fingers tightened around the steering wheel. She'd mentioned that she ran in from the hot tub and threw on some clothes, so this time her no-fuss look wasn't a slap in his face. Just EmmyLou au naturel. And the shockwaves she sent through his body were so strong they bordered on painful.

He shifted in his seat, trying to loosen the shorts that rubbed his crotch like a dull saw.

"Don't talk much, do you?" she asked.

"Don't have anything to say."

"You used to have a lot to say. You used to talk everybody's leg off…oh. Sorry. Really."

The apology knifed through his gut, exposing that sensitive inner layer. "Don't!" He slapped the steering wheel. "That's what I can't stand. 'Sorry.' 'Oh, poor you.' 'Poor Sol.' That's the very reason I've never breathed a word of this to anybody in this town. Having to put up with the bad-leg pity is awful enough. The no-leg pity would send me over the edge."

She remained quiet for half a minute. "So, it's the leg that keeps you from going out? Dating, I mean?"

"That's nobody's business—and what makes you think I don't go out?"

"Taylor's Grove's omniscient eye sees all. I'll mark your answer down as a yes."

He didn't respond. As he'd said a minute before, he had nothing to say.

"I'm relieved to know it's the leg that's your problem, actually," she went on in a casual tone like they were talking about a bad haircut. "The whispers—and surely you knew your secretiveness would cause whispers—they've always been that the little head between your legs got damaged, so it messed up the bigger head on your neck."

"Damn!" Sol brought the truck to a grinding stop. Bentley yelped as he thumped against the back of their seat.

"Hey, watch it! He doesn't have his seat belt on." The swat from the back of EmmyLou's fingers stung Sol's bicep, reminding him how little physical contact he had—except when Creighton-Fullers were present.

"So people think I'm…impotent?"

EmmyLou shrugged. "Well, of course. I mean, studly Mr. Hot-for-Everybody comes home from Afghanistan and gives up the one thing he was best known for? His 'specialty'…" She made air quotation marks exactly like Joe Wayne had done, and Sol caught himself before he allowed it to make him smile. He was too affronted to find anything amusing right then. "…because of a leg?" She held up the prosthesis and waved her other hand toward his torso. "When you've still got a body like that? *Pfft!*" She shook her head with disgust.

Sol took his foot off the brake and pressed the gas again, too confused to know what to say. To have the world's view of him laid out so matter-of-factly was unsettling. The people of Taylor's Grove had been doing more than pitying him all these years—they'd built him into some damaged soul straight out of a melodrama. He let his window down and spat, trying to rid his mouth of the bitter taste.

And though EmmyLou's last comment was shrouded as a compliment, he knew better. She still wanted something from him. Probably for him to forget the bill, which he'd never intended to call her on anyway, so the joke was on her.

A more welcome sight he'd never seen than the turn onto her lane.

They rode in silence until he stopped his truck and threw it into Park at the back of her driveway. "Are we done now?" he asked.

She opened her door and got out, still clutching his prosthesis, then opened the back door for Bentley. "We haven't even started, sugar." She grabbed the crutches and tossed them into the front. "I'll get us a glass of tea and meet you at the table by the pool."

She slammed the door and walked away, the affected but perfected jiggle of her ass drawing his attention like an unsuspecting bug to a Venus flytrap. Once she was out of sight, he threw the truck in Reverse.

Show her you don't give a rat's ass. Go home.

To what? Some TV show he couldn't get interested in? His cot in the kitchen of a house where he knew every sound and every creak and had memorized the number of teapots on the wallpaper above the sink?

A glass of tea with a pretty woman who knew he wasn't impotent offered a change from the excruciating sameness of this life he'd come to live.

Last week had given him a taste of change. Made him hunger for more.

He put the truck in Park, figuring it couldn't hurt to stay for a little while and negotiate...

THE BREAK-'EM-UP BAR and Pool Hall had stood for thirty-two years on the same site and had never allowed any minors. As a result, it predated and was excluded from the smoking bans that had become so popular in other areas. Thirty-two years of various types of smoke had created a veil thick enough to obscure most of the goings-on of its patrons. The standing joke was that the air was so heavy, you could catch your own cold by coughing one night at the east end and returning the next night to breathe in the germ at the west end. Stay for even a few minutes, and you left smelling like a well-chewed cigar.

No one seemed to mind—especially Joe Wayne. The stage was strategically placed so that the guys had to pass right by it on their way to the pisser. Forgetting they'd already tipped him, most tipped several times a night, and the smoke gave him a valid reason to keep the free beer coming. The cold liquid and alcohol cut the smog from his vocal cords even if it made the one in his brain worse.

Nobody here much listened anyway.

The Break-'Em-Up was too loud and boisterous for anybody to hear much past the first row of tables…except for that one time. All wound up in an old-fashioned, foot-stomping bluegrass tune, he'd started to yodel. It took all of about twenty seconds of that crap for two army guys to get to the stage, hoist him up by his hands and feet like a pig headed to a luau, and toss him into the parking lot on his ass.

Coming back in had earned him a round of applause like he hadn't heard since his glory days, though. All in good fun.

"And he ain't gonna wallow, he ain't gonna beg, but Sol lost his heart when he lost that damn leg," he sang and strummed the final chord of the song he'd pieced together this afternoon. Thought he'd try it out tonight for the patrons in the first row.

Three people clapped. One was a guy who laughed real loud and appeared to be applauding the joke someone had just told rather than reacting to the song, never even glancing toward the tiny stage in the corner. The woman on the bar stool with both elbows resting on the bar to push her breasts out to their maximum even stuck two fingers in her mouth and let out a sharp whistle. She'd been giving Joe Wayne the eye, and he knew she'd be his for the taking by the end of the night if he chose—which meant, if nothing better came along. The *something better* appeared to be the petite blonde in the front row with two of her girlfriends who were doing shots of Fireball. Her enthusiastic applause was directed right at him.

"You know any Luke Bryan or Jason Aldean?" she called as the server set another shot in front of her.

"Yes, ma'am," Joe Wayne drawled, and his fingers flew into Bryan's "Crash My Party" before his mouth could recall the lyrics. He hummed a while until the words dug their way out of the fog.

It didn't seem to matter to the little blonde. She swayed with her eyes closed and her shot glass lifted high in the air. Sometime in the middle of the chorus, she let out a whoop and downed the contents of the glass. Then she started to sway again.

Joe Wayne sang as if he believed there was somebody he'd want to crash his party. No images came to mind. Just blurs of women he'd known…and then hadn't.

As he figured might happen—he'd seen it often—the little blonde's swaying got out of control, reminding him of that windshield wiper on his brother's old VW that would occasionally go rogue. She swayed right out of her chair—passing out cold, her butt just one of the many littering the floor.

While the others gathered around to get her up and out to the car she came in, he finished the song to the applause of one.

With a wink in that direction, he strummed a few bars. "Here's a new one I been working on. It goes out to the pretty lady sitting at the end of the bar." His fingers caressed the strings, showing her the tenderness they were capable of. He closed his eyes and willed the words to the front of his brain. "Your hair like satin 'neath my touch. You know I need you, oh so much. Need your lips, your sighs, your heart, pressed close to mine. Give me just another chance, to hold you through this final dance. Pretend you're happy to be with me one last time."

CHAPTER NINE

"Mama wouldn't approve, Bentley." Emmy leaned the fake leg against the kitchen island, but Bentley made a lunge for it. She jerked it out of his reach and laid it across the corner, eyeing it as she poured two glasses of her special tea. "She'd say that holding a man's fake leg hostage is setting myself up to lose one of my own." She took a sip, moving slowly, giving Sol plenty of time to get seated by the pool. Her heart ached at her discovery, but seeing him struggle with crutches would break her. She couldn't let that happen. Had to stay tough and get him to drop that stupid bill.

Besides, some of what she wanted to talk about was for his own good, though they probably wouldn't agree on that, either.

So what else was new?

She released a long breath as she tucked the leg under her arm. "I never expected to be serving leg with my tea. Live long enough, you'll do anything." Getting a firm grip on the glasses, she headed outside.

Sol had donned a T-shirt—throwing Emmy into momentary confusion about whether she was relieved or disappointed—and had seated himself at the table rather than choosing one of the couches surrounding the fire pit. She suspected he'd chosen that seat deliberately to hide his stump of a leg and thus draw attention away from it. Like that was going to happen. His neon-green sneaker was hard to ignore, too, pressed against her breast and caressing her nipple. Putting a bra on would've been a smart move, but it was too late now.

She thrust her breasts out, determined to make the most of the situation, but once again, Bentley preempted her entrance by rushing to Sol, who laughed and leaned over to brush his face against the dog's and accept the affectionate licks.

The sight loosened a swarm of butterflies in her stomach. "Bentley…" she scolded, but Sol shook his head.

"He's fine. He's a good dog."

Obviously taking that as an invitation, Bentley loped into his lap, which drew another deep, oh-so-sexy chuckle from Sol.

EmmyLou's renegade nipples tightened even more at the sound. "Just push him off." She took out her aggravation on the dog. "Bentley, down."

"No, really. He's fine." Sol smoothed one hand along the dog's back, and his chin buckled as he accepted the glass with the other. "Thanks. After my time with Joe Wayne, I expected hard liquor or beer."

EmmyLou shook her head, taking the seat across from him. "Half green tea, half lemonade sweetened with honey." She wedged the artificial leg under the arm of her chair so it wouldn't fall. "If anything's going to keep me awake at night, I don't want it to be something I drank."

Sol seemed to miss her quip, or else he ignored it. His eyes leveled with hers. "Your brother's got a drinking problem."

The sip she'd just taken trickled through the tightness in her throat. "He's always had a taste for the sauce, but I never thought it was in excess."

"It's been my experience, when a guy has to have a drink as soon as his feet hit the floor, he's probably got a problem."

The tea hit Emmy's stomach with a thud. "Is it that bad?"

Sol nodded, his face creased with concern. "It's that bad. He drinks all day *and* all night. And he has a hard time remembering things—like songs he's just written. They're gone almost instantly. I don't know how he gets through a gig."

His mention of Joe Wayne's gigs caused the glass in her hand to tremble, the ice making soft *clink*s. She rested he glass on her lap beneath the table and Sol's line of vision. "My oldest brother Dustin was a mess for years..." Her heart squeezed at the memory. "Until he finally went to AA. He's been sober for six years now, but it nearly cost him everything. Wife. Kids. I'll have him talk to Joey."

Sol gulped down his tea and set his glass on the table, concern gone now, face set in stone with a no-nonsense look. "So what do you want in exchange for my prosthesis?"

"Only a couple of things, actually." She took a quick sip to moisten her dry throat. "Number one, promise me you'll come here to swim instead of by yourself at the lake."

His back went ramrod straight. "Come here?" He gave an amused snort and shook his head, shaggy hair dancing around his face. "You've lost your mind."

"And you've lost your leg." She shrugged, keeping her poker face in place.

"I've always swum in the lake. Since I was Bentley's size. I appreciate your concern, but nothing's going to happen. Besides." He drummed his fingers on the table. "You swim alone here. That's just as dangerous."

"Well." He had her there, but she shrugged again as if she'd thought this all through. "You're right. It's something neither of us ought to be doing. We could swim together. Wouldn't it be

good therapy for you?" His grimace warned her
to lighten the conversation. "And you need somebody to guard your leg to keep Bentley or...or
anybody from stealing it."

"You're referring to people like yourself."

"I did *not steal* your leg. Bentley fetched it. I'm
trying to return it."

"Along with a few demands."

Her jaw clenched at his tone. "Concerns." She
ground out the word.

He looked at the dog snuggled across his lap
with his head resting on the arm of the chair,
and she watched the beginning of a smile before it vanished. "Will we make a schedule? For
my *therapy*?"

"Of course." She would need to plan which bikini for which day.

He drew a long breath, and it hit her that this
was not a man used to giving in. Having to accept the fact that he no longer had half of one of
his legs must've been a hell of a bitch slap.

"All right. Can I have my prosthesis back
now?" he growled.

And the preliminary round goes to EmmyLou!
Her stomach flounced with a happy pirouette
as she held up a finger. "Soon." *On to the main
event.* She cleared her throat as she placed the leg
on the table, keeping it out of Sol's reach. "I've
done the math, and I figure an artificial leg must

run around…oh, say ten thousand dollars? I'll let you have it back for the bargain price of four thousand eight hundred twenty-three dollars." She quoted the exact total on his bill.

Sol leaned back, casually resting his elbow on the arm of the chair not occupied by Bentley's head. A slow, smug grin crossed his face. "I've got a better idea," he drawled. "You give me my prosthesis and keep it a secret, and I won't tell people you're really EmmyLou Fuller, the female half of that singing group The Fullers."

"JOEY TOLD YOU."

EmmyLou's eyes grew so wide, they seemed to take up her whole face. Big, gorgeous eyes that grabbed Sol's heart and floated it into his throat when they filled with tears.

Oh…no. No, no, no, no no…damn! He'd never expected self-assured, get-everything-I-want EmmyLou to cry…and certainly not over something *he* said.

"Hellfire. Don't cry, EmmyLou. Please." He added the last word as her face contorted on an explosive sob. He thought she might be faking, but when she grabbed the prosthesis and thrust it across the table at him, he saw a flash of something in her eyes. Something resembling the terror he'd seen on comrades' faces when the enemy was known to be in the area but hadn't shown himself yet.

"Thanks." He took the object and leaned it against his chair. Putting it on in front of her would expose too much, and right then her tears were eroding his armor. "I won't tell anybody anything Joe Wayne told me." It was difficult to be reassuring and deliberately evasive at the same time. His mouth went dry with the effort. "I...uh... I could use another glass of tea."

She vaulted out of her seat, seeming as eager for a break as he was. "Okay," she managed between quivering spurts of breath. She swiped at her face with both hands before picking up her glass and coming around the table to get his. She paused, looking down at him...her bottom lip caught between her teeth.

The look held no pretense...beguiling in its honesty. He opened his mouth to confess that Joe Wayne hadn't really told him anything except her real name and the fact that they'd been The Fullers, but she laid a hand on his arm. The heat from her touch burned the breath from his lungs.

"Promise me you won't leave, okay? I want you to hear my side of the story."

He nodded, not yet trusting his voice.

She grabbed his glass and hurried inside, her movements waking Bentley, who jumped down and followed.

Sol made quick work of getting his prosthesis attached. Then he picked up his crutches and tossed them in the backseat of his truck, not wanting the reminder of his vulnerability lying around in plain sight.

And he needed to move around, too. Hell, he needed a cold shower.

EmmyLou met him with a full glass when he returned to the pool area. Her tears were dried, though her face still held the blush that seemed to heighten her beauty...if that was possible. "Let's move over there." She pointed toward the chairs and couches surrounding the fire pit. "The furniture's more comfortable, and a happy ass makes for easier talking, I think."

"Sure." Sol motioned for her to lead, noting that the way her ass danced in those shorts probably meant he was about to get an earful.

She settled for a corner of the conversation area that contained two wicker chairs angled toward each other and a small table in between. The chairs were thickly cushioned. He waited for her to sit, and then he sank down into the comfort. Bentley was content to lounge on the outdoor rug.

Emmy was nervous, he could tell. She sipped from her glass...set it down...picked it up and sipped again. He'd never seen her like this, and it made for an interesting study. He kept quiet, giving her time to get her thoughts together, but also protecting his own tongue from blurting out the truth.

He *wanted* to hear her story.

"When he's drinking…and the subject of The Fullers comes up…does Joey hate me?" Her voice quivered, quiet and small—nothing like the EmmyLou the world knew. "I mean…whenever I bring it up, he cuts me off and says we're good…that he understands why I walked away from it all. But I can't help feeling guilty, and deep down I know his drinking problem's my fault. Mama's forever reminding me that if it hadn't been for my *silliness*—" she quirked her fingers with the standard Fuller mannerism "—he'd be…we'd be…stars by now. Millionaires. And he wouldn't be playing those hole-in-the-wall beer joints. Or drinking so much."

"Your mom has no right to say things like that. No right to blame you for…" He sought the word to fill in the blank and came up with nothing. "…for what happened," he finished. "Joe Wayne makes his own choices just like the rest of us."

Emmy toed out of her boots and pulled her knees up under her chin, wrapping her arms around her legs.

Sol tried not to let his eyes wander to the shapely, feminine calves that had been placed within touching distance…tried not to imagine his tongue gliding along that crease on the outside where the muscle was perfectly defined. Had he done that the night they spent together? He couldn't remember. It seemed like a lifetime ago, and technically it was. He'd been a different man then.

"I tried to control the panic attacks." Emmy's words jerked him back into the present conversation. "But the damn psychiatrist wanted to put me on those meds that made me feel like shit. I was seventeen! I had my whole life in front of me, and I just couldn't see spending it in a blur, taking a freakin' pill every time I felt the stage fright coming on—which got to be every time I stepped in front of an audience bigger than my family!"

Stage fright? That was her big secret? It didn't seem to be such a big deal—although for an entertainer, it could have been crippling, he supposed. But the bigger deal at the moment was the mental thrashing his conscience was giving him. He gave her a time-out sign. "EmmyLou, Joe Wayne never mentioned any of this."

"He didn't?"

Sol shook his head.

"Not even when he was drinking?"

Sol shook his head again. "Not even then, and I told you before, he was drinking the whole time." They were sitting closer now than they had been at the large table, and at this distance he could read the wariness in her eyes. "Look." He leaned toward her, resting his elbows on his knees. "All he told me was that Creighton was your middle name…that y'all were The Fullers and you shared the circle at the Grand Ole Opry. And he told me you were the draw and that I should ask you if I want to know more because the rest of the story wasn't his to tell."

Her jaw went slack…the calm before the storm. She lunged from her seat to stand over him, totally oblivious to the devastating effect those unencumbered breasts beneath that skimpy tank were having on his attention span. "You are a spiteful, selfish asshole, Sol Beecher!" Her finger whizzed back and forth in front of his face. "You led me to believe you knew everything about me, lying in wait like a fox on an unsuspecting rabbit, and then you let me spill my guts, gathering information so you can…what? Put a price on it and add it to that stupid bill?" She shook her finger at his nose, shaming him like she would a three-year-old.

Enough! She might not see him as a man, but she wasn't going to treat him like a child.

Sol pushed out of the chair, pulling himself to his full height, which gave him some advantage. He bent his head to bring his face close to hers, forcing her to tilt hers back to maintain eye contact. "I don't much care what you think of me, EmmyLou," he lied. He *did* care, but he wasn't about to let her know it. "But unlike you, I don't go spouting my mouth off at every chance, and I would never *ever* give out any information on people that they wouldn't tell on themselves."

"I'm *not* disloyal." They were so close, he could almost feel the heat flashing from her eyes. He saw the tension in her jaw as she ground out the words, "Yeah, I may talk a lot, but I. Don't. Gossip."

He grabbed the hand she'd used to punctuate her words by poking him in the chest. He heard her sharp intake of breath, noticed how his breath stopped at the same moment as if she'd stolen it. Their eyes were only inches apart. Their mouths closer. He hadn't kissed a woman in a long time... but when...*if*...it ever happened again, it had to be with somebody who accepted him the way he was. He loosened his hold, giving her the freedom to move away.

She did, easing back a small step.

As they glared at each other, an idea occurred to him—something that might defuse the anger. He steadied himself by placing his hands on his hips.

"Tell you what," he said. "Let's change the subject and talk about something else for a minute. Since the bill seems to be bothering you, how about I hire you for the next hour at…" He wasn't sure what the going price was, so he named what he thought might be a reasonable amount. He shrugged. "Does five hundred dollars sound reasonable?"

It was a good thing his hands were on his hips. Otherwise, the force of her palm connecting with his cheek would have landed him flat on his ass.

CHAPTER TEN

"HOW DARE YOU, Sol Beecher." Anger pressed so hard in Emmy's throat, breathing was difficult, not to mention speaking. But she would get this out even if she suffocated in the process. "You take your fake leg and your fake gentlemanly behavior and get off my property right this instant. And don't ever come here again. You are the scum of the earth."

Sol raised his hand to his jaw and wiggled it as if testing to see whether it still worked. Then his hand went back to his hip, and as he shook his head, a smile bloomed on his lips that quickly broke into a laugh. "Damn it, EmmyLou, I want you to sing for me."

"Sing."

"Yeah. Play the guitar, if you still have one. I used to have some of your CDs. Thought maybe you'd give me a private concert if the price was right. Joe Wayne serenaded me every night, but of course, he did it for free."

"Oh God, Sol." Her knees went to jelly as the adrenaline left her system. She plopped back into her chair, covering her face with her hands. "I'm too embarrassed for words."

His easy laugh should've put her at ease, but instead it made her insides quiver pleasantly.

"Then I've achieved the impossible. The things that come out of your mouth had me thinking you were unembarrassable." He sat back down, also. "I could've phrased my offer better, though."

"Yeah, you could've." She leaned back, resting her head against the chair, and closed her eyes. What was she thinking? Sol had made it perfectly clear time after time that he wasn't interested in her. She shook her head at her own foolishness.

"Do you ever sing anymore?" The gentleness in his voice was a surprise. It brushed a soft finger over her bruised ego.

"Only for Bentley." Hearing his name, her pup came to her and laid his head on her lap, looking at her with adoring eyes.

"Lucky dog." Sol's chuckle finally coaxed a bit of a laugh from her. "Now that we're on the same wavelength, I'll pose my question again. I'd like very much to hear you sing. And I'll deduct five hundred dollars from the bill in return. What do you say?"

Great. Her chest muscles had relaxed, and now her abs were squeezing at the thought of singing in front of someone other than family. But it was only one person, and five hundred dollars off the

bill was nothing to sneeze at. If they swam together twice a week, and she sang for him each
time, she'd be debt-free in about a month.

But could she do it?

"I don't know, Sol." Her hand trembled as she
brushed it through her hair. "I haven't sung in
front of anybody besides family in a long, long
time. The thought makes me queasy."

"Suit yourself. But it'd be an easy five hundred."

"I gave back your leg. Can't you just call it
a draw and forget the bill since we know each
other's secrets?" She was herself again, and her
irritation with him returned with it.

"Nope. And by the way, I hope that slap didn't
knock my nose out of place again."

"Crap!" She sat up quickly, catching the bloom
of her handprint on his face. "I forgot about your
nose!"

Using his thumb and index finger, he probed
the still slightly swollen area and gave a shrug.
"It's *probably* okay, but—"

"You're not adding any more to that bill." She
pushed out of her chair. "I'll sing."

THE FIRST VERSE of the first song had been rough.
Sol heard the tremble in EmmyLou's voice—
beautiful as it was— and was reminded of those
first shaky steps he took on his prosthesis. An

uncanny urge grabbed him to stand, take the guitar away, pull her to him and just hold her until
her fear was gone. But he'd resisted the urge. It
was ludicrous even to think such things.

Instinctively he leaned back in the chair and
closed his eyes. On the second verse, her voice
found some strength.

One song blended into another, and finally he
opened his eyes. She didn't seem to remember
he was there, she was so caught up…lost in her
music.

He got lost in her.

This was a different woman sitting beside
him—one who didn't want to be in the limelight,
didn't want any of the attention. An about-face
from the woman he'd known—the man-eater
EmmyLou Creighton with the sassy attitude.

This was EmmyLou Fuller in the raw. Outside
layers peeled away like an apple until the heart
at the very core was laid bare, offering a tanta-
lizing, sweet taste.

Forbidden fruit.

Her repertoire was vast, including recent re-
leases from Miranda Lambert and Carrie Un-
derwood. There was some of the old stuff,
too—Patsy Cline, Loretta Lynn and Dolly Par-
ton. Some he'd never heard before—originals,
most likely.

She finally stopped to take a drink.

"That last one was really nice."

She held the liquid in her mouth a few seconds before swallowing. "Thanks." It was the quietest word he'd ever heard come from her mouth.

"Was it original?"

She nodded, her eyes darting away.

"You write a lot of songs? Because Joe Wayne writes them constantly." Her eyes came back to rest on his at the mention of her brother. "I've never seen anybody come up with stuff as fast as he does." He shook his head. "But then he loses them as quickly as they come."

She caught her bottom lip between her teeth as her eyes drifted away.

Oh hell. Don't cry!

"I told him he should record himself with his phone. I think he was going to try. Maybe that'll help. Where was the last place y'all performed publicly, anyway?" His change of subject might keep him treading on thin ice, but she'd never finished her story earlier.

"Tennessee State Fair. And we didn't actually perform." She took a deep breath and blew it out slowly, resting her forearm on the top of her guitar. "I was petrified before we ever walked out onstage, but I refused to take the medicine. I couldn't go the rest of my life using a crutch." Her eyes met his head-on. "You understand."

He nodded. "I do."

"I had to prove to myself that I could do it."
She paused and swallowed. "But I couldn't. I
opened my mouth and nothing came out. My
heart started beating so fast, I could feel it all
over." She covered her ears and bounced her
hands against her head a couple of times. "I could
hear this pulsating roar in my head, but it wasn't
keeping time to the music." She shrugged. "Next
thing I knew, I was in an ambulance, headed for
the hospital."

While she talked, she hugged the guitar, even
cradling her cheek against the neck.

He was seeing her interact with her best friend.
The intimacy of the moment shook him physically.

"Our press agent spread the news I was suffering from exhaustion, and they canceled the rest of
the tour for the year. There were only three shows
left." She shrugged. "But I never went back. A
few months later, I turned eighteen, graduated
from high school. My boyfriend and I took off
on his motorcycle for a trip across country. I cut
my hair. Dyed it blond. I got colored contacts.
Bought some big ol' glasses. Didn't wear any
makeup." She shook her head, but the laugh that
accompanied it held no mirth. "Thank God the
internet was still pretty new. The Fullers faded
into oblivion fairly quickly."

"Yeah, I tried looking you up on the internet, but I didn't get much," Sol admitted.

That made her smile a little. "Laws protecting minors kept a lot of the media from digging too deep. And social media wasn't a thing back then. We just faded out of sight."

"Any regrets?" Sol prodded. The story was fascinating...or maybe it was the woman who was fascinating.

"None." Her eyes leveled with his as she shook her head slowly. "Well, except for what it's done to Joe Wayne. And Mama's never forgiven me, but nothing I've ever done has been good enough." She shrugged. "I finally quit trying to please her."

There was a pause, and Sol's brain whirred to come up with the right thing to say. But he didn't have words. And as it turned out, Emmy didn't need any further prodding.

"I wanted to be close to my family," she continued. "But not in Nashville. Not even in Tennessee. Dickie—that was my boyfriend—and I camped a few days on Kentucky Lake during our trip. I liked it. Thought it was beautiful. So I decided to move to Paducah. I went through cosmetology school, where I met Maggie Wells." Sol smiled at the mention of his old friend—the one who'd first introduced him to EmmyLou. It was her house EmmyLou lived in now. She'd bought it when Maggie moved to California. "She started the salon, and I bought in." She threw her hands up. "And here I be."

"It's a shame to waste a talent like yours, though. You're as good or better than anybody out there."

EmmyLou rolled her eyes. "Oh pul-leeze. Projectile vomiting onstage might be popular with some audiences, but country music fans wouldn't take a shine to it."

Sol chuckled. The EmmyLou he knew was present after all.

She looked at her watch and then squinted one eye toward him. "Just so we're clear, *you* started this conversation, so the talking counts as part of the hour, right? You're not gonna deduct these minutes from my wages."

He laughed loudly at that. "No, ma'am. No deductions for talking."

"Okay then." Her eyebrow rose as she gestured toward his prosthesis. "Your turn. Show-and-tell."

SOL'S EYES MET her challenge, and for a moment she thought he would refuse. But instead, he started talking.

Probably needed to, she decided.

"When I re-upped—"

"And you did that, why?" She'd always been

curious about Sol's decision to join the army. He hardly seemed the soldier type.

His lips pressed into a straight line. "I just woke up one day—with a little help from my dad—" his grimace eased as the corner of his mouth quirked "—and realized that everything I had had been given to me. Sure, I'd worked my whole life, but for family, and I knew I'd take over the marina someday. I had this need to do something—something that would give meaning to my life, beyond pumping gas and selling bait."

"*And* sleeping with every woman within a twenty-mile radius." Emmy couldn't resist the barb.

Sol's eyebrows drew in, but he grinned. "You get that line from my dad?"

She shook her head. "Common knowledge."

"Obviously, my rudder was stuck in a circle," he acquiesced with a shrug. "So I enlisted and found that I liked it. For the first time in my life, I felt like I was doing something that would make a difference in the world. When the time came, I re-upped and was deployed to Afghanistan with the Tenth Mountain Division. Ghazni Province."

He stopped as if that was the end of the story.

"Go on," she prodded, wanting and yet dreading the rest.

"Five of us went on a scouting mission. We were headed back to the base when a rocket-propelled grenade came out of nowhere and hit the Jeep. I was driving. Lost the lower part of my leg. The guy riding shotgun lost an arm at the shoulder. The three in the back were killed."

The breath she drew stopped at her throat. "God, Sol. That's awful."

"It was weird…seeing my foot lying several yards from my body. Knowing it was mine." His chuckle was brittle around the edges. "My first thought was that I needed to get it so they could reattach it." His shaggy head trembled. "Then I looked down and saw it wasn't any use. Nothing to attach it *to*."

The scene he painted emerged in Emmy's mind, and a shudder rocked her body…shook away the words that had formed in her mouth.

"A year of surgeries and physical therapy followed. When I felt ready, I came back home. I'd warned Mom and Dad that I wanted to be the bearer of my news, and they respected that, but the right time never came."

"Yeah, I was still living in Paducah then, but I remember Maggie talking about Sol Beecher Day in Taylor's Grove. How you never showed up for the parade or the festivities."

"I couldn't do it, and you of all people should understand." He raised a brow, pinning her with a look that dared her to disagree. "Every eye on me. Every speech about me. I couldn't stomach the idea of the attention on me all day long. But…" He raised a finger in the air. "I sent my regrets."

Emmy let out a snort. "Maggie was soooo pissed. I told her to chalk it up as typical behavior from a jerk."

His laugh filled the darkness, warming the air. "I can't imagine you suffering from stage fright. I've never known anybody with a more ready tongue than EmmyLou Creighton."

Her stomach fluttered. *You have no idea how ready my tongue is, Mr. Beecher.* But the words remained poised on her lips, unspoken for once. She wasn't quite sure why this man threw her off her game, but she needed to figure it out, *pronto*.

Throughout his story, his low voice had remained strong, sure—full of emotion and engaging, yet controlled—like it had been at the school the night of the drawing. She'd been envious that he could speak so easily when she was a quivering wreck. Now that the truth of what he'd been through and the sacrifice he'd made were clear, the envy was gone, replaced by a growing admiration of the man's fortitude.

Of the man himself.

An admiration that could prove dangerous if she didn't heed the warnings going off at the back of her brain for the past forty-five minutes—

since they'd stood so close he could've kissed her if he'd wanted.

But he didn't.

Her years of tried-and-true know-how about the male of the species got swept down the sewer when it came to Sol Beecher. She'd been positive he was going to kiss her. Any man she'd ever stood that close to in that kind of situation *had* kissed her. If that wasn't desire in his eyes, what was it? Was he totally oblivious to the electricity when he held her hand?

Evidently he was. He'd dropped it—just like he'd dropped her after one night together.

Ha! There it was—the hint of the old irritation that kept her sane around him.

She drew a calming breath and strummed a few bars. "Now that we have all our secrets out in the open, you got any requests?"

"Nope. Surprise me."

A song popped into her mind—one she hadn't played in a long time. She'd taught it to herself, playing it by ear after hearing her Dad's favorite CD so often. He'd been pleased, but Mama had scolded her. Said she needed to stick with country. From then on, she'd played it only when Mama wasn't around.

"It's not country," she warned.

He shrugged. "You make it all sound good."

She closed her eyes and gave her fingers over

to the memory. They plucked the strings, drawing out the beautifully haunting melody of "I Don't Know How to Love Him" from *Jesus Christ Superstar.*

She'd played this song a thousand times, but tonight, the emotion of the lyrics came to life, honest and gut-wrenching. Somewhere in the middle, she opened her eyes, but she couldn't bring herself to look at Sol. She sang to the stars...to the stillness of the night...to Bentley. By the time she reached the last line, it came out as a whisper.

The final note from the guitar faded away, and she forced herself to look in Sol's direction.

Instantly she wished she hadn't.

The way he was watching her sucked away the tiny amount of breath left in her lungs—an intense gaze with enough heat to shimmer the air between them like highway asphalt in the middle of summer.

If she wasn't careful, it would find the fault hiding deep within her and crack her wide open.

"You realize how amazing you are, right?"

The growl in his voice coiled her insides, and she instinctively hugged the guitar, shielding her heart.

"I'm blown away," he went on. "Maturity has given your voice such complexity."

Oh good Lord! He was commenting on her singing—not her as a person.

"And your range is phenomenal."

On safer ground, her sassiness returned. "Keep bragging on me like that, and I'll have to up my price."

He grinned. "No more bragging, then. I want as many of these private concerts as I can get." He started to clap, then paused, placing hands on the chair arms, and pushed to a standing position before resuming his applause.

She nodded in gratitude at his standing ovation, the struggle it took making it sweeter. "Thank you. Thank you very much." Now that the mood had lightened, she kept it there with her Elvis impersonation.

"I should be heading home now, seeing as how I'm already up on my feet." He hitched a thumb in the direction of his truck.

Once again, his words caused a confusing range of emotions from genuine disappointment to utter relief. "Yeah." She stood, too, arranging the strap on her guitar so that the instrument hung between them. "I've got an early day tomorrow."

She walked him to his truck as she would any guest…like Mama had taught her was the proper show of Southern hospitality. It let your guest know you enjoyed the visit and wanted to prolong it as much as possible.

Oddly, it felt fitting this night.

He climbed into his truck without any preamble except leaning down to snuggle Bentley's head with his own. "It may not've started that way, but the night ended up pretty nice. Thanks."

She leaned on the edge of the door so he couldn't shut it just yet. "About the swimming. Maybe Sundays in the afternoon and Thursdays like tonight? In the evening?"

His eyes scoured the ground and focused on something out the windshield. "My swimming's not pretty. I'm awkward with my prosthesis off."

"Pfft." She gave a sarcastic snort. "You're awkward with it on, too."

That garnered a chuckle as he finally slid his eyes her way.

"Sunday. Two o'clock." She stepped back and shoved the door. "C'mon, Bentley."

Sol started the truck and backed it around.

She waved to the receding taillights and then blew out a long breath, the weight in her chest finally lifting.

She shifted her guitar to her back as she returned to where they'd been sitting. "Never in my life did I picture myself singing for Sol Beecher. Like I said, live long enough, you'll do anything."

Bentley wagged his tail, tilting his head sideways with an adoring look.

"Can you carry these?" She laid her boots together and held them out.

Bentley immediately sank his teeth into the soft leather, holding his head up proudly to show off his accomplishment.

Emmy kissed the top of his head. "You're such a good boy." She grabbed the glasses, and the two of them went inside.

She should have been sleepy, but Sol's visit had her all keyed up. She tried a pleasingly hot shower and even got into bed, but sleep wouldn't come.

Every time she closed her eyes, Sol's handsome face appeared just inches from hers, and with it came that intense desire she'd felt for him to kiss her. Was she crazy? He sure made her feel that way.

"He's a master at smoke and mirrors, Bentley." The dog opened his eyes but didn't raise his head. He was used to pillow talk. "Been hiding in plain sight for eight years."

A twinge of guilt caught between her shoulder blades.

"Yeah, I know. I have, too…for longer."

She sank into her pillows with a sigh, the words of the last song she'd sung jogging laps around her restless mind until it wore her into a fitful sleep.

CHAPTER ELEVEN

"HEY, DICKHEAD."

Joe Wayne kept his eyes closed, hoping he wasn't the dickhead being referred to. The vibration from a door slamming nearby made his head feel like a set of billiard balls had just been broken apart by a hard-hit cue ball.

"Yo! Joe Wayne. Time to haul ass off that couch and help me clean up this mess."

A hand grabbed his T-shirt at the back of the neck and jerked him to a sitting position.

"Shit...fire!" Joe Wayne rubbed his throbbing jaw. Shit-o'-day, it was sore.

"Yeah. You got a bruise." He recognized the voice and the belly protruding at his eye level with the shirt and its missing button. A hairy navel winked at him in a stupid-ass game of peekaboo. Bacon Ramsey was owner of the Break-'Em-Up. "Kathy Anne may be little, but she throws a mean punch."

Joe Wayne wiggled his jaw, which didn't feel broken, as his memory swam aimlessly through the mire of still-waiting-to-be-metabolized whiskey silt clogging his system. "A woman did this?"

"You don't remember the catfight?" Bacon shuffled over to his desk and picked up two coffee cups, running a finger through both handles. "Best of the century, so far." He peered into the cups, squinching an eye with a look of dissatisfaction before lifting them up to his nose. He sniffed, and a moment of uncertainty passed. "Kathy Anne showed up just as you wuz finishing your last set. Apparently, she wuz under the *expression* you wuz going home with her." He shrugged, and his face relaxed as he picked up the whiskey bottle and poured some into each cup. "And Martha said you wuz going home with *her*. Push came to shove, and all hell broke loose."

"Thanks." Joe Wayne's hand shook as he accepted the proffered cup. He downed the contents, closing his eyes in a silent welcome to the burn that assured him he was still alive in spite of the SOS his brain insisted on sending out every day. "So if two women was fighting over me, how'd I come to spend the night on this piece of shit?" He smoothed his palm over the vinyl that still held the impression of his shoulder.

"You got Kathy Anne around the waist and pulled her off Martha." Bacon lumbered back to his desk and snatched up the bottle, adding another splash to his own cup and Joe Wayne's. "Whooee! *That* let the devil loose in her. And when you let her go, she came out swinging. You tried to calm her down and called her Sunshine. Big mistake."

Joe Wayne shrugged. "I call 'em all Sunshine." He swished the whiskey around in his mouth, letting it clear his sinuses before he swallowed.

"That's fine when there's just one of 'em. But you pissed off Martha 'cause she said that wuz your pet name for *her*. And damn if you didn't call her Sunshine right then. That's when Kathy Anne coldcocked you. You went down for the count—course, you wuz wobbly anyway—and a couple of guys carried you in and dumped you there." He pointed to the couch.

"What happened with the women?" Joe Wayne was alert enough now to be curious.

"Found other guys to take 'em home and kiss away the bruises." Bacon let out a laugh that jiggled his belly enough to work another button loose.

That was suitable motivation to bring Joe Wayne to his feet…slowly. "Sorry about the ruckus. I thought sure we was gonna make it through this time with no fightin'." He ran a hand through his hair. "Damnation! Even my head is sore."

"Guys carrying you bumped it pretty hard on

the doorjamb on the way in." Bacon oozed his way back to his desk and set the bottle down. "But don't be frettin' 'bout the damage. Those ladies didn't hurt nuthin' much. They sure 'nuff made a mess of the place as they was chasin' each other around, though. Tables and chairs flyin' all over the place." He made a sweeping hand gesture toward the other room. "They even managed to knock the speakers off the stage, so we gotta get everything set up again 'fore you leave."

"Leave? I thought I was singing tonight."

Bacon squinted at him, raising his lip enough on one side to bring a flash of gold from his teeth. "We ain't open tonight, dickhead. Today's Sunday."

"Sunday?" Joe Wayne sat back down hard, which sent a pain slicing through the back of his skull. "Where did Saturday go? Did I perform?"

"Yeah. You wuz good. Only forgot the words three or four times."

Joe Wayne's stomach churned. He'd lost partial days before but never an entire day.

"Who'd I come with?" He vaguely remembered a woman pushing him into a shower, but that was Friday night, wasn't it?

"You shacked up with Martha." Bacon wasn't paying him much attention then. He was searching his desk for something. "Leastwise, she wuz the one brought you in both nights. I'm betting in your condition, you didn't do her much good." The big guy's stomach rolled as he laughed. He pushed a pile of papers to the side, uncovering a set of keys. "Hallelujah." He dropped them into his pocket. Coming around the desk, he swept a finger from Joe Wayne toward the office door. "Let's get to it. We got a couple hours' work 'fore I can get you on your way."

Joe Wayne eased back onto his feet and gained his balance. Those first few steps were always a bitch.

"Where you headed next?"

"Thought I'd visit my sister in Kentucky. Taylor's Grove. Ever hear of it?" Bacon shook his head in answer. "Not too far from Paducah," Joe Wayne followed Bacon into the barroom, coming to a sudden stop.

Calling the place a mess had been an understatement. Not a table or chair sat upright. Cans and bottles littered the floor. The speakers had indeed been knocked off the stage. It looked like some of the wires had been torn loose, too.

"Smartest thing you ever done was replacing all those wooden tables and chairs with this plastic stuff." Avoiding leaning over and the pain that would ensue, Joe Wayne lifted one of the chairs with the toe of his boot and set it upright. "This is gonna require a couple of beers, Bacon." He rubbed his head, already weary.

Bacon grabbed a couple of cold ones from the bar. Twisting the caps off, he set one within Joe Wayne's reach, and the world brightened. "Want me to call Katmandu? They're always looking for somebody cheap."

Joe Wayne had heard of the bar, though he'd never played it. It was about as rough as these places came. He'd always considered himself too good. He was Joe Wayne Fuller, damn it! He'd performed in the circle at the Grand Ole Opry when he was fifteen years old.

Nobody should reach his peak of success at fifteen.

He grabbed the beer and swigged it down in three gulps.

"Hell, no," he answered.

He wasn't *that* desperate...yet.

"How MANY LEGS do you have?" Emmy stood up and lifted her face to the sun, running her palms against her scalp to force the excess water out.

She'd waited patiently for Sol to finish his last set of laps before trying to engage him in conversation. When she'd suggested they swim together, she'd expected a lazy and carefree afternoon, mostly just relaxing by the pool. But it was obvious Sol had viewed it as physical therapy time.

The man had been swimming nonstop for the better part of an hour. Twenty laps of one stroke followed by twenty laps of another. The last twenty he'd done the butterfly, and the sight of his powerful upper body muscles pulling his torso out of the water had been something to behold.

But she'd invested a lot of money in the pink-sequined bikini she'd bought especially for this occasion of their first swim together, and it was high time Sol Beecher did some beholding of his own.

While he lounged on the steps in the shallow end, catching his breath, she'd eased down the steps into the deep end and done a leisurely breaststroke until she'd reached the rim, a few feet away from where he sat.

"Only one leg," he answered gruffly, but then the corner of his mouth twitched. "But I have three prostheses, if that's what you're asking."

"Wouldn't it simplify things to call them your leg? *Leg*'s a lot easier to say than *prosthesis*."

His eyes met hers levelly. "Would you ever think of a wig as your own hair?"

She shrugged and ran her fingertips across the top of the water, twisting slowly so the sun would catch the sequins better. "If I had to wear it all the time, I think I'd forget about it eventually."

"No, you wouldn't. Trust me. It might get more

comfortable, but you'd never reach the point that you could completely forget about it."

She'd made up her mind to maintain the semi-peace they'd reached Thursday night, so she dropped that line of discussion and tried a new one. "Why three? You keep a couple of spares in case a dog runs off with one, or what?"

That brought a genuine grin. Mmm! The man was gorgeous when he smiled. "I have two for everyday use. This one fits better than the other, so I use it most of the time." He nodded to the apparatus standing by the nearby chair. "I also have a waterproof one for the shower."

"Wow." Emmy imagined trying to negotiate a shower while standing on one leg. "I can see how tricky it would be trying to soap up…even with a bar to hang on to." She raised her left foot and ran her hands into her hair, pretending to wash it. Sure enough, she lost her balance and had to set the foot down. She'd lost his attention again—he was looking off toward the woods—so she pulled herself out of the pool and sat on the edge.

"Does it hurt?" she asked. "You kind of always have a bit of a scowl on your face and then sometimes—well, more like all the time—you grimace when you move." She did her best impression of his facial features pulled into a hard frown.

He shook his head, and the sunlight sparkled

in his eyes when he grinned. "Do I look like that, honestly? Because you look like a lizard right now." He swept his hand through the water, dousing her good.

The unexpected face full of water made her gasp. "Lawd, Sol Beecher." She did her Scarlett O'Hara impression. "Your sweet talk just charms the breath right out of my lungs." She wiped the water from her eyes and kicked, sending a retaliating splash his way and exchanging Scarlett for Rizzo from *Grease*. "But how 'bout it, karma chameleon? Does it hurt?"

He shrugged. "The prosthesis doesn't hurt, no. And the wound's long healed. But the knee hurts most of the time." He lifted his injured leg out of the water. "Don't get me wrong... I'm thankful they were able to save my knee. Having the joint makes mobility easier. But having to lift my leg with the thigh muscle for every step without the help of a calf muscle puts a lot of extra burden on the knee. It takes the brunt of all the balancing actions that used to be shared by the calf and the ankle. Stairs are a real bitch—I avoid them if at all possible."

"But your house is two stories..."

He grimaced. "I sleep on a cot in my kitchen."

Emmy didn't try to hide the fact that she was appalled. A house like that and Sol was sleeping on a cot in the kitchen? What a travesty. "Can't somebody come in and make accommodations?"

"You want me to install an elevator?"

"No, but they have those machines. Those chairs you can sit in and they take you up the stairs."

"I'm not eighty," he growled. "Besides, I've got an agent looking for a house for me. Something small with one story."

"But that's your family homestead."

"The operative word there is *family*," he said, all his earlier sarcasm replaced with regret. "It's a home meant to house more than one person."

"Yeah. I hear ya." She tossed her head toward the house behind them. "I bought this one with the idea that I'd settle down and have kids someday. Sometimes *someday* never comes, I guess."

"My God, EmmyLou. It's not like you're over the hill."

"So? Neither are you." The conversation hit a nerve. "And you tell me all your parts are still in good working order, so there's no reason why you should let yourself go the way you have. Get a haircut. Dress up a little. Get back out into the world instead of living like some kind of recluse."

"Haircuts are for people who give a shit." Sol started moving backward up the steps, one at a time. "I'd better go. I don't like the direction this afternoon has taken."

Emmy stood up. "What? You say you don't want people feeling sorry for you, but you don't like it when somebody tells you like it is, either." He stopped on the top step and threw an angry glare her way. "Give me the evil eye all you want. You know I'm right. You said it yourself with the haircut wisecrack. Maybe it's time you started giving a shit."

Sol ignored her as he worked his way into the seat he'd put at the edge of the pool when he arrived—a place to remove his prosthesis and ease into the water. His ignoring her worked to her advantage, as she stepped closer and snatched the artificial leg just as he leaned back.

"Damn it, EmmyLou. Give me my prosthesis." He held his hand out.

"Nope." She snuggled it between her breasts. "Not until you let me cut your hair."

"I like my hair the way it is."

She shrugged. "I don't. Makes you look creepy. Like those guys who hang out on park benches with a paper sack and an empty bottle to spit their tobacco in."

"And I guess you're going to charge me some outrageous price for this haircut that will have to come off my bill."

"What an excellent idea! Don't worry—I'll give you a discount, sugar." She winked.

Sol threw his hands in the air and leaned back

in the chair. "Fine. Cut my hair." He pointed a menacing finger at her. "But this is the last time you hold my prosthesis hostage. No more snatch-and-demand. Agreed?"

"Oh, all right." She started to hand it to him, then drew it back. "But this one last time, I'll hang on to it until after the haircut. And I want you to know, this is a first for me. I've never had to wrap myself around a man's leg to keep him from leaving. Most of them *want* to stay." She cocked a brow. "I'll go get my stuff."

She had his full attention now, so she decided to make the most of it with a grand finale exit. Pretending she was wearing a top hat and using the prosthesis as a cane, she choreographed a routine worthy of the Rockettes, singing and prancing her way inside.

She grabbed the small bag of tools she kept at home and returned poolside. Sol grumbled only a little when she wrapped the cape around his neck. She arranged a couple of beach towels to catch the hair as it dropped and then began combing out the tangles with her fingers.

"Your hair is gorgeous," she said, evaluating the wavy texture as she ran her hands from the nape upward.

"Thought it was creepy."

"It is creepy, the way you let it get so shaggy. But you could be a hair model." She moved around in front of him and leaned down to run her fingers through his hair from that angle, lifting the top and sweeping it back to one side, away from his face. He grunted, and the sound pulled her attention away from his hair long enough to drop her eyes to his hands. They were gripping the arms of the chair, knuckles white beneath the bronze skin.

From being touched?

She raised her eyes to his, saw the cool exterior kept in place for the world. But deeper, beyond the icy, uncaring facade, she caught a glimpse of the flame, like a pilot light, waiting for the gas to be turned up.

The flash of encompassing heat, she realized, was her own furnace.

Just one kiss. What could it hurt?

A warning bell went off in her head, and she straightened, realizing it wasn't a warning bell at all, but her phone. Either way, it was a timely occurrence that had saved her from making a huge mistake.

She cleared her throat and said, "Hello?"

"Hey, Emmy." It was Bree. "Are you busy?"

"Well, I have company..." She threw a sidelong glance at Sol, whose fingers no longer had a death grip on the chair.

Bree snorted. "Of course you do. Well, Kale's going to fire up the grill later for hamburgers, and we're making homemade ice cream. We thought you *and* your guest might want to come over for dinner. Audrey and Mark are coming—and, of course, Tess and the dogs. We're gonna play cornhole, too. What do you say?"

"Let me check." Emmy twisted the phone away from her mouth. "Bree and Kale have invited us over for hamburgers and cornhole—" Sol was already shaking his head. "Come on, Sol."

"*Sol?* As in *Beecher*?" Bree's tone was total disbelief.

"Yep. Beecher man is here for a swim and a haircut." She winked at him and grinned. He didn't return the gestures. Just shook his head harder. *You go*, he mouthed, pointing. *Not me.*

"Well, I'll be. I *never* would've thought *you* and *Sol*."

"Whoa! Don't go getting any skewed ideas. He helped my brother out when he was at the beach house. I'm just paying back the favor." *No hanky-panky, damn it*—although she failed to voice that part.

"I'm glad to hear y'all have made peace. Tell him we're excited to have him. It'll be like old times."

"Yeah. He says to tell you he's excited about it, too." Emmy laughed when Sol threw his hands into the air.

"How 'bout five or five-thirty? We'll eat around seven. Oh, and bring Bentley."

"We'll be there. Shall I bring a little apple pie moonshine?"

"Bring anything you want. Just no food. We've got that covered."

"See you then!"

Emmy hung up, meeting Sol's angry look with a triumphant smile.

"I'm not going." He shrugged, rugged jaw set like a piece of granite, looking every inch the spoiled brat…and yummy hot…and still creepy, due to his hair. Instantly the style she would give him popped into her mind. She would retain the bad boy look, but civilize it a bit.

"Quit being so pissy when you and I both know you're going to go." She picked up her scissors as she walked behind him and started running the fingers of one hand through his hair, massaging his scalp. "And do you know why?"

"No. Why don't you tell me?" The sexy growl was back in his voice. The massage would tame it to a purr soon.

"Because it's time for you to stop living like that wild boy they found in the woods some-where. France? I don't remember. It's not impor-tant. But what *is* important is that today's the day you take your rightful place in Taylor's Grove society again, Mr. Beecher. And I'm just the person to help you do it. Welcome back."

He grunted.

"You ever notice that you grunt when you're disgruntled?" She lifted a lock of hair and let it fall, noting the natural lay of it without combing. "What's up with that? Maybe we need to make up a new word for you. Gruntled."

"You ever notice that you talk a lot?"

"Everybody notices *that*. I think better when I'm talking." She leaned down and whispered in his ear. "Now, just relax and let my hands work their magic."

Yep. His grip tightened again. "I have a sneaky suspicion Delilah said something similar to Samson—and the whole time she was talking, she was planning his demise."

Emmy smiled at the idea of wielding that kind of power over Sol Beecher. "It'll be over real soon… Samson," she cooed…and made the first snip right above his ear.

THE FIRST HALF hour at Bree and Kale's had been an awkward mix of feeling like the new kid on the block and being welcomed home like a long-lost relative. It wasn't that Sol hadn't seen these people regularly for the past eight years, but rather that he hadn't *interacted* with them on any level except superficial niceties in a long time.

And of course, there was the initial anxiety that one of the dogs would hump his leg or one of the kids would hug it and expose his secret. That had kept him busy with one or the other on his lap except when he was eating or playing cornhole.

It became evident with the first pitch of the beanbags that as far as Kale, Mark and Emmy-Lou were concerned, the Cornhole World Championship was at stake. And though it took Sol a few throws to find his balance and the right trajectory, once he did, that old competitive spirit emerged and he, too, was out for blood.

But damn, it was hard to maintain focus on anything except the perfect curves of Emmy-Lou's body in those short shorts and T-shirt. After the haircut—which he grudgingly had to admit looked good—they'd swum right up until time to leave, so her makeup was minimal, and she'd traded those high heels she usually wore for flip-flops. Still, she was the prettiest woman he'd had the privilege to spend time with in so long that he couldn't remember the others.

Being around her was pure hell, but he'd lived through hell before.

"So Daddy runs out on the upstairs veranda in the middle of the night…" EmmyLou was in the middle of another one of her stories. Sol couldn't remember when he'd laughed so much. Being with her and Kale was like catching a performance at a comedy club. "…and this old coon was hanging right there by their bedroom window—a full story off the ground, mind you. Daddy catches the coon's eyes with the flashlight and yells, 'Get out of here, you stupid sonofabitch!' That coon lets go and drops down to the ground with a *splat* and runs off. But all the commotion wakes Miss Janie, our next-door neighbor. She comes running out in her gowntail to see who the man was that Daddy had caught Mama with!"

EmmyLou's speech was always animated, but Sol could tell when the moonshine started to kick in. She got louder and funnier. It was hard for him to imagine the woman ever suffering from stage fright. She never seemed to be at a loss for words.

Once the laughter died down, Mark stood and stretched. "I'm sure Kale's about to top that one with his own coon story, but we need to get Tess to bed." The little girl was conked out with her head in her mom's lap.

"Want me to take y'all home?" Sol offered. "My truck's got a backseat."

Although they lived close enough that they'd walked, Audrey readily accepted. "That would be great. I hate to wake her up, but she's getting almost too big for Mark to carry that far."

The new stepdad didn't seem to mind, though.

He'd already gathered Tess up in his arms, and she'd latched her arms around his neck and her legs around his waist. Her sweet face was in perfect repose against his shoulder.

Sol's ribs squeezed at the sight. Wife…kids… things he'd taken for granted in his future until the damn grenade went off. Oh yeah, they were still possible, just not probable.

The thought of dating—trying on women until he found the one in a thousand who could look at him without pity and still see him as a whole man—it made him tired just thinking about it.

"You're gruntin' again." EmmyLou's poke brought him out of his reverie.

"Are we ready, then?" he asked, and her head wobbled on a nod.

They said their goodbyes and loaded the truck with the dogs in the truck bed and the Dublins in the backseat for the drive that only took a couple of minutes—time filled with EmmyLou's endless chatter.

But as soon as they'd let the passengers out and seen them in, she got quiet. So quiet Sol thought maybe she'd passed out, even though she hadn't had that much to drink.

He glanced over to find her soft profile bathed in moonlight. She was staring out the windshield at…nothing.

He reached over and brushed a finger down

her arm. "You okay?" He hoped she wasn't about to be sick. He'd cleaned his truck inside and out just yesterday.

She shrugged but didn't look at him, then rolled her head to face him. "Apparently not."

"Are you sick? Should I pull over?"

"No, I'm not sick," she snapped.

"But you said you weren't okay. What's wrong?"

"I said 'apparently not.'"

He hadn't been with a woman in a long time, but he could still recognize that double-speak they were all so good at. He pulled the truck to the side of the road and put it in Park. Turning to face her, he propped his left arm on the steering wheel. "What does that mean? Have I done something to offend you?" A quick mental scan of the afternoon and evening didn't bring anything to mind. Everything had gone well. He'd had fun, even. And he hadn't uttered anything but compliments about the overpriced-but-good haircut.

She faced him, arms locked across her chest, pushing her amazing cleavage almost too high to ignore. "It's what you *don't* do that offends me."

He studied her for a minute. "You're crazy, you know that? You and your brother both. Certifiably nuts."

"No, we're not. And you leave Joey out of this. At least, we don't *ignore* people."

"Are you trying to say I ignore you? Because

that just confirms you're crazy. You're the most *un*ignorable person I've ever been around."

"But you ignore me as a *woman*." She huffed and threw herself against the seat back, arms still crossed.

"*I do not* ignore you as a woman."

Her head jerked his way, the angry glare still pulsating. "But you don't even try to kiss me. You treat me like a hunk of cow tongue."

Sol couldn't believe his ears. EmmyLou was a known tease, and this was her at her finest. "You want me to kiss you." He didn't offer it as a question.

"I give you every kiss-me look, I know, but you're like a piece of granite."

"Well, you've got the hard part right." He snorted. "Hell, Emmy, I had to swim all afternoon because a cold shower wasn't available."

"See? Here I sit, not an arm's length away, all but begging you to kiss me, and you want to argue about it."

"I'm not arguing about it. I just can't imagine that you're being sincere."

"So now you're calling me a liar?"

"No. I'm saying that you have all those other men wanting to kiss you, so why fixate on me unless you want to prove something?"

"So you *don't* want to kiss me?"

Sol pinched the bridge of his nose and squeezed

his eyes closed. "God Almighty, you can be annoying. I don't want to be toyed with."

He threw the truck into Drive and pulled back onto the road, fuming. The tentative friendship he and EmmyLou had found this week had all been a farce. She'd never liked him. Hell, she'd announced that to the whole auditorium the night of the drawing, hadn't she? Since the one night they'd slept together all those years ago, she'd had a hard-on for him—not the good kind.

The heat of their silence made the air in the truck heavy and hard to breathe. He understood that old saying, "Like a fish out of water." That was precisely how he felt as he turned onto her lane. He brought the truck to a stop in her driveway and cut the engine. Without a word, he got out, determined to walk her to the door so she couldn't throw not being a gentleman in his face.

But she was already out before he even closed his door. She came around and met him at the front. "You're right. I do toy with guys. It's called flirting. Maybe you've forgotten? 'Cause it must not happen very often down in that hole you've dug for yourself to live in. It's supposed to be fun. A way to show interest. And I know you haven't forgotten what *that* is…." She stepped against him and slid her arms around his waist in one fluid movement. And then her lips were pressing his, warm and inviting.

The jolt that zinged through him was strong enough to shake the dust off his libido. Without a thought or a consideration, his arms held her to him, and he answered her mouth with the fervor it demanded.

Being toyed with might be okay...

She tasted of cinnamon with a hint of apple and vanilla from the moonshine she'd been drinking. A touch of smoke from the barbecue grill lingered in her hair. Sol had never tasted a more intoxicating blend—or drunk from a more enjoyable vessel.

The kiss heated, its vacuum pulling him deeper into a sweet oblivion where nothing existed except EmmyLou Creighton's luscious curves. He'd enjoyed the sight of them all afternoon—and now the rest of his senses were getting their chance. His hands explored and she responded in kind. The sound vibrating from the back of her throat was part moan, part whimper, and total desire.

All of his finely honed instincts about women came bursting out of dormancy.

He was no longer being toyed with. This was no game. But what in the hell did EmmyLou want with him?

This afternoon, she'd mentioned repaying his kind treatment of Joe Wayne. Was pretending to be attracted to him her way of paying it forward? Making him feel like a man again?

He broke the kiss and set her away from him. "EmmyLou…" He had to pause to catch his breath, which was coming in short spurts. "You don't have…to do this."

She squinted one eye. "Do what?"

"Treat me like a charity case."

"You think I go around taking guys to bed because I feel *sorry* for them? Lord help me, Sol. I give up." She shook her head and walked toward the back of the truck, lowering the tailgate. "And you call *me* crazy. C'mon, Bentley boy." Bentley jumped down and headed toward the back door with EmmyLou following him.

Sol intercepted her at the stone pathway, grasping her arm. If she got very far ahead, no way in hell could he catch her. "*'Taking guys to bed…?'* Are you implying you're attracted enough to me to…to…?" Saying it aloud would invest too much in his tentative hope. He dropped her arm and rubbed the back of his neck, finding it odd not to get a handful of hair.

Bentley let out an impatient bark and chased it with a whine.

"To find out if there might be something between us? Something besides chemistry?"

She felt chemistry?

"Something that makes me crazy and scares me to death at the same time? Something that makes me look forward to Thursdays and Sundays because I know you're coming to swim? Something that—"

"Makes you put on makeup?" His heart kicked in his chest.

"And makes me fix my hair." Her voice grew softer. "And wear my sexiest new bikini."

Sol had heard enough to be convinced...for the moment. With the smoothness he'd perfected in his early twenties, he swept an arm around her waist and claimed her mouth with his.

The sigh she expelled on his tongue held both contentment and heat. When she relaxed in his arms, the heady sense of power surged south.

Bentley's bark grew more insistent. By the time they'd reluctantly broken the kiss, he was standing on his back paws, front paws perched against EmmyLou's hips.

"Jealous." She leaned over and gave him a peck on his head.

He dashed to the steps again.

The short respite gave Sol's vision a chance to clear. Over EmmyLou's head, he saw what had Bentley stirred up. "What the hell?" Sol pushed EmmyLou away and behind him. A dark figure lay sprawled out on her back steps. A man. Was he hurt? Dead?

"Oh my God!" EmmyLou brushed past Sol on a run. "It's Joey!"

She got to him before Sol did and checked his

pulse. She straightened up, her face a mixture of relief and anger with a bit of sadness tightening the outside corners of her eyes.

"He's drunk and passed out," she said. "Think you can give me a hand?"

Sol nodded, feeling his newly healed nose getting once again out of joint.

CHAPTER TWELVE

"JOE WAYNE." EMMY SHOOK her brother, but not nearly as hard as she wanted to. "Wake up."

"Don't." His eyes remained closed. "I nee' sleep it off."

"You need to get some food in you to soak up the alcohol. Come on." She clamped her fingers onto his jaws and shook. "I've made you a waffle. Blueberry. Your favorite."

"Not hungry." He threw an arm across his eyes and rolled onto his side.

She and Sol had gotten her brother as far as the couch last night, but there was no way to get him up the stairs to one of her guest rooms, so that's where he'd stayed.

It wasn't a surprise for him to show up unannounced, and she usually didn't mind. Joey got passes on lots of things that would warrant lectures from her if it was anybody else doing them. But his timing last night had been the worst. Just when she and Sol had finally made a step in what she hoped might be the right direction, Joey showed up and all hell broke loose.

They'd had to get him out of those filthy, stinking clothes—not an easy feat, and one that would've been nigh to impossible if Sol hadn't been there to help. And though she'd wanted to bathe him as well, she'd settled for double-sheeting the couch and hoping none of his body parts touched anything other than the sheets.

Then there had been the mess outside. He'd invaded the patio bar, emptying a six-pack of beer and throwing the empty cans into the pool. She wouldn't dare consider what else he might've done in the pool. He'd consumed an entire quart jar of her homemade apple pie moonshine and had broken two others.

"Leave it," Sol had told her. "Your brother needs to learn to clean up his own messes. Then maybe he'd think twice before he makes them."

She knew he was right, but it was her property that the night wildlife would be attracted to—skunks and raccoons, or worse, coyotes and bobcats. If they started coming around, she'd never be comfortable letting Bentley outside. "I can't leave moonshine all over my patio," she'd snapped, her frustration level nearly reaching its breaking point. "You go on home and I'll deal with this myself."

He hadn't. He'd stayed and helped her clean up. But by the time it was all done, neither of them was in the mood to do anything except chew Joe

Wayne's rear end—and since it wasn't available, anyone's rear end would do.

The last straw had been finding Joe Wayne's motorcycle parked on the far side of the house instead of in the drive. Furrows cutting diagonally across her front yard indicated he'd missed the driveway and plowed across her newly seeded lawn and through two flower beds.

Sol started pushing the heavy cycle back around to the driveway, and she could tell by the way he was limping that his leg was hurting him terribly.

"You're limping, Sol. Just let me do it." She stepped up to take the handlebars, but he held firm.

"I can do it."

In the dark, he didn't see the hole where Bentley had dug up the mole. He stepped in it, turning his ankle and pitching over onto the hip on his good side.

Emmy could only watch helplessly as Sol and Patsy crashed simultaneously to the ground, thankfully in opposite directions.

She went over to him, but he refused her help, shaking her hands off. His embarrassment and humiliation came out loud and clear as he cursed and grunted his way to an upright position.

Emmy stood back, watching until he was on his feet. "You hurt?" she asked.

"No" was all he said. He grabbed Patsy's handlebars and uneventfully finished pushing her to the drive. Then he got in his truck and drove away.

Emmy was actually relieved to not have to deal with the awkwardness of a goodbye.

She couldn't remember another day that started out with such promise and ended on such a pile of shit.

"Joe Wayne Fuller." She gave him one more shake. "I've got to get to work. Are you planning on staying with me for a while, or are you just passing through?"

His answer came as a snore.

She gave up and went back to the kitchen, wrapping the waffle in a paper towel, but leaving it on a plate on the counter. Joey could warm it up later.

She went to the kitchen door to call Bentley back inside, and he came running, abandoning his squirrel chasing duty. She exchanged his underground fence collar for the lighter one he wore to the salon and called a last goodbye to the snoring heap on her couch.

There was no reply, of course.

He'd probably been to Nashville, so maybe he'd mentioned his plans to Mama or Daddy. She punched the button and gave the Call Mama command.

"Yes, EmmyLou?" Her mom's voice held her I-don't-have-time-to-deal-with-you-right-now tone.

Emmy got right to the point. "Joe Wayne showed up at my house last night. Any idea what his plans are?"

"Well, why don't you ask him?" Irritation.

"He was passed out on my back steps last night when I got home, and he slept on the couch. I can't get anything out of him this morning."

A dramatic sigh. "I don't know why you would be asking me? I'm getting ready for my bridge and brunch club, and I don't have time for this adolescent behavior."

"Mama, Joey's drinking goes way beyond adolescent behavior. I'm worried about him."

"Finally, you're worried about him? You walked out on him at the most important time of his life, ruining his career."

Here we go. "Mama, don't start—"

"Of course, you don't want to hear it. You never want to talk about your failures. You always want to act like it's something *we've* done. But when you walked out, the excessive drinking started. So, as far as I'm concerned, it's your turn to deal with it. Your father and I are tired of cleaning up the messes you kids caused. You've made your bed and now you have to li—"

Emmy punched the button and hung up without saying goodbye.

Maybe if the day *started* on a pile of shit…

THE POUNDING INSIDE Joe Wayne's head grew louder...and then it sprouted a voice.

"Damn it, Joe Wayne. I know you're in there. Open the door."

Joe Wayne sat up and peered through bleary vision at his surroundings. EmmyLou's place. He remembered having plans to come...just couldn't rightly recollect getting here.

The pounding started again. It was on the door.

"Joe Wayne. Wake up. It's Sol."

Sol? Word really did get around fast in this town. He stood up. The room swayed, and he waited for it to settle. "I'm coming. Just don't hit that door again!"

When he opened the door, he found Sol Beecher standing exactly the way he had left the man down in Florida—hands on his hips and a scowl on his face.

"Howdy thar, Mr. Beecher." He held the door open, squinting against the brightness of the sun. Sol nodded in greeting as he passed. No hi, no kiss my ass, no nothing.

"Get some work clothes on," Sol ordered. "I've got a truck full of dirt and some bedding plants out here to fix those ruts in EmmyLou's yard."

"Whoa." Joe Wayne covered his eyes and felt for the door to shut out the light that was making the inside of his skull throb. "I haven't ate breakfast yet."

"It's twelve-thirty. That you haven't eaten's your own fault."

"Blame Johnnie Walker, not me." He laughed at the joke, but his friend evidently didn't get it. "Have a seat, Sol. Make yourself comfortable."

"I'm not here to visit, knucklehead. I'm here to help you fix EmmyLou's yard where you tore it up last night. Now get your ass in gear, and let's get on it."

Joe Wayne searched his memory, but last night's arrival didn't exist in it. He went to the front window and looked out. There was a deep indentation in the grassy area by the road. But toward the middle of the yard, the area that had obviously been recently seeded and strawed and well-watered had a deep rut cutting through it just off-center. "Damn!" He gave a low whistle. "I did that?"

"Yep." Sol had come up beside him. He slapped Joe Wayne on the back, hard enough to jar his teeth together—and start a corkscrew winding through the back of his head. "But don't worry. It's repairable. I brought my tiller and everything. Just go change clothes. Your stuff's in Emmy-Lou's bathroom."

"How do you know where my stuff's at?"

"I put it there." Sol gave him a shove that got him started.

"You were here last night?" He turned and walked backward, giving Sol a grin. "In my sis's bedroom?"

"Only long enough to get your stuff put away." Sol moved toward the kitchen. "I'll fix you a sandwich."

Joe Wayne found his small bag of toiletries and a pair of his shorts and a T-shirt on a chair in the bathroom. He wanted a shower, but he'd only have to take another one later anyway. And what he really craved was a drink. He hurried to change clothes.

Sol met him at the kitchen door and handed him a sandwich, thick with roast beef and Swiss cheese, and a bottled water.

Joe Wayne looked at the bottle, then at Sol. "I'll need beer for this job."

"Not in this heat. You just need to keep chugging the water." Sol steered him out the door. "Alcohol will make you sweat more. You'll get dehydrated."

"I didn't say alcohol," Joe Wayne protested. "I said beer."

Sol raised his eyebrows, which meant he was about to make a point. "And I said no."

Joe Wayne opened the water and drank the entire bottle. "Got more?"

Sol rolled his eyes. While he went back for more, Joe Wayne gobbled down the sandwich.

He wasn't sure when he'd last eaten solid food, but it hit the bottom of his belly pretty hard, so he must've been drinking his meals for the last few days.

Sol came back with two bottles of water and one of those round coolers with a spigot on the front. "This should do it."

"You got beer in that?" Joe Wayne asked.

"Ice water."

"That's the biggest damn disappointment of my day so far," he said, meaning every word.

They went around front and examined the damage, which he had to admit was more extensive than he would've thought possible. Then they unloaded the tiller from the truck and started to work.

Sol guided the tiller through the soil that had been packed down tightly under Patsy's weight while Joe Wayne was forced to do the pissy-ass work of planting the replacement flowers in the beds he'd slaughtered. The sun blazed down on his back and neck, and sweat poured off his face, sprinkling the flowers with his salty spray. He needed a beer in the worst way. That's the only thing that would make this hell job bearable. A cold beer gliding down the back of his throat. Mmm! His hand holding the trowel started shaking. EmmyLou surely had some beer in the fridge.

When the urge became too strong to ignore, he stood up. Catching Sol's eye, he gave a gesture he assumed meant *Need to piss* the world over and thumbed toward the house. Sol nodded like he was asking permission—which he wasn't.

He went in the front door, sprinting into a run as soon as it closed.

The beer was right where he expected it to be. A twelve-pack with a couple already gone. He opened a can and downed it in three gulps. Then he grabbed another and repeated.

"Oh, yeah." He belched the words, noticing that just those two drinks had cooled him enough to stop his hands from shaking.

With the eight or so remaining, he should be able to get through the rest of the job.

But if he ran out?

There was sure to be some whiskey, or Emmy-Lou's prized moonshine, around here someplace.

And the liquor cabinet was indeed well-stocked with anything he might have a craving for.

Relaxed and satisfied, he headed back outside.

EMMYLOU JUMPED OUT of her car and ran to Joe Wayne, hugging him tightly. "Oh my goodness! Look at what y'all have done!"

Then she loped over to Sol for the same. A tight hug. An innocent, brotherly hug.

Great.

Sol had hoped to be finished with the yard before she got home from work, telling himself he wanted it to be a surprise and allow Joe Wayne to take the credit. But truth was, the lingering effects of last night's kiss and the abrupt turn of events had left him in a mental and physical limbo. The kiss had been sultry and hot and better than any kiss he remembered. The hug just now? Standard fare.

Of course, last night's kiss had been fueled by white lightning. If EmmyLou hadn't been a little tipsy, he wasn't sure she would've ever started the conversation that led to it. And it wasn't lost on him that as soon as the Joe Wayne episode started, and she sobered up, the sensual mood evaporated with the moonshine.

Sometime in the middle of his sleepless night, he'd decided to play it cool and wait for her to make the move again.

If she didn't, he wouldn't cmbarrass her by making a big deal out of last night's one-hit wonder.

"I figured I'd have to hire somebody to come in and retill that—Bentley, stop jumping on Sol— since I don't have a tiller." She'd let the dog out of the car without his leash, and he was running crazy, happy circles around the three of them, stopping to give their legs doggy hugs while she tried ineffectively to rein him in.

"We still got to finish putting the straw on."
Joe Wayne put his arm around her shoulder and
gave her another hug. "Sorry about the mess,
sis. Guess I'd had a little more than I realized."

EmmyLou's happy face dissolved, and she
pushed free of her brother's hold. "You smell
like a brewery."

He cut his eyes to Sol and away. "I've had a
couple. It's hot out here."

"I should've known," Sol said. "All those trips
to the bathroom…"

Played for a fool.

Sol shook his head, almost as disgusted with
himself as he was at Joe Wayne.

"You shouldn't have been driving last night,
Joey." EmmyLou jerked her sunglasses off, revealing her eyes, pinched with worry. She swiped
the glasses through the air as she spoke. "You
could've killed somebody. Or yourself."

Joe Wayne gave a sheepish shrug. "I hadn't
had that much till I got here." His eyes darted
away and around the yard.

"And why didn't you call and let me know you
were coming?" EmmyLou wiped her eyes and
replaced the glasses, settling her fists on her hips
in a motherly stance, though from Sol's perspective, the curve of those hips in that body-hugging
lemon yellow minidress was far from motherly.

"My phone got smashed up in a catfight. These

two women was fighting over me." Joe Wayne took off his cap and used the tail of his shirt to wipe the sweat from his face. "One got hold of it and made use of a hammer somebody'd left laying around."

"Joey, Joey, Joey." EmmyLou's head rolled back, and she gave a long sigh. "What am I gonna do with you?"

"Feed me, I hope." Joe Wayne flipped the cap back onto his head.

She laughed softly, her anger melting away. "Okay, sugar. I'll get supper started."

Sol watched the exchange with interest. Em-myLou's voice, her actions, everything looked and sounded like she was dealing with a fifteen-year-old rather than a grown man.

When she walked between them, she hesitated, brushing her hand across Sol's arm. "You staying for supper?"

"No, better not. I want to finish this job. And I smell like a goat. Not fit for mixed company."

She grinned, lifting her eyebrows above her glasses. "I've got showers."

Not a good option without his other prosthesis. "But I'd have to put these dirty clothes back on."

"Finish up. Go home and clean up. Be back by seven." She started walking away.

"I really shouldn't impose," he said, and she turned to listen. "Y'all need to catch up."

She tilted her head. "You got other plans?" Her smirk said she knew she had him.

"Well, no but…"

Her chin lifted defiantly. "See you at seven. C'mon, Bentley."

Sol forced his eyes to check out the section of ground that still needed straw rather than watching the sway of that yellow minidress.

"Well, I'll be." Joe Wayne punched his bicep. "You and EmmyLou."

"There's no me and EmmyLou."

"You said you was here last night when she found me."

"I came over to swim yesterday afternoon." He kept his face sober as he met Joe Wayne's knowing smile. "Friends called and invited her to dinner, and she insisted I go with her. That's all."

Joe Wayne's hands slid into his back pockets, and he rocked from his toes to his heels and back. "That's all, huh? And how'd you finagle an invite to swim?"

Sol wasn't about to go through *that* story, but he was fairly certain EmmyLou would relish the telling. "EmmyLou thought it would be good therapy. For my leg."

Joe Wayne's knowing grin ruptured into a cackle. "I'll just bet she did."

"Shut up, dumbass." Sol pulled out his pocket knife and sliced through the twine, loosening the last bail of straw. "Let's get this done." He wasn't sure if he was looking forward to the upcoming evening or not.

Two nights in a row of being in EmmyLou's proximity might be more than his starving manhood could take.

CHAPTER THIRTEEN

EMMY'S STOMACH MUSCLES ached from laughing. Usually she was the one telling the funny stories, but Joey and Sol made quite a pair with their tale of what really happened at the beach, in all its glorious detail. It was obvious the men held a genuine affection for each other that touched her heart. Watching them together, she saw Joey bringing out the kid in Sol, while Sol brought out the man in Joey.

Both of them needed a little more of each, respectively, in their lives.

"Y'all are seriously gonna arm wrestle to see who gets the last pork chop?" she asked, not sure which category this last competition put either of them in. Only one thing came to mind that would be better for Sol—and watching his biceps bulge under the pressure into mounds of rock caused that other thing to settle into her brain and declare squatters' rights.

She silently rooted for him…was glad he won easily.

And she pacified Joey with an extra piece of Kentucky pecan pie—his favorite.

Sol seemed so much more relaxed than he'd been the night before. His secret wasn't a secret here, so tonight called for no pretense. Oh, he'd been smooth last night, but she'd noticed how he carefully picked up the dogs and the kids.

Life would be so much easier for him if he'd just tell the truth about his leg. Then again, maybe she couldn't see things too clearly with that big ol' log in her eye.

The only thing that seemed to bother Sol tonight was Joey's drinking. Every time her brother poured himself a shot, Sol's sensual, full lips pressed into a straight line.

She'd talk to Joey about his drinking. Tomorrow.

Tonight, she had different plans.

"So, Sol…how much would you be willing to pay for a private concert from The Fullers?" She shot a pointed look toward Joey as she finished wiping off the counter. "You're responsible for part of the bill he gave me, you know, Joey. And we've entertained you all through dinner with the curious incident of the leg in the nighttime." Sol laughed at her allusion even though she'd referred to his prosthesis as a *leg*. "It's time you earned your keep around here."

Sol rubbed the stubble on his chin. She was glad he hadn't shaved when he went home to shower. Now that his hair was short, the stubble made him look hubba-hubba instead of derelict.

Fact was, it made him impossible to resist… almost. Or, he would have been if he ever did anything that needed resisting.

But he hadn't given her a smidgen of a look to suggest he remembered the heated kiss last night.

"Five hundred per Fuller is the going price, as I recall," Sol said. The corner of his mouth twitched, and her lower parts twitched in response.

"Sold for one thousand dollars an hour." She accepted the offer, but Joe Wayne's head tilted like Bentley's when she asked him questions.

"He's gonna pay us a thousand dollars to sing for him?"

"No," she explained. "He's going to subtract a thousand from the bill he gave me. That brings it down to—"

"Three thousand two hundred twenty-three," Sol filled in the total.

The amount wasn't nearly as much as it had been when he first presented her with that damn bill. Three more concerts—if Joey stuck around—and two more haircuts.

And then what? Would Sol keep coming over, or would he slink back into his cave and hibernate for the rest of his life?

She couldn't let that happen. Yesterday she'd

told him she was the one who could help him become social again, and that was what she intended to do.

"Shit-o'-day." Joey's use of their Pawpaw's favorite expression put a grin on Emmy's face. "For five hundred dollars, I'd sing buck nekkid on Main Street."

"Heaven spare my eyes from such a sight." Sol shuddered. "I still remember you in that T-shirt and thong. And let me tell you something—you make an uglier woman than you do a man." He tilted his face toward Emmy and winked. "How your parents could produce a woman who looks like you and a man who looks like him is beyond me."

Joey was on his feet. He moved behind Sol, grabbed him in a choke hold, and planted a kiss on the top of his head. "You just can't admit you love me, bro...or anybody else." He shot a lopsided grin toward his sister. "I'll go get the *gee*-tars."

As soon as he got out of sight, Sol rose from his chair and came over to lean on the counter she'd just wiped off. His eyes were soft around the edges, but his mouth was firm. "EmmyLou." His voice was almost a whisper. "He's had ten beers and four whiskey and waters that have been more whiskey than water."

His gentle concern brought tears to her eyes.

She nodded, tried to blink them away. "I know. It's gotten out of hand. I'm going to talk to him tomorrow."

He laid his hand over hers and squeezed. "If you need any help…"

Argumentative banter with Sol came easily, but this serious talk threw her into a tizzy. "Thanks," she muttered, glad to hear Joey's footfalls coming down the steps.

Sol removed his hand and eased away.

She grabbed the dishcloth and wiped the counter again until the tears he'd brought on were gone. God help her, this man wrung emotions out of her like she was a wet mop.

"Y'all coming?" Joey yelled from the small sitting room at the front of the house. "It's raining outside, and the caustics are better in here anyway."

"He means acoustics," she explained to Sol.

He chuckled, and the pleasant sound jerked her body into a different realm from where it had been a moment ago. "He butchers the language better than anyone I know. And coming from Taylor's Grove, that says a lot." They shared a smile, and he gestured in the direction of Joey's strums. "Ready?"

She nodded. But when she walked past him and his hand touched the small of her back, his question took on a completely different connotation.

IF HE EVER found one of those geniuses in a bottle, Joe Wayne would ask for only one wish: to sing again with sis onstage. Her voice had a way of quieting his insides almost as good as the liquor. Hell, if he could've convinced her to hit the sauce like he did before a concert—and convinced Mama to stay off her ass—they could've been winning those CMA Awards and standing onstage with Blake and Brad and the whole crew.

Despite the changes age brought to their voices, they still blended in the most perfect harmony. They was the Everly Brothers...if one of them had been a sister.

He was getting a little woozy—probably from working so hard all afternoon in that hot sun. "Do 'Stone's Throw from Your Heart,'" he suggested. He'd written that one just for EmmyLou and always considered it one of his best—a plaintive tune she crooned in the most perfect way about a young girl whose mother ran the local saloon and house of ill repute. Too bad it hadn't come to him during their heyday. Nobody but family had ever heard it.

Without hesitation, EmmyLou's fingers plucked the strings as she closed her eyes and hummed the introduction before starting to sing. "I watched you play in the mayor's yard from my window just above the bar." She began soft, her voice sweet and innocent. "And how I wished that

I could be your friend. Sometimes you'd smile and wave at me. I'd dream of love that couldn't be. I know so much more now than I did then."

Joe Wayne's eyes cut to Sol, and he leaned back to study the interesting look on his friend's face…and to steady his head, which had started to swim. At first, he assumed Sol was caught up in the song, but something in his heart told him it wasn't the song at all that had him ensnared.

EmmyLou was plucking the guy's heartstrings as surely as she was the guitar strings. And yet, something between them was a few sandwiches short of a picnic. Was it the damn leg thing? Because that seemed a really stupid reason not to be together.

"But people kept on throwing stones, hurtful words like sticks and stones that built the wall and kept our love apart. Our narrow street was wide in ways that rule the world and life's parade and kept me just a stone's throw from your heart."

Sitting back, Joe Wayne felt the flask in his back pocket, which he'd filled earlier. Just being aware of it made him crave a drink. EmmyLou had only one more verse to go, and then he'd sing again. He needed something to prepare his throat. Hell, they'd been going at it strong now for well over an hour. He pulled out the container and screwed off the lid, had it just poised at his lips,

when Sol looked over and caught him—or that's
how it felt—like he was some damn snotty-nosed
kid caught with his hand in the cookie jar. Sol's
mouth pulled down at the corners. Joe Wayne
held out the flask in offering.

Damn if Sol didn't take it and keep it without
even taking a drink.

Joe Wayne grinned. He liked Sol, but the guy
could be such an ass.

"You wrote that, Joe?" Sol clapped. "It could
be a big hit."

"Not unless EmmyLou comes out of hiding.
Nobody else could touch it."

EmmyLou shook her head. "And we all know
that's not gonna happen."

"What about that one you were working on
at the beach? 'Lonely People?'" Sol hummed a
few bars.

Joe Wayne flew into the song, singing the entire thing and forgetting the words only a couple
of times. He also fumbled the strings a few times
when his fingers started to twitch. *I need a drink.*

EmmyLou squealed with approval when the
last chords faded away. "I *love* it, Joey! Call Tate
and let him hear it."

Joe Wayne shrugged. He hadn't told Emmy-
Lou about his last conversation with their old record producer…when the gruff old bastard had

referred to Joe Wayne as "not so much a has-been
as a never-was."

The comment had cut him deep, but he had to
admit Tate was right. Without EmmyLou, he'd
never been much of anything.

The memory brought a need for a drink in the
worst way.

"Tate can kiss my ass," was all he said in answer. "But that room upstairs is calling me, and
I'm gonna bid you good folks good-night." He
stood and leaned down to kiss EmmyLou's forehead. Then he held out his hand to Sol for his
flask. The smart-ass grinned and shook his head.

Joe Wayne laughed and slapped him on the
back as he passed. "Don't y'all kids stay up too
late, you hear?"

He walked at a normal gait even though he
wanted to run—that bottle of whiskey he'd filled
the flask with was waiting in his room.

ONCE JOE WAYNE LEFT, Sol felt the awkwardness
descend on him and Emmy like a wet blanket.
A wet electric blanket that sent a shockwave
through his body every time his eyes met hers.

She was giving him that kiss-me look again,
and damn if his body wasn't itching to comply,
although just a kiss couldn't begin to scratch
his needs.

And with her brother upstairs, this was hardly the time or the place.

"I'd better be going." He stood. "The concert was great. Expensive, but great."

She grinned as she stood and put her guitar in the seat she'd vacated. "Worth every penny."

"Yeah, it was," he agreed.

He'd parked his truck around back, so they headed toward the kitchen.

"You sure you have to go? Got a hot date waiting for you at home?"

"Last night was the closest thing to a hot date I've had in eight years." He meant it as a joke, but it had sounded funnier in his head than out loud.

The rain had stopped, and he was surprised when Emmy followed him out, walking him to the truck. Both of them kept their hands sequestered in their pockets. He wondered if she did it for the same reason he did—to keep from reacting to the jolt that went through him when their elbows brushed. To keep from pulling her against him and losing himself in one of her kisses again.

"Thanks for fixing the yard." Emmy grinned at him. "I know you tried to give the credit to Joey, but there's no way he would've ever come up with the plan or the stuff to fix it. Bless his heart. He means well."

"Yeah, he does." Sol couldn't keep the melancholy from his tone. That someone he cared about so much was battling alcoholism at such a young age hurt him more than he cared to admit. He'd seen it with buddies from the service…saw what they went through. In many ways, it was worse than losing a leg.

Alcohol could steal the very life from you a sip at a time.

"Thanks for supper." They'd reached his truck and still she was with him—which felt pretty great. He leaned against the driver's door, and she just kept standing there with her hands in her back pockets, looking at him with that dreamy expression.

Oh, what the hell.

Sol reached his hand to her waist and watched the spark light her eyes and the smile touch her lips. She stepped closer, so he took the liberty of putting his other hand on her waist. She responded by laying her arms across his shoulders. For a few still moments, they looked into each other's eyes, scanned each other's faces.

What was going through her head? Had she really thought this through?

"In case your memory's failed you since last night, this is my *yes* look," she said softly.

He grinned. "Then I need to get you comfortable, because this may take awhile." He shifted his hand to her neck and let it slide into her hair, cradling her head when she tilted her mouth up in offering.

His brain told him to go slow. It would be too easy to let these urges run away with him…take him too far ever to return to his simple life. But damn! With the first touch of his lips to hers, he wanted to possess every inch of this woman. Her mouth met his and pressed closer, somehow remaining soft and luscious, opening an invitation his tongue readily accepted.

His free hand stroked her back, his thumb finding a warm strip of exposed skin between her top and her shorts. She shuddered, and he felt more than heard the moan that vibrated deep in her throat.

Had he gone too far?

The answer came when her hands found the bottom of the back of his T-shirt and slid underneath—the first to touch him there in so long. He gasped at the forgotten sensation, losing his breath.

He pulled his mouth from hers but couldn't bear to lose the contact to those nerve endings, too long suppressed. His lips moved down her jaw to her neck and earlobe, encouraged by the sound of raw pleasure she made as she lifted her chin and gave him easy access to the tender places along her hairline. Her hips swayed against him in an erotic dance that would be his undoing if he wasn't careful.

And being careful was the last thing he wanted to think about right then.

It took every ounce of fortitude he had, but somehow he stopped his hands and mouth from their determined exploration and shifted his body away from her enough to clear the head attached to his neck. The move brought him up against the door of his truck, and he was glad for the support as Emmy leaned on him, resting her cheek on his shoulder, her warm breath feathering his neck.

He was aware of his heart kicking in his chest like a wild horse fighting captivity. Emmy must've felt it, too. She moved her hand to rest over the spot, taming the beast with her gentle touch.

"Emmy." He wasn't sure what to say. Too many emotions converged at the central intersection of his brain, bringing logic and speech to a halt.

"Do you want me, Sol?"

The hesitancy in her tone threw him. Experience had taught him that people generally projected their own emotions onto others. He took a deep breath and shifted to the side so he could look her in the eyes. He wished he hadn't when he saw the flicker of fear. She was having second thoughts. Had it finally caught up to her that this flirtation could develop into something serious?

If she wasn't careful, she'd end up saddled with a man who would never be whole.

"Do you really have to ask?" he questioned.

"It's just that…" She took a step back, and his heart sank. "You're not like other guys."

He hadn't expected her to be that direct, but he should have.

"We slept together all those years ago." She eased back a little more, and he saw the shine in her eyes even in the meager light of the cloudy night. "And the next morning, you couldn't wait to get rid of me. Then you never called me again." Her voice grew stronger. "I've never had another guy treat me like that. It made me furious. Made me dislike you, and yeah, I'll admit I've bad-mouthed you a lot. What I'm trying to say is that I don't want to start something we can't finish, because you are the very worst thing that has ever happened to my ego."

Sol's heart leaped at her words. She wanted him. Wanted to give this thing between them a go. He took her hands. "EmmyLou Creighton Fuller, if you can't see how much I want you, then you don't know your ass from a hole in the ground."

Her eyebrows drew together in question. Not at all the reaction he'd expected, but why should that ever surprise him with this unpredictable creature? "That saying's always confused me.

I mean, most people take it at face value and assume you're talking about an actual hole in the ground. Like one you'd dig. But *ass* is another word for *donkey*, which is another name for *burro*, b-u-r-r-o. But a *burrow*, b-u-r-r-o-w, is a hole that an animal digs in the ground, so if you don't know your ass from a hole in the ground, could it mean that you don't know a burro from a burrow?" Her eyes grew wide. When she tilted her head, he realized she was expecting an answer.

"I…uh." The strangeness of what she'd just expounded on surprised the hell out of him. He erupted into laughter and pulled her tightly against his chest, locking his hands behind her back. "I have no idea how to answer that." When he caught his breath, he went on. "But I'm sorry I ever made you doubt yourself or your desirability. I just thought you were such a fake with the perfect hair and perfect makeup. I didn't think anybody would be able to dig through all those false layers. And honestly? There were too many other women for me to want to take the time to do that."

She pushed her palms against his chest and wiggled out of his hold, moving back to look him in the eye again. "And what about now, Sol? Because I still wear the makeup and do the hair. It *is* a huge part of me—probably always will be."

"I've gotten to know the real you." He ran a finger down her arm, hoping his touch conveyed what he felt in his heart. "I've seen what's under the makeup and the hair spray, and I like what I see. I'm…interested, EmmyLou. Interested enough to want to give this—" he wiggled his finger between them "—a good, solid try."

His answer seemed to please her. The worry in her face softened into a smile. "That's a good place to start." She took his hand and swung it as she tilted her head toward the house and gave him a wicked smile. "And if you want to take things a step further, we can go in and I'll screw your leg off."

In typical EmmyLou fashion, she meant to be funny. His brain screamed that to his heart as it plummeted to the area around his feet…or rather, *foot*.

But the simple truth was that with this comment, she'd told him she was aware of his prosthesis. It was close enough to the front of her brain to be in her thoughts as she contemplated making love to him.

The woman he was looking for was the one who could *forget* his prosthesis. That obviously wasn't EmmyLou.

He stepped to the side to gain some distance from her and watched her smile dissolve into worry again.

"That was a joke." She poked him in the ribs.

"I know." With one hand on the door handle, he recognized the moment his intention dawned on her, and he raised his other hand in a stop gesture.

"You're leaving? Did I…did I hurt your feelings? 'Cause you know I'd never do that in a million years on purpose."

"No. You didn't hurt my feelings." He swung the door open. "Your comment just made me realize that the prosthesis is a major issue with you. If it's in your head at a time like this, it'll *always* be there."

She shook her head furiously in protest. "You know me. I was just trying to be funny. I treat everything as a joke—"

He slid into the seat. "And that's one thing I *really* like about you. But…" He swallowed the grief piling up in his throat. "I think you and I may be better off as friends than as lovers." He pulled on the door slightly, and she stepped back, allowing him to close it.

So many emotions flashed across her face that he couldn't keep up with them all. But none helped ease the pain he felt—pain inside, for a change. He tore his eyes away as he started the car and backed out of her drive.

The short distance to his house somehow seemed like the longest drive of his life.

CHAPTER FOURTEEN

THANK GOODNESS THE alarm on Emmy's driveway woke her at eight thirty-three or she might've missed her first appointment at ten o'clock. The night had been a fitful one, thanks to Devil-Man, Sol Beecher, who'd obviously made it his sole purpose in life to drive her to the brink of insanity.

But maybe that's him.

She shot out of bed, detesting how her heart two-stepped into a happy rhythm at the idea that he had come to make up and start over.

Said heart slowed to a dull thud at the sight of the familiar yellow van from Kerry's Grooming and Doggy Daycare making its way slowly up the drive.

"Oh Lord have mercy." She'd forgotten that Topher Kerry was picking up Bentley today for his monthly grooming. She hurried to slip on some shorts and a tee and make herself look like she'd been awake for a while. She shook her fingers through her hair, loosening the strands from sleep mode. Then she ran the makeup brush all over her face, leaving behind enough of the powder to take off the shine.

By the time the young man reached her doorbell, she had Bentley's collar and leash on him and his gluten-free treats ready for travel.

"Morning, Topher." She held the door for him as Bentley's tail beat a greeting on the nearby wall.

"Hi, Miss Emmy." The twenty-one-year-old's blush always made her feel like Mrs. Robinson even though she'd never done anything around him that could even remotely be taken as flirting.

"I've got everything ready to go. Here's his bag…and his leg. Oh crap! I mean, leash. Not leg." She was the one blushing now as Topher looked at her with an expression that said he was totally reevaluating her hotness and replacing it with senility. He'd opened his mouth when footfalls on the stairs drew their attention.

Joe Wayne came sauntering down, scruffy and swollen-eyed. "Morning." He wiped his hand down his face.

Emmy could smell the liquor on him from three feet away.

Topher's eyes widened as his quizzical look bounced between her and her brother.

"Hey, bub." She tilted her head. "Topher, this is my brother Joey. Joey, Topher Kerry, Bentley's dog groomer."

"Topher?" Joey scratched his head. "Sounds like something you'd chew up and spit out."

Topher grinned. "Short for Christopher. You know, like Topher Grace?"

"That a church song?" Joey didn't bother to cover the big yawn that stretched his mouth wide.

"No, it's a movie star," Topher answered, and Joey shrugged, obviously unimpressed. "Did you remember that we're closing early today?" The young man turned his attention back to Emmy while Joey sprawled leisurely on the stairs.

"Gah! No, I'd forgotten." She had appointments until five. Venting her frustration, she let go with a loud cat hiss, causing Bentley to bark and Joey to groan.

"Soooo, are you going to come pick him up, or shall I bring him back here?"

No way could she get off by three-fifteen, which is what it would take to be in the town of Benton by the four o'clock closing time at the groomers. "Just go ahead and bring him home. I hate for him to miss playtime, but it'll be only this once, I guess."

"I'll take him out to play when he gets home," Joey offered.

A twinge hit her between the shoulder blades. Joey's heavy drinking disallowed him from any kind of duty with her precious pooch. "No, that's okay. It'll be too hot outside for him. We'll swim tonight when I get home. Besides," she added, hoping to discourage any inkling Joey might have of ignoring her, "he can be a real handful, and you have to change his collar, and it's just too much for you to deal with. Thanks, though."

"I'll have him back around two," Topher promised.

EmmyLou bent down, squeezed Bentley's neck for a big hug and kissed the top of his head. Bye, baby dog. Be good for Topher." Sol needed a dog. It might help him learn about real love.

Had she just allowed *love* and *Sol* in the same thought?

Noooo! That cannot happen ever again.

She needed to get some food in her stomach to stop it from squeezing so hard.

"Ready, Bentley?" Topher tugged Bentley's leash and clapped his hands.

Bentley nearly jerked the kid's arm off when he shot out the door and down the steps.

Emmy watched until the van disappeared. Then she turned to Joey. "I overslept, so I've got to rush. There's plenty to eat. Just help yourself." She went over to the steps where he was still sitting, stooped down and brushed the hair out of his eyes so she could see them. "Don't drink too much today, okay? I'm worried about what all that alcohol's doing to your liver…and your brain. And you know it shrinks your testicles, right?" She'd read that on the internet sometime around three this morning in an attempt to get her mind off Sol.

Jocy gave her a lopsided grin. "If I get back the voice I had at fifteen, maybe I'll become famous again."

Emmy laughed and ruffled his hair as she stood. "Just remember—" she shook her finger in his face "—Bentley doesn't need to go out. But *if* you take him out, either he has to be on leash or you have to put on the collar with the signaling device."

"Got it." Joey pushed to his feet. "How long did Sol stay last night after I turned in?"

"Not very long. Maybe fifteen minutes."

Thirteen minutes of heaven and two minutes of hell. Way too long and not nearly long enough.

JOE WAYNE PIDDLED away the morning.

He swam a little until the pool water got so warm it felt like a bath. The heat made him thirsty, so he went looking for beer, but all he found was a case in the pantry. He made quick work of loading it into the fridge. Since he'd been the one to drink all the cold yesterday, he figured beer-cooling was part of his responsibility here.

And dog-sitting, but Bentley wasn't home yet.

While he waited for the beer to reach a palatable temperature, he made do with a bottle of wine from the cellar in the basement, which Emmy kept set to fifty-eight degrees. He didn't care for the sour red stuff his sister was so fond of, but the white kind poured over ice wasn't too bad.

Of course, none of it was as good as whiskey. But he'd seen the concern in Emmy's eyes, and he hated that she was worried about him. So today there'd be no whiskey drinking.

He wandered out to the pool area again, red plastic cup in one hand, bottle in the other, and stretched out on one of the long chairs in the shade.

Patsy caught his eye. Standing there in the sun with the light gleaming off her chrome parts. She had to be the most beautiful cycle ever built. And she was all his.

He filled his cup again, draining the bottle, and walked out to where she stood, smoothing his hand over the worn leather seat, heated by the sun.

"Lots of women have taken me for a ride, but none have ever given me the thrill you do, baby." He threw his leg over and sat down. "I may not have much, but I have you." He downed the contents of the cup and tossed it away.

A ride was what he needed. Him and Patsy and some hot asphalt. He wouldn't go far. The kid would be bringing Bentley back before too long.

Careful to stay on the path and not run over any of the flowers in Emmy's garden, he guided Patsy to the driveway and took off down Emmy's lane and then the state road. Instead of turning right to go toward town, he turned left. He'd never gone that way before, but he trusted his sense of direction.

No one was around, and he revved her up to top speed, but only until he saw the truck parked out by the road at the end of the driveway up ahead.

"That's Sol's truck, Patsy, sure as shootin'."

He slowed down as he passed.

Sure enough, the mailbox said Beecher, and there was Sol, stripped to the waist, putting up a section of new white fence to replace a dilapidated old split-rail.

Joe Wayne made a U-turn at the For Sale sign and brought Patsy to a stop by the truck.

"Hey, Joe."

Sol's greeting wasn't overfriendly. 'Course, it usually wasn't. But his sour-faced look was puckered up a hell of a lot more than normal.

"Hey, Sol. This your house?" A pretty, but old, stately home sat way back on a piece of shady property.

"Yep."

"She was a queen in her day." It was hard to see her through the trees, but Joe Wayne could tell even from this distance that she needed a lot of repair work.

"Yep." Sol didn't stop his work.

"'Cause of your leg?"

"Yes." Sol didn't look at him, but he trailed the end of the word out into a hiss. He was pissy—as usual. The guy needed to drink more. Might help his attitude.

The bottle of whiskey back in his room popped into his mind. The one he wasn't touching today for Emmy's sake.

Joe Wayne's mouth went dry, but he spotted the cooler by one of the shade trees. "Got any cold beer in that thing?"

"Nope, just bottled water. But help yourself."

"Naw, I'm not thirsty," he lied.

"How's your sister this morning?"

"Emmy's always good. She overslept and was rushing around like a chicken with her head cut off, but she just takes life in stride, you know?"

"Yeah."

"I guess that was one good thing that came out of Mama staying on her ass about stuff all the time. She finally turned a deaf ear to most of it. Now she don't much care what other people think."

"You're wrong about that." Sol finished a section, and rather than stopping for a break, he grabbed the post hole digger and slammed it into the ground. "Don't you see how she keeps herself fixed up? She thinks she has to be perfect, has to look pretty all the time to be loved."

Joe Wayne thought back through the years, realizing he couldn't go back far enough to recall a time when Emmy wasn't fully decked out. But then, he had a lot of fuzzy years. "Her looks was the only thing she ever got right with Mama."

Sol stopped and looked at him real weird-like. Then he grabbed that post hole digger and slammed it twice as hard as the time before. So hard he staggered.

"Whoa there," Joe Wayne cautioned. "Gonna hurt yourself."

"Go piss up a rope," Sol growled.

The man was in a mood, and being around people in a mood made Joe Wayne crave a drink real bad. Maybe the beer would be cool enough to be halfway enjoyable by now. If it wasn't, he'd have to settle for more of that god-awful wine.

"I'd best be going. The groom's bringing Bentley home soon. I pulled doggy duty this afternoon."

Sol grunted something. It might've been "See ya," or it could've been "Go to hell." With Sol, it was hard to tell.

"Later, man."

Joe Wayne got astride Patsy and took off in the direction he'd started out originally. He found a dirt road and drove for a while between two corn-fields that already had stalks taller than he was. Last night's rain was a million-dollar shower to the farmers. He checked his watch. It was almost one, so he headed back the way he'd come.

When he passed Sol's house again, his friend was nowhere to be seen, so he didn't stop this time.

He got back to sis's house and immediately went to grab a beer.

He flipped the top, took a big swig, and almost gagged. Nothing was worse than lukewarm beer. He walked over to the sink to pour it out, but couldn't bring himself to waste the beloved brew.

"What the hell." He downed the contents and went looking for another bottle of wine.

Bentley still wasn't home, so he went back out-side to wait, and it was then that he noticed how filthy he'd gotten Patsy during the ride down that dirt road. It just wouldn't do for the love of his life to go around looking like that, so he pulled her over to the hose and spigot—still at the back of the house, but on the side away from the drive, where there was afternoon shade—and found EmmyLou's cleaning supplies in the garage.

Damn, it was hot—even in the shade.

"Helloooo!"

Two paws hit his ass before he could swivel around to the voice.

"Hey, Bentley." He stooped down to receive the happy face licks from his favorite nephew, who was all spiffed up, complete with a shitty little blue bow tie. That damn thing was coming off as soon as Tofu got out of sight.

"Bentley was a good boy today." The kid smiled and handed him the leash. "Sorry I have to run, but we're leaving for Disney World in two hours!"

Joe Wayne managed a smile, though he couldn't imagine anything worse than having to pay ten dollars for a dollar-and-a-half beer. He'd go broke in one afternoon. "Have fun," he called as Tofu jogged back to the yellow van.

"I still got to wax Patsy," he told Bentley as he removed the prissy bow tie. Bentley licked his cheek in thanks. "But I tell ya, Bentley, I got to have some refreshment to finish this work. Let's go check on the beer."

They went inside, and Bentley immediately went to his water bowl and drank while Joe Wayne gulped down another not-yet-ready beer.

"That's disappointing," he told Bentley as he threw the can into the trash. He rubbed his hand across his sweaty head. "I can't take another bottle of that gut-rotting wine, but I got to have something to keep my energy up."

The bottle of whiskey was still in his room.

And he hadn't told EmmyLou he wasn't going to drink it. That was just going to be a surprise.

Oh hell, there were plenty of things he could do around here to surprise her.

Fix supper and have it waiting, for instance.

And she'd probably rather have that as a surprise anyway.

He made for the stairs, Bentley loping along beside him, leash dragging behind him. What a good dog.

He retrieved the bottle from beneath the bed where he'd put it for safekeeping and swigged a little just to fortify himself for the task at hand.

"Ahh!" Bentley tilted his head at the sound. "Sorry, fella. You're too young. Gotta be twenty-one in this state, which EmmyLou insists ain't a state at all, but's a commonwealth, whatever the hell that is."

Back down the stairs and out into the heat they went. He didn't have the foggiest notion where EmmyLou kept that other collar she said Bentley would need, so Joe Wayne was careful to keep the leash hooked around his wrist the whole time he polished Patsy. Every time he got a drink for himself, he turned the hose on and let him drink from it. He even wet the dog down with it a couple of times to make sure he stayed cool.

By the time he finished the chore, he was so

hot, he was actually dizzy from the heat. A cool shower would have been wonderful, but he wasn't sure he had enough energy to climb the stairs. And the pool would be even hotter than it had been this morning.

He'd taken off his T-shirt early on, so now he shucked out of his shorts down to his boxers and turned on the cold water from the hose, letting it drench him and Bentley from head to toe and nose to tail.

The cool-down was exactly what he needed, but the shock made the world sway around him. "I need to lay down, Bentley." He grabbed the bottle and staggered toward the back steps, leaving a dripping trail behind him. "Nope. Can't go in like this. EmmyLou'll tan both our hides. C'mere."

The chair he'd sat in this morning was still there in the shade. They could just lie on it and nap while they dried off.

He sat down on the warm cushion, making room for Bentley between his legs. The wet leash was scratching his wrist, so he took it off but kept it firmly gripped in his hand.

"We'll just sit here and dry off. Won't take long. And then we'll go in and fix a nice supper for EmmyLou." He rested his hand on the furry body and closed his eyes.

Won't she be surprised?

SOL WORKED AS long as his knee would let him, but finally had to call it a day.

He'd come in for lunch and rested a little while but headed back out around two, determined to get that second section in the ground and concrete poured around it. The fence was something he should've taken care of a long time ago.

The second section *had* gone quicker than the first. But at this rate, he'd be done…sometime in September, maybe.

Post hole digging was good therapy. Slamming the apparatus into the dirt helped work off the frustration he felt about the way things ended with Emmy last night. He'd almost convinced himself that he hadn't overreacted—had every right to respond the way he did to EmmyLou's humorous proposition—because she obviously *was* thinking about his leg, though maybe it hadn't necessarily been in a *bad* way.

But damn it to hell, he didn't want his leg to be the first thing that always came to mind when he was with somebody. That was the reason he'd kept it a secret all these years. And sure enough, the *one* of two people who *knew* and was the one person who *mattered*…

There was the rub.

Emmy *mattered*.

More than he ever thought possible, and certainly more than he wanted.

He leaned against the kitchen counter and took another long drink of ice water.

The thought of not kissing her again was like facing another amputation.

He carefully set down the glass before pounding the end of his fist against the granite counter. The sound echoed.

It took him a couple of seconds to realize the echo was someone at his front door. Who in the hell? No one ever came out here anymore, except Joe a few hours ago. He grabbed the sweat-soaked T-shirt he'd thrown over the back of the chair and jerked it on as he made his way toward the front of the house.

Through the window in the front door, he could see a woman's shape.

Nell Bradley?

She pounded again, harder this time.

He pulled the door open, and the elderly woman instantly dissolved into tears.

"Oh, thank Heavens you're here, Sol! I've hit a dog. Is it yours? I'm so sorry! He just ran right out in front of me and I couldn't stop. I tried to swerve!" She was blubbering, wringing her hands and almost hysterical.

He'd never seen Nell like this. She was known in Taylor's Grove to be always cool-headed and calm.

"I don't have a dog, Nell." He stepped out on the porch and closed the door behind him. "But I'll go take care of him." He jerked up the rug from in front of the door. "It's probably a stray, or one somebody dropped. They do a lot of that along these back roads."

"No." She shook her head and cried harder as they hurried down the steps. "He's wearing a collar and a leash. And the collar has a tag on it, but I couldn't read the print. It was too small."

Sol's stomach, which had grown queasy at the thought of having to deal with this situation, now turned completely over. "Was it a bright blue collar and leash?"

"Yes! Do you know who he belongs to?"

He broke into an awkward run. "That's EmmyLou Creighton's dog. Bentley."

"Oh dear! I thought maybe he was your dog since he was in front of your house."

Joe had said he was dog-sitting this afternoon. If Bentley had his collar and leash on, had something happened to Joe?

Sol pushed into a harder run, trying to ignore the pain that made the knee covered by the prosthesis band feel like it was on fire.

They reached the road. When Sol saw Bentley lying off to the side on the grass, a cry convulsed in his throat, but he held it in.

At their approach, Bentley raised his head and struggled to get up, yelping in pain at the movement.

Seeing the dog alive lifted the weight of dread from Sol's chest but replaced it with urgency.

"Do you think he's hurt too badly? He's not moving, but there doesn't seem to be any blood." Nell's voice was more like her normal self now.

"Easy, boy. Good dog. Let me see."

Bentley lay still as Sol pressed softly along the rib cage. The dog's heart was racing faster than his own and the heavy panting was coming in spurts, but nothing up there seemed to be broken. As Sol's hand moved lower, Bentley whined.

"I think it's his hind leg or his hip or pelvic bone." Sol prayed it wasn't his spine. "I need to get him to the vet."

"You don't have to do that. If you'll just help me get him to my car, I'll take him." Nell's words finally drew Sol's attention to the woman, dressed in a suit and a hat—obviously on her way to some event.

"I'll take him, Nell." Sol spread out the rug behind Bentley as he talked. "Emmy's a good friend of mine and Bentley's used to me. Easy, boy. This might hurt a little." He slid his arms under the dog and lifted him only enough to get him onto the rug, which he wrapped around him. Bentley yelped when he lifted him, but he didn't snap or growl. "Good boy. You're such a good boy."

Sol gritted his teeth as he made it to a kneel. He had to get to a standing position while jostling the dog as little as possible. He hated to do this, but… "Nell. This is my bad leg. Can you give me a hand?"

"Oh, sure. Of course." She locked her arms around his elbow, and that extra bit of stability was all he needed.

"Thanks. Now, could you open the passenger door of my truck?" Luckily he'd left the truck out by the road when he finished working. He laid Bentley gently on the seat and hurried around to the driver's side.

"Are you taking him to Benton? I'll follow you."

"Nell." He took her hand. "You're dressed up, obviously going somewhere."

She shook her head. "We're having pictures made for the Marshall County Garden Club. I'm the president and I'm receiving an award, but that's not important—"

"Go. I'll call you as soon as I know anything definite. I don't think it's too bad—" That was a lie. He had no idea if there were internal injuries. But he would have to call Emmy, and she was going to be hysterical. One upset woman was all he had the wherewithal to deal with right then.

"If you'll give me EmmyLou's number, I'll call her."

"Better let me handle that, too. But give me your number, and I'll call you later." He let go of her hand so she could get the phone out of her purse and made use of the time by getting in, starting the truck's engine and letting down the window. Nell gave him her number as Bentley settled his head in Sol's lap. Sol flipped on the air conditioner and pointed all the vents toward his canine friend.

"You're an angel, Sol. I don't know what I would've done if you hadn't been home." She gave him a motherly peck on the cheek through the window.

"I'll call you," he assured her as he drove away.

He couldn't in good conscience leave town without checking on Joe, despite the angry little voice in his head warning of what he was probably going to find.

Out of habit, he pulled all the way to the back of Emmy's drive. From there he could see Joe sprawled on the chaise.

"Ought to leave without even checking on your sorry ass," he grumbled as he climbed from his truck, which he left running. He had to make sure the guy was breathing.

Joe was breathing all right. Sol's ears picked up the loud snore from several yards away. Furious, he made an about-face and hurried back toward the truck, pausing only long enough to vent some of his frustration with a loud yell.

"That's right! Let me be the one to have to break the news to EmmyLou, you good-for-nothing drunk sonofabitch!"

He pulled out his phone, finding Emmy's number as the last that he'd dialed. He punched the button, and the pressure pushed all the way into his gut.

CHAPTER FIFTEEN

WHEN SOL'S NAME came up on her caller ID, Emmy's heart did a twirl and dip that would've made Derek Hough proud. She paused, her finger hovering above the Accept command on the screen. More than any man she'd ever known, he deserved the title of *jerk*...the way he jerked her heart around. Did she really want to talk to him?

No. She did not.

Screw him...and his fake leg...and his fake life. She moved her finger over and touched Ignore.

A minute later, her phone rang again. Sol.

"Thought about it and decided you're horny after all?" she said to the stop sign beside her. "Well, too bad. If you're gonna get this woman hot and bothered, you gotta come through with more hot and less bothered, Mr. Perpetual Cold Shower."

Again she touched Ignore. The call had barely disconnected when it rang again.

"Oh, for Heaven's sake." She touched Accept. "Leave me alone, Sol! I don't want to be your friend." She shouted the words partly because she had the top down and wanted to be heard over the wind but mostly because she felt like screaming at the asshole.

"EmmyLou, where are you?"

"Emmy, EmmyLou, where are you?" she sang to the tune of the Scooby-Doo theme song. "We've got—"

"Emmy, listen to me."

"No, but thank you for calling." She went to end the call.

"Do not hang up on me, EmmyLou Creighton. This is serious." The old sour Sol was back. Cool and calm, but sour as a pickle. "Are you on your way home?"

"Yes, sir! Coming into Taylor's Grove this very minute, sir!" she barked.

"Pull into the diner parking lot. I'll be there in two minutes."

"No, I—"

He'd already ended the call.

"If you think I'm going to drop everything and come running every time you snap your fingers, Mr. Beecher, you've got another think coming," she muttered, but she turned right anyway. Leif Mabrey, the diner's delivery boy, was on the way to his car when she pulled in.

"Hey, EmmyLou." He held up his armload of

boxes and sacks. "Can I take *your* car to make these deliveries?"

"I'd let you, sugar, but if the smell of Patti's cooking got in my upholstery, I'd stay hungry all the time."

The kid laughed as he got in his car and couldn't resist a bit of showing off by squealing his tires as he exited the lot.

Sol pulled in right behind him and blocked Emmy's car. He let his window down and motioned to her. "Get in."

"Forget it." She put her finger on the ignition button.

"EmmyLou. I have Bentley."

She peered at him in her rearview mirror. "What? You're kidnapping my dog to make me talk to you?" She got out of her car, slamming the door. "You are one sick bas—"

"He's been hit by a car. I'm taking him to the vet."

In one leap, she was at the window. The sight of Bentley lying across the front bench seat wrapped in a rug with his head in Sol's lap caused her knees to go weak. "Oh Lord have mercy." The world spun around her.

"Get in the backseat, sweetheart. I don't want to disturb him."

Emmy jerked the handle so hard, a pain ran

up her arm, into her shoulder. "What happened? Oh Lord help, Sol! My baby!"

"You'll have to sit down so I can see to back out."

She lowered her rear end but kept her arms and head draped over the seat. "How did…this…happen?" Sobs wracked her breathing, and Bentley turned his head to lick the hand she had lying on him. "He…he's got on…his collar and leash."

"It's his back end." Sol made eye contact with her through the rearview mirror. "He ran out in the road in front of Nell Bradley's car. It happened right in front of my house, and she came asking for my help. She feels horrible and wanted to take him herself, but I thought it would be better if I took him since he knows me."

The tears were coming too fast now for her to see Sol's face. "He was at…the groomers. That's all…the way…in Benton. How'd he get…in front of your house?" None of this was making sense.

"My guess is he got away from Joe."

"Oh God." With instant clarity, she understood. "He's drunk, isn't he?" She leaned her face on her arm and wept into it.

"Yeah, I'm sorry. I stopped by to make sure he was okay and found him passed out on one of the patio chairs. He probably had Bentley outside with him." Sol took the hand she had on Bentley and kissed it. "I think he'll be okay."

"Bentley…or Joey?"

"Bentley."

His tone said it all, and no amount of tears could ease the ache in her heart.

"Shitfire!" A wave of frigid water startled Joe Wayne awake. He flew up in his seat, the cold water and the quick motion making his head feel like a cherry bomb had gone off inside it. "What the freakin' hell you doing, EmmyLou?"

His sister stood over him with an empty bucket. "I'll tell you what the freakin' hell I'm doing! I'm waking your ass up so I can whip it all over this backyard! Do you know where Bentley is?"

She was slinging the bucket as she talked. He leaned back to avoid contact with the hard plastic. "Oh shit." He wiped the water out of his eyes with the crook of his elbow, then looked around. "Bentley. Come here, boy." He clapped a couple of times, let out a shrill whistle. "He was just here a minute ago, sis. Helped me wash Patsy."

"He was not here a minute ago, Joey! Want to know how I know that? Because two hours ago the vet took him into surgery to set his broken leg from where he got hit by a car!" She was yelling so loud the words felt like they were splitting his skull.

He closed his eyes, trying to focus past the pain to what she was telling him. "I didn't let him off his leash—just like you told me. We was going to fix you some supper, but I guess I fell asleep." He slid his legs off the chair, straddling it as he stood up, but his brain wasn't quite ready to make the transition. He fell back into the seat, jarring his head so hard he could've puked for a nickel.

"You didn't fall asleep. You passed out drunk. You're still drunk." EmmyLou hauled the bucket over her head and threw it into the yard. He was thankful she didn't aim it at his head, 'cause he would've lost his lunch for sure.

She was probably right about the drunk part, although it was kind of hard to tell with his head hurting so bad. But her words finally drilled into the part of his brain that understood. "Bentley's hurt? And it's my fault?" A giant fist landed right in his gut, loosening everything inside. He leaned over the arm of the chair and hurled.

"Oh, Joey. No!" EmmyLou's wail sounded like a coyote when there was a train coming.

Sol must've been somewhere close, because all of a sudden he stepped into Joe Wayne's range of vision. His arms came around EmmyLou, cradling her head against his chest. She sobbed real loud, and that was damn hard to take. Joe Wayne hadn't seen her like that since Mawmaw died.

"Go in and clean up, Joe." Sol tilted his head toward the house. "I'll take care of things out here."

Joe Wayne took his time getting up and managed to get a sort of firm footing. He patted EmmyLou's back. "Sorry about Bentley, sis. I'd've never done nothing to hurt him on purpose. He gonna be okay?"

Sol nodded over her head. "He'll be okay. It's you I'm worried about."

"I ain't worth worrying about. Just a worthless, stinking piece of shit."

Emmy cried harder, and he stepped up his pace to get out of hearing range. Her crying made his heart hurt even more than his head. Once inside, he had to slow down on the stairs and hold on real tight to the banister. He showered and changed clothes, but it didn't make him feel any better.

How could he have done this? Poor Bentley. Hit by a car. Broken leg. What if his leg made him all grumpy, like Sol? He'd been such a good dog. Thinking of him going around with a frown on his face the rest of his life made Joe Wayne so sad he could have cried, too.

The flask he'd filled up and left beside his bed was calling to him.

Nope. Not gonna happen.

But EmmyLou was surely waiting downstairs to tear into his hide again. 'Course, he deserved every bit of her anger.

He needed to prepare for the long lecture he

was facing. And her tears. There was sure to be lots more of those.

Just a little nip would get him through.

But once the flask was at his lips, he allowed the nip to become a gulp. If a little helped, a lot would help even more. Another gulp and he replaced the lid.

Oh yeah, the edge was gone and he was ready to face the world. The woozy, wobbly world.

He leaned heavily against the rail and got to the bottom of the stairs without falling. EmmyLou and Sol were talking quietly at the kitchen table when he walked in, probably discussing him, judging from the way they shut up as he approached.

"Sit down, Joey." Emmy pointed to the chair across from her. "We need to talk."

"I'll be going now." Sol stood, but EmmyLou shook her head.

"Would you stay? Please?"

Sol sat back down, and Joe Wayne could tell by the look on his face that she could've asked him to jump to the moon right then and he would've tried.

Joe Wayne had seen that look before, and it meant more than "I want to be your friend."

As soon as Joe Wayne took the seat, she looked at him and squinted. "You drank some more upstairs, didn't you?"

"No," he lied.

"Yes, you did. I smell you, Joey. You've got that damn whiskey up in your room."

"Just a little flask. It's almost all gone."

"No more." EmmyLou looked him in the eye all serious-like. "Your drinking's gone too far. It's out of control, and you're out of control, and it's got to stop."

Might as well be truthful. "I don't want to stop." He drummed his fingers on the table and shrugged. "I can stop anytime I want. But it helps take the edge off, you know? Helps me relax when I perform."

"You haven't performed in days, except for last night in front of Sol, and that was like family." She laid a hand on his. "One way to measure if you're an alcoholic is to ask yourself if your drinking causes problems. It does. Lots of problems."

"And it becomes a physical addiction, Joe Wayne." Sol's tone was low, but not gruff. "Your body craves it. Has to have it."

Joe Wayne laughed at that. "My body craves a lot of stuff."

EmmyLou and Sol, neither one cracked a smile.

"We want to help, Joey." EmmyLou squeezed his hand. "You need to nip this in the bud now, before it gets any worse. Before you hit rock bottom. There's a detox center in Paducah. Sol just called them, and they said they have a place for you. Tonight."

"You think you're taking me to some hospital?" He stood way too fast and had to grip the table to keep steady. He'd never let his anger toward EmmyLou show before, but this time the alcohol numbed his brain enough that he told her how he was feeling. "Just drop me off and let somebody else deal with me? Oh yeah." He snapped his fingers like an idea had come to him. "That's how you do it, ain't it? You take off and leave. Let somebody else deal with the fallout."

He watched the anguish settle in her eyes and wished to hell he hadn't said that, but he wouldn't take it back.

"I'm sorry for every time I ever let you down, Joey. But this isn't letting you down. It's helping you up." Her voice cracked. "I don't know the first thing about alcohol addiction or what to do to get you through it. It takes days to detox, and I can't close the salon to be here with you."

"It can be dangerous, too." Oh great. Sol wanted in on this. "People have died coming off alcohol."

"I ain't coming off or going in or taking on or acting out." He hit the end of his fist on the table, knocking over the salt shaker. "And I ain't standing here listening to no more of this bullshit." He started toward the stairs, taking it slower than he would've liked.

EmmyLou came out of her seat, too, and ran to block his way, barring the steps. "Then you can't stay here. I will do anything in the world to help you." He snorted and looked away. She turned his face back toward her. "I love you, but I can't stand to see you do this to yourself. And I refuse to be an enabler. If you won't get help, you go upstairs and sleep off your drunk. And in the morning, you pack up your stuff and go. I'm spending the next couple of hours getting rid of all the alcohol down here and locking the wine cellar."

A twinge of panic made his heart beat fast. "This is pure bullshit." He pushed her arm out of the way and shoved past her.

"I mean it, Joey."

He flipped her off.

Once back in his room, he sat on the bed and let the room quit spinning. She didn't want him? His own sister was kicking him out?

To hell with her. He wouldn't stay where he wasn't wanted.

He started gathering his things…slowly.

He was out of here.

"THE WINE CELLAR in the basement has a keyed lock on the door. I'll make sure to lock it up when I get back inside."

"Must be some pretty expensive wine you keep down there if the door has a lock on it." Sol set the load he carried in the back of his truck, sliding the half case of beer off the box of hard liquor. He reached for the box of mason jars filled with Emmy's homemade moonshine, but she was already pushing it deeper into the truck bed.

"I guess Maggie wasn't taking any chances with a teenage son running around."

Sol noticed how Emmy's voice always took on a wistful tone when she spoke of her best friend and former business partner. "You still miss them a lot, don't you?"

"Yeah." She sighed. "But she loves California, and Russ is doing great at that college in Chicago, though who'd want to live in that freezing-ass city in the winter is beyond me. I knew Russ would be fine, though. He's a great kid." A small chuckle bubbled out of her. "But even good kids get into mischief when they have their friends over. My daddy says, 'One boy's a boy, two boys is half a boy, and three boys is no boy at all.'" To Sol's surprise, she turned around and gave a little hop to sit on the lowered tailgate. "We had four boys in our family, so what does that tell you about how things were around our house?"

She obviously was in a talkative mood, so Sol hopped up beside her…though not too close. Getting too close to EmmyLou Creighton stirred his body to the point of pain, and his heart…well, he didn't even want to think about that right now. The woman just confused him so, it was hard to tell which way was up. And tonight, he wasn't up for the confusion.

He was tired.

"Were they all like Joe Wayne?"

"Thank the Lord, no. I think I've told you before about Dustin's drinking problem. Trace is kind of quiet. Mama always said he talked a lot until I started talking, but then I never shut up, so he couldn't get a word in edgeways, and he just quit trying."

"Seems to me your mama places an awful lot of blame on you for things that aren't your fault." He watched the quick frown bloom on her mouth before she shrugged and went on about her brothers.

"Knox, he's the baby. He's kind of different. More…sophisticated. He lives in Gadsden, Alabama."

On she talked without Sol hearing much of what she said. He'd become fixated on her mouth. Full and ripe and luscious. So kissable.

His heartbeat kicked up at the thought, warning that his mind was leading him into dangerous territory. He scooted away from her and swung up into the truck bed, backing away so he could lean against the wall and stretch out his bad leg.

She did the same, using the opposite wall as support. The bit of distance between them gave him a chance to take some deep breaths without the scent of her perfume filling his nose.

She was deep into a story now about her brothers filling the beach house bathtub with salt water and hiding a small stingray for a few hours. Sol's mouth managed to make appropriate sounds, but his memory jumped back to his teenage days, when his and his friends' trucks were party central. Friday and Saturday nights would find them and their girlfriends in the middle of somebody's field with the radio blasting and the beer flowing. They'd laugh and dance and make out, and at the end of the night, they'd head in separate directions across the field, making sure their trucks were far enough away from everybody else's that no one could see or hear what was going on in the backseat or sometimes in the truck bed under the stars.

It had been way too many years since he'd sat in his truck bed like this. EmmyLou had a way of making him remember things he'd lost. It was like she pulled him back to his old life—to the person he used to be. To the person he sometimes wished he could be ag—

A roar split the peacefulness of the night.
Motorcycle engine.
Emmy jumped up. "Joey! He's leaving!"

Sure enough, Sol could make out the dark form at the far side of the house, sitting astride Patsy and revving the motor.

"He's too drunk to ride. He'll kill himself! Or somebody else!" EmmyLou took off with Sol scrambling to catch her.

"Don't try to stop him. You'll get hurt!" He screamed to be heard over the roar as horrifying images flashed through his brain of what might happen.

But none of them even came close to what actually happened.

Sol watched it all unfold in front of his eyes as if in slow motion. Frame followed frame as Joe Wayne revved the engine and took off across the patio, evidently aiming for the driveway. Emmy stopped her forward motion and leaped to the right as he crossed the area where she stood in front of the pool. Her brother made a sharp turn to *his* right, curving around the shallow end of the pool and away from her, but he wasn't able to straighten out the front wheel in time. The curving trajectory had all the markings of a stunt gone wrong, and Sol could only watch in horror as Joe Wayne and his beloved motorcycle plunged into the deep end.

CHAPTER SIXTEEN

"Joey!" EmmyLou yelled. "Quit diving down there. You can't get it up."

He didn't hear her. He was already underwater again, tugging at the motorcycle's handlebars. She continued to tread water until he surfaced. This time, when he did, she grabbed his arm.

"Joey, listen to me." The eyes looking back into hers were wide with shock. "You can't do it. We'll have to call a wrecker."

"Help me, y'all!" Her brother's eyes jumped from hers to something over her shoulder. "She's gonna die down there!" He filled his lungs with a gulp and dropped beneath the surface again.

She turned and found Sol treading water behind her.

He shook his head. "No way. Not even with all three of us. Even if we got it to the surface, we couldn't get it out. And if we try to pull it out with my truck, it'll tear up the patio." He took a couple of awkward strokes that moved him to the side, and she realized he'd jumped in wearing his prosthesis. "When he comes up, I'll grab him. Maybe between the two of us, we can hold him long enough to talk some sense into him."

Joe Wayne surfaced again, sputtering and out of breath. Sol grabbed him around the waist and hauled him up against the side. Emmy moved in and flanked him from the front, locking arms with Sol and effectively pinning her brother... for the moment.

"If y'all would just help me..." He sounded about three years old, his voice trailing off into a pitiful whine.

"Patsy's too heavy, Jocy. We can't lift her out." She tightened her hold around him to a hug. "We'll have to call somebody."

"I'll call Benny Troutman." Sol's voice came from behind Joey. Emmy couldn't see him. "He has that wrecker service in Draffenville. If he can't do it, he'll put me on to someone who can."

Sol to the rescue again. What would she have done without him today?

Joey was shaking now, though not from the cold. "I've done it now, EmmyLou. First Bentley. Now Patsy." He started to cry, and the sound wrenched her heart. "She's all I got in the world. And now she's gone, and it's all my fault."

"She's not all you have in the world. You have me. Our family. Everyone loves you." Emmy felt herself moving backward. Sol was guiding them to the shallow end.

"She's all I got that's *mine*," came the answer. "Or she was. Now I got nothing."

When her feet touched bottom, she held on to her brother's hand and led him out of the pool. He wandered over and plopped down on the couch, still crying like a baby, burying his face in his hands. Emmy sat beside him, pulling him close.

Sol didn't sit. He limped on past them to the driveway, where he pulled his phone out of his pocket and made the call. His phone was in a waterproof case, thanks to his work at the marina, she supposed. How much would a drowned cell phone have cost her in payback?

And the prosthesis he was wearing wasn't his waterproof one, she was certain.

The way things were going, she might never get out of Sol Beecher's debt.

"I got no insurance, EmmyLou." Joey's voice was quiet, sad. "Had to let it lapse when things got lean. I can't pay for a wrecker, and I ain't got the money to get her fixed. You don't want me here, but I got no place to go and no way to get there if I did."

"That's not true." She hugged him tighter, pressing her cheek to the top of his head. It had been years since she'd held him like this, and in an odd sort of way, it felt good. As if she was doing something good for him for a change. "I didn't say I didn't want you here. I said I didn't want you here if you were going to drink. Sol and I got rid of all the alcohol in the house, so, if you stay, drinking's not an option."

He let out a pitiful groan in reply.

"You want me to take it in or what?" The wrecker guy addressed Sol again, but Joe Wayne felt too upset to give a rat's ass anymore.

All through the entire process of getting Patsy out of the water, which had taken several hours and a whole damn crew of men, Joe Wayne watched everybody turning to Sol for the answers, ignoring him completely.

None of them understood what Patsy meant to him or what he'd lost tonight.

"Benny's brother works on motorcycles, Joe." Sol was talking to him? *Would wonders never cease?* "Has a shop in Benton. You want him to take it there?"

It. They all referred to Patsy as *it.* She was just a motorcycle to them.

Joe Wayne had no idea how much it would cost to have her repaired, but cost didn't make much difference when there was no money anyway. He shook his head. "Naw. Better just leave her here." Someday he'd take her out into one of the fields here on EmmyLou's place, dig a hole and give her a proper burial. That would be easier than watching her rust and fall apart piece by piece.

"Send this bill to me, would you?" Sol kept his voice low, but Joe Wayne heard.

He should have protested, but what would be the use? He was too frazzled to think. His head was busting at the seams, his gut felt like a mule had kicked him, and the only thing keeping him going at this point was the thought of that flask up in his bedroom.

Emmy thought she'd gotten rid of everything, but the flask was still there, hidden under his pillow.

Enough to take the edge off tonight. But what in the hell would he do tomorrow?

His hands shook just thinking about it.

SOL HAD NEVER seen Emmy like this.

Quiet. Downright solemn. Defeated.

Despite the fact that she'd been surrounded by a crew of men—some of whom had tried their darnedest to flirt, especially the one they called Luke who seemed overly proud of his six-pack abs—she sat most of the night huddled on the patio couch next to Joe with her knees drawn up under her chin and her arms locked around her legs.

He saw her on the phone a couple of times. Once after he suggested she call her insurance agent. The wrecker had done some major damage to her garden and pool area—all repairable, but expensive. Gasoline had leaked into the pool, too, so it would probably have to be drained and cleaned and then refilled.

Joe was downright pitiful. What he needed was for someone to kick his ass up around his ears. Maybe that would jar some sense into him. But he wore an expression similar to Bentley's this afternoon, and Sol didn't have the heart. Besides, everybody knew how a one-legged man would fare in an ass-kicking.

Emmy finally stirred, getting up from the couch as Benny and his crew were leaving. "Thanks, y'all. I'm sorry you had to come out this late, but I sure appreciate it."

"I get called out a lot later than this." Benny patted her back. "I'm just happy a dead body wasn't involved like a lot of the scenes I'm called to."

Luke the flirt had disappeared to his truck, but now he returned, flashing her a smile along with a business card. "Here's my number. I'm with the fire-and-rescue team. Call me if you ever need assistance...with *anything*."

Sol's hand doubled into a fist. With the mood he was in, it would take very little for him to punch Luke right in his toothy grin.

Emmy just gave the asshole a vacant stare and slid the card into the pocket of her still-wet shorts. "Thanks." She turned her focus to Joe, who was on his knees over by his cycle. "Joey," she called. "Could you move your bike over to the driveway? Or put it in the garage." Without another glance Luke's way, she went to the keypad and punched in the code to raise the garage door.

Luke's grin dissolved, and he stalked away.

Sol followed Emmy to the garage, locating a tarpaulin and spreading it out on the floor. The cycle was no doubt leaking oil and gas along with the water that still dripped from everywhere.

Joe parked the cycle on the tarp and then stepped back, drawing a reverent sigh. "Sorry 'bout the mess I caused, sis. Patsy and Bentley. Everything. Thanks for your help, Sol." His shoulders hunched in a slow shrug. "I'm going to bed now." He didn't give her a hug or even another look before he walked away. Sol understood. Sometimes pain ran so deep, even the slightest sympathetic touch could shatter you from the inside out.

He'd been there.

They stepped back outside, and Emmy pressed the button and closed the garage door.

He checked his watch. Past midnight. "You should go on to bed, too." Without thinking, he lifted his arm to her shoulder for a quick hug. Her muscles didn't give with his squeeze, so rigid with tension. "Hey. Relax. It's not the end of the world."

Her eyes scanned her garden, patio and pool area that had been beautiful a few hours ago and now looked like a hurricane had gone through them. She didn't say anything, but she didn't have to. Her emotions were all over her face.

"Here." Both of them were still in damp clothes, so he didn't want to take her inside. Instead he guided her to sit down on the couch where she'd spent the better part of the last three hours. He stepped behind her and started massaging her shoulders.

"Ow." She groaned, but tilted her head to one side for more. "That hurts so good."

Her sexy tone had Sol reminding himself he was doing this for *her* pleasure, not his own, though touching her brought him a sense of *pleasure* he couldn't deny. He tried for conversation.

"You called Carl?"

She nodded.

"Will your insurance pay?"

She drew a long breath. "Nope. His exact words were, 'I'm sorry, EmmyLou, but we can't insure against stupidity.'" Her imitation of Carl's nasally tone was spot on.

Anyone who didn't know him might've been shocked at the agent's abrupt manner. Everybody in Taylor's Grove was used to it.

"Well, Joe's gonna need a project to pass his

time while he's here. Make him earn his keep by putting things to right. It'll be good for him."

"I guess." She paused and then added, "I'm so worried about him, Sol. I've never seen him so…despondent."

He continued to work his thumbs into the iron bands that were her neck muscles. "It's the alcohol, sweetheart. Everybody thinks it's an upper, but it's not. It's a mood enhancer. Whatever you're feeling, it just makes you feel it more."

She reached up and took his hands, tilting her head back to look at him. "Come and sit. Tomorrow I'll work myself in with one of the massage therapists at the salon." She let go of one hand but continued to hold the other as he came around and had a seat.

He didn't sit right beside her, choosing to keep a safe arm's length away. She was exhausted, and he didn't want a repeat of last night's horrible finale between them.

She patted his hand. "You're a good friend, Sol."

Her words were kind, but the idea of being a good friend—or maybe of being *only* a good friend—stung his heart just the same.

"And because you're a good friend, I'm going to say what's on my mind."

He grinned. "Like you don't usually."

She didn't return his smile. "Of course I do.

The people I have to watch what I say around are people I don't choose to be around."

"Okay." He wasn't sure what she was driving at.

"I want to ask about your leg."

"Oh." He pulled his hand loose and laid his arm on the back of the couch.

"See..." She flicked a finger toward his arm. "I'm concerned because you jumped in with your prosthesis on, and I know it's the one you don't use in the shower, and I'm just wondering if it's ruined now and how much that's going to cost you. But if I say anything, you think all I think about is your leg."

His fatigue suggested he keep things light. "My insurance is better than yours. It *does* cover stupidity."

She still didn't smile. "You're not hearing me. Or you don't want to hear me. I like being around you, but I don't want to feel like I'm walking on eggshells every time I'm with you. And it's hard not to, because *you* may think I'm constantly thinking about your leg, but the truth is, *you're* the one who's always thinking about it. Some people wear their hearts on their sleeves. You wear your leg."

He challenged her verbosity with his own lack of it. "I do not."

"Yeah, you do. I've been reading online what it's like to live with a prosthesis."

Whoo, *that* tightened his jaw. "Trust me. Reading about it is *nothing* like living it."

"Lord have mercy." She dropped her head back and wiped a hand down her face. "You feel so sorry for yourself all...the...time." She lowered her chin to level her eyes at him. "There are people out there with fake legs—sometimes both of them—who, believe it or not, run marathons, snow ski, water ski. They do whatever they want to do. Live full lives. It's not your leg that's your problem, Sol. It's your attitude. You say you don't want people feeling sorry for you because of it, but when I made a joke, you puffed up like a bullfrog. You can't have it both ways. People will feel about it the way you make them feel about it."

He was too tired to argue with her, and plus, she made some sense. The regret he'd felt earlier when he remembered what he'd said the previous night twisted in his gut. "Look, I'm sorry about how I reacted last night. Or rather, how I overreacted. I get so damn tired of my missing leg being right out front all the time. I'm not just a leg. I'm a man."

"Then act like it." Her quiet tone held no fire, no anger. "Quit letting it define you."

Was he doing that? Had he been so focused on ignoring his leg that it never left his mind?

"But that's not what I called you around here to say, Sol. I want to thank you. Time after time, for the past couple of weeks you've been there for me. For Joey. For Bentley." She brushed her damp hair out of her eyes but held the contact steady. "I don't know what I would've done if you hadn't been here today. I want our friendship to last. It means a lot to me."

He tried not to obsess over her word choice. *It*…not *you*. He'd had so many great friends once upon a time. And he'd let the damn leg kick those people from his life. He wouldn't lose Emmy, too.

More and more, he was starting to feel that he was in her life for a reason. Maybe he was her guardian angel.

Lord knows she and Joe Wayne could use one.

With all these words poised on his tongue, "Me, too" was all he got out before footsteps pulled their attention to the back porch steps.

Joe Wayne. The damn whiskey flask in his hand.

They swung around to face him, and Sol wondered if she could read the haunted look in Joe's eyes as well as he could.

"I been sittin' on the bed upstairs thinking," Joe said. His Adam's apple bobbed like a ball stuck in his throat. "I went up there to finish off what was in this here flask. But I got to thinking 'bout what you said 'bout hitting rock bottom."

He paused again. "I'm there, sis. When Patsy hit the bottom of that pool, I sank with her." He unscrewed the lid and poured the contents onto the patio. "I'm quittin', but I'm doing it on my own like Dustin did. I can't go to no botox."

"Detox." Emmy eased off the couch and took his hand that held the flask. "And you know I want you to get clean and sober like Dustin. But Dustin had Katy. I can't stay home with you, Joey, and I won't leave you to try and get through that alone."

Sol's stomach tightened with a double-fisted grip. Joe Wayne was in a bad way, like so many other buddies he'd known. Some he'd even lost to this damn disease. Even if it was hard to admit, Joe Wayne *was* a buddy. Hell, Sol had been worried enough about him this afternoon to stop and check on him on the way to the vet.

And EmmyLou was in way over her head on this one.

Guardian angel. Wasn't that really just another name for *good friend?*

The finger poking Sol's heart punched faster and harder until it bumped the words he was holding back right up into his mouth.

"Go get your things, Joe." He stood up and motioned toward the house. "You're moving in with me for a couple of weeks."

CHAPTER SEVENTEEN

EMMY TUCKED THE broom handle under her arm as she grabbed her phone. Her heartbeat had already soared to maximum speed, the same thing it had done every time her phone had rung the past two days—ever since Joey went to stay with Sol.

The caller ID said Bree.

"Hello?" She pushed some air into her voice.

"Did your brother really get drunk and drive his motorcycle into the pool?" Her friend's easy laugh didn't loosen the tight coil that her stomach was in.

Emmy dropped the broom handle into her free hand and swept the hair on the floor from her last cut into a pile. "I shouldn't be surprised that you heard about that, seeing as how we live in Taylor's Grove, but *how* did you hear about it?"

Bree snorted. "The local paper deemed it worthy of the Not-So-Newsy column. You know that gossip stuff? Which I usually don't read, of course."

Another round of terror, though from a different source, burned Emmy's belly. Did everybody know Joey's real name now, too? "Oh dear Lord. What does it say?" She braced herself as the sound of paper rustling came across the line.

"Joe Creighton, brother of Paducah salon owner EmmyLou Creighton, took his motorcycle for a swim Tuesday night in his sister's pool near Taylor's Grove. Alcohol might have been involved." Bree's laugh was light. "I've got to meet Joey sometime, Emmy. I always figured your stories about him were exaggerated, but now this? All I can say is, he must be quite a character."

"Yeah, he is." Emmy dumped the full dustpan into the trash and sat in her chair.

"You okay? You don't sound like yourself." Bree's concern turned apologetic. "Oh no. Did the article upset you? I never would've called if I'd known it would do that. I thought you'd find it funny."

"Oh, sugar, don't feel bad that you called me. I need to talk to somebody, and I'm glad it's you." Emmy checked out the dark circles under her eyes in the mirror. "Yeah, the situation upsets me." She still had a few minutes before her next appointment and preferred to discuss this in private, so she went to her office and closed the door. "Sinking his motorcycle in my pool was a wake-up call for Joey. It proved to him, finally, that he has a drinking problem."

"Emmy, I'm sorry. I didn't know."

"I know. There're people who would've been ornery enough to call me about it just out of meanness, but that's not you."

"No. You know I love you. But now I'm concerned about you *and* Joey, and I don't even know him. Can you convince him to get help?"

Tears stung Emmy's eyes. "He wouldn't go to detox. Says he wants to do it on his own like our brother Dustin did."

"Isn't that…dangerous?"

"It is. And I'm so worried about him." She grabbed a tissue from the box on her desk and dabbed the tears as they caught on the rims of her eyes. "But Sol insisted Joey stay at his house. He says he's been through this before with friends from the service."

"Sol again." Emmy heard the question in Bree's tone. "Did I miss something? Are y'all…?"

"No, there's nothing to miss. Although, truthfully? I wish there was." The fact that she could admit that openly was as much a shock to her as she was sure it was to Bree.

"EmmyLou Creighton. I've never known you not to get the man you wanted. Have you told him how you feel?"

"Well, I haven't put it in the Not-So-Newsy column, but I've done everything else. One minute he's interested, and the next he's as cold as those bass Kale brings home."

"He's not the easiest person to communicate with…and that's so weird because he used to be really outgoing. Mr. Party Animal. Remember?"

"Yeah. He's still the animal, but it's more like a lone wolf…and I can't seem to make him want to howl."

Bree chuckled. "I was glad he came with you Sunday night, though. It wasn't exactly the old Sol, but it was the closest to him that I've seen in a long time. I think you're good for him."

"I think I *could* be with half a chance, but I *know* he's good for Joey."

"They met down at the beach house?"

"Yeah. Joey's drinking got him in some trouble down there, too, and Sol helped him out."

"I dunno, kiddo. Sounds like he's working hard to be your hero." In the background, Emmy heard Kale's rich voice and Isaiah's bubbly little boy laughter. She smiled around the lump it formed in her throat. "We'll keep all y'all in our prayers. I know this is a hard time," Bree went on. "And speaking of hard time, I just heard about Bentley this morning from Nell Bradley. You should've called me! Is he going to be okay?"

"I get to bring him home from the vet today. His back right leg was broken. It happened in front of Sol's house and Nell was too upset to deal with it, so Sol took Bentley in his truck and picked me up on the way."

"Seems that everything happening to you these days involves Sol. Maybe somebody's trying to tell y'all something."

"Yeah, well, if the Man Upstairs can't get through to him, I don't even know why I'm bothering."

Bree laughed. "You might want to stay away from him during lightning storms."

"That lightning rod he's got should make him an easy target." She was referring to his prosthesis, but Bree wouldn't know that.

A shocked giggle burst from the phone. "Emmy, my friend, you are too much. I'm supposed to be cheering you up, and you're the one making me laugh."

Taryn knocked softly and stuck her head in the door. "Your appointment's here."

Before Emmy could say anything, Bree spoke up. "I heard that. I'll let you go. Plan on me bringing supper to your house tomorrow night. There'll be enough for three, in case you want to invite somebody to join you."

"Thanks, Bree. Love you, sugar."

"Love you, too. Bye."

Emmy sat for another minute, gathering her wits. She was itching to call and see how Joey was doing, but that should probably wait.

Instead she plastered on the *I'm okay* smile she'd perfected so many years ago.

Her public was waiting.

"QUIT SLAPPING YOUR arm so hard, Joe." Sol's calm voice wormed its way into Joe Wayne's ear. "You're making bruises."

Joe Wayne pushed his hands under his legs to hold them still. "I can't help it. If you'd give me just a little—just a sip—it'd help. I know it would." They were crawling all over him. "God Almighty!" He screamed at the top of his lungs and grabbed the front of the cushion he was sitting on, squeezing it in fisted hands. "These spiders—I know they ain't real—but they look real and they feel real and my hands just slap 'em whether I want 'em to or not." He jumped up. "Gotta move. Gotta move. Need to walk." He thrust his hands into his pockets and paced, making laps around the ground floor of Sol's big old house. Living room, dining room, kitchen, utility room, back hall, den, study, front hall, living room...

"How long's it been now?" He passed Sol, who'd gone into the kitchen to fix him another one of those drinks that would put electric lights back into his body. Sol kept insisting that was important, but Joe Wayne thought it sounded dangerous.

"Forty-one hours." Sol caught up with him in

the utility room and handed him the bottle with the blue stuff that was the color of a Bombay Sapphire gin bottle but tasted disappointingly like Juicy Fruit gum. "Seven more hours and the worst will be over. You feel like eating a little something? I'm going to have some of those berries Emmy brought over this morning."

Joe Wayne vaguely remembered seeing his sister come in with a basket. Had that been just this morning? In his head, days had passed since then. "No," he grumbled and took a gulp, then screwed the lid back on. "I don't want berries. I don't want this blue piss you keep sticking in my hand." He thrust the bottle at Sol, who stepped away. "I don't want nothing but a drink."

"You *have* a drink." Sol turned around and headed back to the kitchen.

Joe Wayne slapped at the imaginary spider on his hand, watched it hop to his elbow and his shoulder, felt it sprint across the back of his neck and into his hair. He swatted at the creature with the plastic bottle. Once…twice…then a third time out of frustration and anger. "You know what I mean. Whiskey! Just give me half a shot to mix in here. I know you got some here someplace." He stalked through the den, bumping his shin hard against the recliner foot he'd left out.

"Sorry, bud. It's all gone." Sol held out a bowl

of berries as Joe Wayne passed through the kitchen. "Want these instead?"

He only meant to push the damn berries away with the bottle, but it swatted the bowl hard, sending the bowl and its contents across the room. Strawberries, blueberries, and blackberries flew every which way, and he felt like a cattle prod was poking in his stomach. "Shit-o'-day, I'm going crazy." He whispered the words, but they were a shout inside his skull. He dropped to his knees, wrapping his arms around his head. "I'm sorry, Sol. I can't take this no more."

His friend was already on the move to the utility room for the broom. "Yes you can. Take deep breaths and calm down."

Joe Wayne lowered his hands to his knees and tried to force air into his lungs, but it kept getting caught in his neck, and he prayed that the imaginary spiders hadn't eaten through the flesh and left their imaginary eggs in there. He stood up fast and gulped down the drink to drown the sons of bitches. But he hadn't gotten a good breath, so he choked. The drink spewed down his front and across the floor.

Sol finished gathering the berries and dumped them in the trash while Joe Wayne caught his breath and took the wet rag from his hand and wiped up his own mess. He'd noticed that getting down on his knees made Sol grimace harder than anything else.

Joe Wayne rinsed the rag in hot water in the sink and then pitched it in the dirty pile on the utility room floor by the washer. The pile was getting big. He'd made a lot of messes the past forty-one hours. 'Course, nothing like what he'd made of his life.

He sat down at the table, suddenly exhausted, and clasped his hands together to keep from slapping or scratching. "How'd you do it, Sol?"

The way his friend's eyes tightened told him he knew what he was asking about. Sol shrugged. "One day at a time. But it didn't start like that." Sol took the seat across from him. "At first, it was one minute at a time. Seriously. I would tell myself, 'Okay. You can stand this one more minute.' One became two. Two became five. Five became fifteen. Then thirty. Then an hour. Eventually, I reached the day stage. Sometimes I'm still there. And every now and then, I even have to start back with a minute, but not very often."

"Never having a drink the rest of my life. Never. Forever. Them's some of the scariest words ever invented."

"You can't focus on the scary words, Joe." Sol leaned forward, his palms flat on the table. "You've got to fill your brain with good stuff. Fill it so full, there's no room for the scary."

Joe Wayne's fingers ached from clenching them so hard. But if he let go, he might fly apart. "There's so much more scary than there is good. I'm a country singer. I sing in bars. Bars have liquor. How am I supposed to make a living if I can't be around the stuff? Not much call for country music singers anyplace else."

"You're thinking too hard, Joe. Your head's way out there a month from now. Just concentrate on today. This minute. When it comes time to think about a month from now, I'll be there to help. I promise. And you know Emmy's going to be there. And your family. Dustin said he'd help you. You don't have to do this by yourself."

Joe Wayne's heart swelled with gratitude. "I appreciate what you're doing for me." He willed his hands to loosen their hold on each other and held one out to shake Sol's. "I'm sorry about the mess I've been making in your house. And I'm real sorry 'bout the berries and the bowl just now."

Sol shook his hand and gave him an almost-smile. "If you haven't noticed, I'm using paper and plastic with you. If you broke any of my mom's good dishes, staying clean and sober would be the least of your problems."

Joe Wayne laughed, and he realized it was the first time in over two days that he'd done that.

He promised himself to do it again within the next two hours.

And during the next two minutes, he would fix a bowl of berries for him and his friend.

LUCKILY SOL SAW Emmy coming up the walk, before she had time to knock on the door or ring the doorbell. He'd never realized how much she and Joe favored until he recognized the look of raw fear in her eyes when he opened the door so quickly. It was the same look he'd seen in Joe's eyes repeatedly the past two days.

"Is he—"

Sol silenced her with a finger to his lips. He stepped onto the front porch and closed the door quietly behind him. "He's asleep on the couch," he explained. "For the first time since we got here."

"Oh." Her shoulders slumped in relief. "I was afraid he was still out of his head."

"No. I think most of that's passed."

Her fingertips tapped his arm—a light touch, but his nerve endings danced to life, oblivious to the fact that his body hadn't rested in almost forty-eight hours. "You look frazzled." She scanned his face. "Shouldn't you be sleeping, too?"

"I will. But I've never been able to sleep while the sun's shining."

"Bentley's home." Her smile beamed so brightly, it seemed rather like the sun itself. Maybe that was why his heart warmed at the sight of it.

"Now, that's great news." He gave her a quick hug. "Is he going to be okay?"

"Going to be fine. You should've seen him. So happy to be home. Hopping around with that cast stuck out."

Her giddy laugh drew a chuckle from him. He imagined she did some hopping around, too. But before he could get that thought out, she held up a familiar box.

"I went by the diner and picked y'all up some supper. Grilled turkey on Patti's homemade rye with her homegrown tomatoes and Bob Farley's fresh Bibb lettuce. He's got a bumper crop this year, so he's been giving it away. Patti threw in some fresh sliced peaches for dessert. You hungry?"

"Famished," he admitted, taking the box and giving her a grateful peck on the cheek. "I've been trying to keep small, light meals coming for Joe because I read that was the best thing. But wow, it's kept me hopping."

"You and Bentley." She stuck one of her legs out straight and hopped in a small circle.

He laughed, despite the fact that she hadn't been here five minutes and she'd already brought up his leg.

"Well, I'll let you go eat." She gave a small wave and moved toward the steps.

"Don't go," he blurted, and the force of the words surprised them both.

Her eyes widened. "You sure?"

"Sure I'm sure." Did he sound desperate? Too bad. Her smile made it worth it.

He walked her around the house to the back patio, where she gave a delighted squeal that grabbed him and hung on like a bream on a cricket.

"Wow, it's like somebody brought down a piece of Heaven and plunked it into your backyard! These your grandma's flowers?"

"Yeah. Her flowers were always prize winners at the county fair, but I never thought much about them." Her comment made Sol look at the garden with a new perspective. "Fact is, I never really paid much attention, but they are pretty, aren't they? What are those purple things?"

"Those are garden phlox. Deer love them, and I've learned to let them eat on them some…long as they don't get too greedy. It's like nature's pruning, you know? I get two blooms instead of one."

"The swing okay?" He nodded his head toward the old wooden structure that occupied center stage. "Might draw a song out of you. Grandma used to sit there for hours with the hymnal in her lap, singing at the top of her lungs."

Emmy patted his back. "That's the perfect spot." She opened the box and handed him two wrapped sandwiches, leaving two in the box. "You go sit and I'll fix you something to drink. I want to check on Joey, too."

"Wake him and I'll skin you alive."

"Would that involve taking off my clothes?" Her grin was positively wicked.

"It definitely would." He tried to maintain a straight face but couldn't keep the twitch from his lips. That impish gleam in her eyes said she was well aware she was torturing him.

Torture felt damn good.

She shrugged. "Might be worth the flaying."

"Might be," he agreed as he headed toward the swing. Her laugh followed him.

She disappeared inside, and he unwrapped one of the sandwiches and took a giant bite. Grandma's flowers, Patti's sandwiches and EmmyLou Creighton's ass beside him in the swing. Didn't get much better than that.

He was almost through the first sandwich when she returned with two tall glasses of lemonade.

"I figured you didn't need the caffeine." She handed one over, but she didn't sit. He tried not to show his disappointment.

"Joey's snoring like a hog." She set the glass on the ground beside the swing. "I'll be right back."

He finished the sandwich and unwrapped the second one before he realized it was probably for her. He rewrapped it and waited.

She appeared around the corner of the house with a bag from a sporting goods store in her hand.

He didn't even try to guess what was in it. With EmmyLou, one had to be ready for surprises.

Case in point, she sat next to him—right next to him—not hugging the opposite arm of the swing, her thigh pressed against his.

Much more of this interaction and his erection would become painful.

"Got a present for you, but first you have to eat your supper. Did your mama say that to you? Mine did, all the time. But most of my mama's presents turned out to be some kind of lesson. She tried every kind of professional known to man to make me perfect." The grin she flashed him didn't reach her eyes. "Didn't work."

He held out the sandwich. "I disagree. You seem pretty perfect to me. Every mama's dream."

He watched the shadow cross her refined features as she shook her head and pushed the sandwich back toward him. "I've got a salad waiting at home."

While he ate, she pointed out flowers and gave him names that held vague familiarity. She told him about her day and about Bentley's happy reaction to getting to ride in the car.

"And do you believe, Nell Bradley paid the vet bill? Bless her heart."

"Well, she should have."

"No, she shouldn't. Bentley shouldn't have been out to start with." She paused. "Anyway, the pool is drained, and the guy is coming to clean it tomorrow. Then I can refill it. Is the idea of swimming with me again putting that smile on your face?"

He hadn't even realized he was smiling.

"No, I was smiling because I followed your segue from Bentley to Joe to Patsy to the pool without even having to think about it." He scrunched up the wrapper and put it in the box with the other one.

Emmy picked up the mysterious bag and held it toward him almost shyly. "Now you can have your present. It's thanks for all your help. I can't repay you—Lord knows I'm way too indebted to you now—but I thought this was something you could use."

The bag was soft. Obviously, clothing. "You got me a Speedo, didn't you? So you can fantasize I'm an Olympic swimmer when we're in the pool."

"Even better." Only a hint of a smile played on her lips. "I got you one of those one-piece, halter-neck swimsuits for guys. The kind with the thong back. Wearing it will let *you* fantasize about the first time you saw Joey."

He'd made the mistake of taking a drink as she delivered her punch line with the timing of a trained comedian. He spewed it almost as far as Joe had earlier. Had any woman ever made him laugh so much?

After they got everything wiped off, he opened the bag and found two pairs of men's cargo pants. One khaki. The other gray.

"I guessed thirty-four, thirty-four?"

"You guessed right," he said, but his face must've shown his curiosity at the strange gift.

"One of my clients had some on today. He was showing me how they worked, and I thought, 'Wow! That would be perfect for Sol.'"

He held them up. "They're nice. Very light and cool. Thanks."

Her smile widened. "Look." She lifted a flap that went around the leg just below the cargo pocket. In an instant, the lower leg peeled away, making it a pair of shorts. "When you jumped in the pool with your prosthesis on the other night, it got me to thinking how you can't get it off quick in those jeans you always wear. But when Dante came in this afternoon with these on, it hit me that they were exactly what you need. If you get hot, you could just peel them off and be in a pair of shorts in about thirty seconds. And then if somebody came by, you could be back in long pants in the same amount of time. Of course, you'd have to keep the bottoms close. But you could stick them in those big pockets. The material's so thin, they wad up to nothing."

Okay, she'd been thinking about his leg again. But the gift was so kind, he couldn't be mad about it. "Thanks, Emmy. These are about the coolest things ever. I've seen them before, but I never thought about buying any." He pecked her cheek. "I'll try them out tomorrow. Unless you want me to strip here and try them out tonight."

She shook her head and stood up, but her smile was pleased. "When you decide to strip in my presence, I want you to have all your stamina." She gave him a wink. "Take my glass in when you get done, will ya?"

She strolled off without looking back, leaving him with a stuffed belly and a grin on his face... but a groin full of need.

CHAPTER EIGHTEEN

"GOING WAS HARD. I ain't denying that." Joe Wayne took a huge gulp of the ice-cold water Sol had poured into his cup. It tasted clean and refreshing, and he could almost hear his insides applauding. 'Course, his brain protested, still craving that other taste. But at his first Alcoholics Anonymous meeting, which Sol had driven him to in Benton this morning, they'd told him he had to accept what he couldn't change. That meant accepting he was a drunk. Like his brother Dustin told him, he'd just have to learn to be a sober drunk. "But hearing those stories of people just like me...it helped. I swear."

"It's worked for a lot of people." Sol set his cup down and hoisted another bag of ready-to-mix concrete into the wheelbarrow. "I attended a group for people who'd lost limbs as part of my therapy. It helps to know you're not alone. That other people have gone through what you have and survived. That's the key. Figuring out you really can live through it."

Joe Wayne followed with the garden hose over

his shoulder. He couldn't pay the concrete company to fix the patio he'd messed up, but he could do at least part of the repair with Sol's help. It seemed to him, he could do a lot of things with Sol's help. "Eleven days ago, I wasn't sure I could live through it. Wasn't even sure I *wanted* to."

"You'll still get that feeling every now and then." Sol slit the bag open with his pocket knife and dumped the contents into the wheelbarrow. "When you get lonely and depressed. I've found keeping busy gets my mind off it."

Joe Wayne turned the hose on and handed it to Sol. It was his turn to mix the concrete. "I got powerful feelings, that's for sure. But this morning, they was talking about finding purpose in your life, and that's the part that worries me more than a little." He began mixing with the shovel. "I ain't sure I got a purpose. I mean, I'm thirty-three years old, and all I ever done is sing in bars. That don't seem like no higher calling to me."

"Your higher calling may be your songs, Joe." Sol held up his hand. "I think that's ready, don't you?"

Joe Wayne lifted a shovelful and turned it over to let it plop back down into the concoction. "Yep. Heavy mud."

They started putting globs of the mixture into the empty space where they'd pulled out the broken concrete. Once they had enough, he grabbed the trowel before Sol had a chance and dropped to his knees to smooth it out. He could tell it pained his friend something terrible to work on his knees. Besides, he was the one who'd done the damage to the patio, so he should be the one doing the grunt work. They had to work fast. It didn't take the concrete long to set in this heat.

"I need a little more here." He pointed out a thin spot, and Sol added another shovelful. "I never thought my music could be my calling. Comes too easy. Shouldn't a calling be something that makes you suffer? I mean, this one woman kept talking about doing pennants for the bad stuff you done, and she talked like that could make you suffer, and like it was a good thing to suffer. But I don't see how hanging up pieces of material could make you suffer, unless she was talking about making a Yankees fan hang up a Red Sox pennant."

"She was talking about something different. P-e-n-a-n-c-e, not p-e-n-n-a-n-t-s. Doing something good to make up for the bad."

"Like fixing EmmyLou's patio?"

"Yeah."

"It does make me feel better. It's not really suffering, though. I like thinking that the sweat drops pouring off me are drops of love for EmmyLou getting added into the mix. They're gonna be there forever."

He looked up in time to catch a weird expression on his friend's face—sort of a half smile with some worry mixed in. "You've got the heart of a poet, Joe. No wonder you're a songwriter."

"What about you, Sol? What you got the heart of?" Getting his friend to talk about himself was like picking fly shit out of black pepper. Nigh to impossible.

Sol grunted. "I don't know. I never really thought about it."

"Well, think about it." He changed his question around the way that doctor on TV always did. "If you had a higher calling, what would it be?"

"Not songwriting. That's for sure."

Joe Wayne drew the trowel toward the board they'd put in to separate the slabs, leveling the concrete to a smooth edge. He sat back on his heels and looked up at his companion. "It appears to me you pour a lot of your sweat into stuff for my sister, too, and I'm just wondering why? She says y'all don't date. Just good friends. But she seems happy around you, and you seem happy around her. Fact is, I seen a lot of your moods the past two weeks, and you're at your best when she's around."

"You think too much."

"Maybe." Sol's face was tightening up into his pissed-off look, but he wouldn't walk off and leave in the middle of the job. "Do you think

EmmyLou might be part of your higher calling? She seems to make you suffer, so that part's taken care of. But she also makes you happy." He shrugged. "You think she's one of the things you should make a pennant for?"

Sol laughed, and Joe Wayne looked up in time to see him shake his head and wipe his face with his bandanna.

"Hey, can I use that?" Joe Wayne snatched the cloth from his friend's hand. It was pretty ragged, so ripping it in half didn't take much effort, but it gave him a triangle.

"What the hell, Joe?"

Joe Wayne tossed one piece back at Sol's face but spread the other over the wet concrete and pressed it in with his hands.

"Have you completely lost your mind? What in tarnation are you doing?"

Joe Wayne shoveled enough of the wet mixture on top of the bandanna to cover it. Then he began smoothing it out. "Don't know what you was talking about earlier, but I do know that a pennant's a triangle piece of material. Like that." He pointed to the piece he'd added to the concrete. "And it's soaked by the sweat off your brow, which we already 'stablished means love when you give it willing-like and not for pay, like you're doing today. I've just taken care of the pennant thing between you and EmmyLou. And

I've even made it permanent." He stood up and clapped Sol on the back. "The rest is up to you."

Sol shook his head, but a slow grin broke on his face. "You're crazy. You know that? I could take you to the mental hospital, and they'd accept you immediately."

Joe Wayne grinned and pointed his trowel at his friend and then the pennant. "Sol, you need to start learning to accept those things you can't change."

"FIRST THE REFRIGERATOR went out, and now the oven."

Audrey shook her head, which brought a warning *"Annnht!"* from Emmy. "Don't move your head until I get this last pin in," she instructed. "Getting this mass of hair of yours into a French twist is a feat in itself, but trying to hit that moving target head of yours when you talk could make it an Olympic sport."

Audrey's daughter, Tess, giggled. "Hold your head still, Mama, or Miss Emmy's gonna have a hissy fit."

"You got that right." Emmy threw the little girl a grin and a wink that were both returned. "Sounds like the school's kitchen needs a redo."

Audrey sighed. "It does, but there's no extra money. And now with school starting back in a couple of weeks, they'll have to borrow the money and start the year in debt. I worry that it won't be long until consolidation is beating at our door. The old, small community school like Taylor's Grove Elementary is fast becoming a thing of the past."

"That's too bad." Emmy put a couple more pins in for good measure. "I went to a big school, and we had lots of stuff like swimming pools and tennis courts. But little schools have advantages all their own. Small classes, low teacher-student ratios."

"What's ratio?" Tess's head tilted in question, making the pink flowers Emmy had tucked around the crown play peekaboo from among the curls framing the precious face. Having a little girl would be pure bliss…no matter what Mama said.

"Ratio is how many students each teacher has," Audrey explained.

"Like how many kids are in Dad's class?"

"Exactly," Audrey answered.

Emmy pointed to the little girl. "Are they really making you practice dropping flower petals tonight for that wedding tomorrow? Because I'm thinking anybody as smart as you wouldn't need to practice something as easy as that."

"I'm just practicing so I get to wear two pretty dresses. The one for tonight is yellow with purple flowers across here." Tess swiped her fingers across her waist. "But the one I get to wear tomorrow's my favorite. It's pink and fluffy and I feel like a princess in it." She twirled, and Emmy's heart twirled with her.

"You'll be prettier than the bride—tonight *and* tomorrow." Emmy grabbed the can of hairspray and doused Audrey's head, then handed her a mirror and spun her chair so she could see the updo.

Audrey's little squeal brought a smile to Emmy's face. "You're a magician, Emmy," she gushed. "Nobody's ever been able to get my hair into a smooth French twist."

"If you want to wear it up tomorrow, don't wash it. Just brush it out tonight, and I'll put it back up when I do Tess's."

"How much do I owe you?" Audrey pulled her wallet out of her purse, but Emmy waved it away.

"My gift to Mark's cousin—two gorgeous girls for her wedding party."

Audrey shook her head in protest. "I can't let you do that. You don't even know Annie."

"But I know y'all." She wagged her finger between the mother and daughter. "Mark's going to be the proudest man there."

"Well, thank you." Audrey stood and gave her a hug.

Emmy swooped Tess up, and the little girl's sweet hug around her neck brought a lump to her throat. She put her down and tapped Tess's freckled nose. "Have fun tonight in that pretty dress, and I'll see you tomorrow. And don't y'all forget—pool party at my house next Saturday."

"Did they get the repairs done?" Audrey checked her hair in the mirror one last time and smiled.

"They're finishing up today. I hope." Her phone rang with Sol's name showing on the screen. "That's them now. Keep your fingers crossed."

Audrey crossed two fingers on both hands and used the others to wave bye as Emmy answered her phone.

"Leave the door unlocked," Emmy called after them. "Hello?"

"Hey, Emmy. It's Sol. Are you busy?"

"Just finished up. Is everything okay?"

"Everything's fine."

Her heart, which had started beating fast at the sound of his voice, should have slowed down at that news, but it didn't. "That's good to hear."

"I was…um." He paused and began again. "I know this is short notice, but I was wondering if you'd like to have dinner with me tonight?"

"You're asking me out? On a date?" She eased into her chair.

"Well, um. Yeah. I'm in Paducah. Actually, I thought I might get a couple more pairs of those pants you bought me. I really like them. And I thought, if you wanted, you could go with me and then we'd grab a bite afterward."

"Sure. That sounds fun." She stood and untied the neck and waist of her cape and slipped it off. The outfit she had on beneath was cute, but she'd bought that new dress on sale today during lunch. "Do you want me to meet you somewhere? Or are you coming by the salon to pick me up?"

The bell on the door tinkled, and oddly, she heard it through her phone. She leaned over to look at the front door of the salon, but all she saw was Sol.

Gorgeous…handsome Sol…cleaned up, clean-shaven, hair combed and wearing a white short-sleeved shirt that made his tanned face seem two shades darker…and warmer. He wore the gray pants she'd given him, and he held a bouquet of flowers.

Her eyes scanned him up and down several times as he approached. If she'd thought her heartbeat was wild earlier, she'd obviously had no idea what it was capable of. "Hot damn" was the only thing her befuddled brain could manage to push out of her mouth.

Sol was right in front of her by then. "That was supposed to be my line." His smile was warm enough to melt the clothes right off her as he handed her the flowers—a beautiful mixture of white daisies, blue delphiniums, yellow zinnias and feathery, pink astilbes—all bound with a wet paper towel around the stems.

"These are from your grandma's garden." He nodded. Shifting her focus for a couple of seconds from the man to the flowers helped clear her head a little, though not much. Just enough to put together the question her pulse insisted she ask. "They're beautiful. Thank you, but…why?"

"You enjoy them so much in the garden, I thought you'd like having some here."

"I do. I will. But… I mean, why dinner? Why this?" She waved her hand to take in his dressed-up state. "Why now?"

He took the flowers from her and laid them on her work station. "I think it's time to give this thing between us a good, solid try." He took her hands, which had dropped to her sides, and stepped closer. His hands were large and warm and calloused from years of hard work. He was all man. A man she was already aware her heart yearned for and would lose itself to if she didn't proceed with caution.

"I'm not saying no, mind you." She wiggled their hands without letting go, yet inching away from him enough to catch her breath. "But what's changed?"

"You told me I wear my leg on my sleeve, which I categorically denied, of course. But these past two weeks with Joe showed me you were right. My time with him took my attention away from my leg. And you know what?" She shook her head. "It feels great. Makes me realize it's time to let my attention be somewhere else. On someone else. And I can't think of anyone I'd rather give my attention to than you."

"Are you going to go all psycho if I say something about your leg? Because I do think about it sometimes." She didn't want him having any false notions about her. "Not all the time. In fact, not very often. But sometimes I worry if you're in pain."

"I've told you before, I don't want my leg to define me."

She looked into his eyes, read the hope and desire burning so fiercely in them, and felt her heart slow to a normal rhythm. "I can honestly say you're not just a leg to me. You are hair." She loosened her hand from his grasp and ran her fingers through the top of his hair. "You are eyes." She trailed the back of her finger down to brush his eyelashes and then farther down to trace his lips. "You are the most kissable mouth God ever produced." She wriggled her other hand free from his grasp and stepped into him to clasp her arms around his waist. "You're all man to me, Sol. I've never wanted anybody more than I want you."

"I'll settle for *want* right now." He leaned down and touched his lips to hers. "Who knows where that might lead us?"

Then he kissed her so thoroughly, so deeply and with such passion, her heart skipped—plunging recklessly down a path that, until this moment, she'd been afraid to wander.

SITTING IN THE beer garden of Max's Bistro in Paducah with a plateful of luscious food, a glass of good wine, Emmy's musical voice in his ear and her hand absently stroking his arm while gestures brought her stories to life—Sol felt like a man reborn.

He might be her guardian angel, but she was simply an angel. Food, drink, clothing—she'd literally given him all of those things…and so much more.

Having her as his closest neighbor made him question if he really wanted to sell his house after all. Knowing he might see her sometime during the day made getting up and putting on his prosthesis a hell of a lot easier. And helping Joe through this tumultuous time had given him a sense of worth again—not only his own self-worth, but also a renewed belief in the value of life.

Though he never felt nearly so alive as he did during the hours spent with Emmy.

He cut another bite of fillet and dipped it in the béarnaise sauce. "The other day you mentioned all the lessons your mom made you take. I'm curious. How many kinds of lessons does a kid need?" The bite he put in his mouth was perfect, but not as pleasurable as Emmy had tasted on his lips at the salon.

She rolled her eyes and set her fork down, freeing both hands to count. "Well, there were voice lessons and guitar lessons. Piano, tap, clogging." She switched to the other hand. "Ballet. I guess the pageant stuff could all come under one umbrella—walking, smiling, waving, makeup and hair. I discovered I was really good at those last two, and I liked doing them. A lady helped me with my public—" there were the air quotes "—persona. Which basically was just a lot of telling me not to do the things that came naturally and to remember that *everything* I said or did would be judged and could make or break my career. *Our* career."

"That's awful. The public would've loved the real you." He cut another piece of steak and offered it to her on his fork.

She didn't comment on what he'd said. Instead, she took the bite and rolled her eyes again as she chewed, but the expression on her face gave the movement a totally different meaning than the last time. "Mmm. That is too good for words."

A comment about feeling the same way about her came readily to his tongue, but she started talking again.

"I put my foot down with speaking lessons. Talking. Diction. Can you imagine what high school would've been like if all of a sudden I started sounding like I grew up in Chicago? Mama wanted me to lose my Southern accent."

"What in the hell was she thinking?" Sol dropped his fork and grabbed her hand. "Your accent's pure gold, you hear me? It's everything a woman should sound like. Sultry and sassy and sexy."

"Not to mention sharp and shrill and syrupy sweet. And those are just the S-words."

He kissed her fingertip. "Tell a joke if you want, but it's true. Your voice makes me want to close my eyes and just listen." The admission eased the tension in his jaw only a little. Her mother's silliness still aggravated him. "What about Joe? He could've used some lessons. Grammar and vocabulary. How did he get by?"

"Joey was mostly ignored. I got all the attention—good or bad, so he was left with no expectations." She shrugged as if it was no big deal, but to Sol, it was the entire anatomy of her stage fright and Joe's alcoholism laid open.

Helping Joe with his alcoholism was something he'd at least had some dealings with. He hadn't the faintest notion how to help Emmy with her stage fright.

"Do you think he's okay, babysitting Bentley?" The worry wrinkle had formed between her eyes. "Would it look like I don't trust him if I call again?" She pulled out her phone.

"Yes, it would." He eased the phone from her grip and laid it on the table. "There's no alcohol in the house, and he has no transportation to get any…except walking, which would be a long walk since Taylor's Grove doesn't have anyplace that sells liquor. He's fine, Emmy, and he needs to feel like he's paying you and Bentley back. Making amends is an important part of his twelve-step program. Give him a chance."

Then he changed the subject to his own teenage years and growing up in Taylor's Grove—for once drawing laughs from her with his stories. They finished their meal and shared dessert in pleasant repartee. When he finally looked around, the place had cleared out and the servers were sending pleading looks their way as they cleaned off tables and rearranged chairs.

Once he'd taken care of the bill, he leaned forward and whispered close to her ear, "Guess we better get out of here."

She nodded. "Too bad. I could have sat here all night."

"Me, too."

She didn't speak another word until they'd exited through the gate on the street and were headed to his truck. She ran her arm through his and hugged it. "You don't remember, do you?"

Her tone caused the skin on his neck to prickle like it used to in the service when he needed to tread with caution. "Remember what?"

"This is where you brought me for our third date fourteen years ago. The night we slept together."

He came to a dead stop. "Seriously?" His brain worked to scratch up a whiff of a memory but came up with nothing.

"Been waiting for you to mention it all night." She shrugged and started walking again. "I was sure that was the reason you chose Max's, but I guess not."

The hurt in her voice twisted his gut. "Damn!" He opened the passenger door for her to get in, then went around and climbed in the driver's side. "I'm sorry, Emmy. I was such a numskull back in those days. All I cared about was getting a woman into bed."

She became inordinately quiet—just like she'd been that time on the way home from Bree and Kale's. No way was he going to have a repeat of that night. So he talked openly, like he'd never done with anyone before, about all his sordid young man ways, and how different he was now—during the entire drive back to the parking lot of her salon and her car.

She didn't say a word when he brought the truck to a stop.

"Say something, Emmy."

When she shook her head and reached for the door handle, a surge of panic split his insides. He touched her arm. "I would never hurt you, Emmy. Never again. You mean too much to me."

She covered her face as her mouth contorted into…a smile? Not just a smile but a laugh—and a belly laugh at that. She wagged her finger in his face. "Do you know how long I've waited—" she wiped the tears streaming from her eyes "—to hear you admit what a jerk you were back then?" Laughter again. Then she leaned across the seat and took his face in her hands. "You are so precious." She kissed the edges of his mouth, coaxing them into a smile. "But Lord, you are soooo easy to play." She kissed him several times on the lips before she leaned back in her seat, grabbing her stomach as the giggles kept coming. "We didn't ever go to Max's. You took me to The Brass Lantern in Aurora."

He was laughing now, too, mainly at her loud, boisterous sounds. "You play dirty, EmmyLou Creighton." He had to raise his voice to be heard over her. "Do not think I will forget this. Getting a man to make those kinds of admissions is an act of war." He climbed from the truck and went around to open her door.

Once she was out of the seat, she pressed against him, kissing him in a way that could only be described as hot and heavy. At least, that's what it did to him—made him hot. And heavy.

"Want to come by my place?" she asked, sliding into the seat of her car.

The look she gave him said she knew he did.

And he did. But what he wanted to do with EmmyLou required a place where they could be alone…and Joe was at her house now. It also required a bigger area than a cot…which was all he had to sleep on at his house.

Making love to EmmyLou for the first time in fourteen years would require someplace special. And some planning.

"I would like nothing more." He leaned down and kissed her. "But tonight's not the night. Can I call on you tomorrow evening, Miss EmmyLou?"

"If by 'call on' you mean doing the down and dirty, sugar, then by all means."

And with that they ended their evening. But he chuckled most of the way home and was crawling into his cot before he realized his leg hadn't come into the conversation all night, except the one time at the salon, and he'd been the one to bring it up.

EmmyLou. The woman of his dreams.

He dozed off, planning their special date for tomorrow night.

CHAPTER NINETEEN

JOEY CAME OUT of the building with a grin on his face and a woman on his arm.

"Who but my brother could manage to pick up a woman at an AA meeting?" EmmyLou half turned to check on Bentley in the backseat. His head hung out of the convertible, his tongue lolling to one side with a look of pure contentment thanks to the pain meds. "If he follows through with that ninety meetings in ninety days thing like Dustin suggested, we may be in trouble."

Bentley's grunt reminded her of Sol, whom she hadn't heard from yet today, but she wasn't worried. Tonight was the night she'd been waiting for since the night Bentley stole the man's prosthesis.

Or maybe she'd been waiting her whole life.

"You're a good dog, Bentley." She scratched his belly, and his front paw lifted to give her free access. "You're also very, very spoiled."

"EmmyLou, this here's Chevron."

"Siobhán," the young woman corrected him, casting a shy grin toward Emmy. "It's spelled S-i-o-b-h-a-n, but it's pronounced *Shuh-von*." A pretty little thing, she had short black hair and big brown eyes framed by lashes so long and thick they had no need of mascara. She couldn't have been much over legal age and looked like she wouldn't tip the scale at a hundred pounds soaking wet.

Emmy held out her hand. "Glad to meet you."

"You, too." Her handshake was as shy as her smile.

"We was talking 'bout guitars, and she was saying how she's been trying to teach herself, and I told her that I could give her some lessons if she liked."

"I'll bet you did." Emmy's protective sense when it came to Joey went on alert. "How old are you, sugar?"

"Twenty-six, ma'am." *Ma'am?* "And I've been sober thirty-eight months."

"Over three years." Emmy retracted her claws. "Wow. Congratulations."

Siobhán's chin rose a fraction, and this time she looked Emmy in the eyes. "Thanks."

"Anyway," Joey broke in, "I was thinking that this could be part of my giving back to the world process—where I do nice things for people just for the good feeling it gives me, which is supposed to feel better than any drunk I ever been on. I invited Chevron over for a lesson this afternoon and maybe a swim afterward."

"Well." He had Emmy on the spot. Inviting this woman to the house when they didn't know her from Adam? Still, thirty-eight months was a long time, and Joey needed to surround himself with people who wouldn't be a threat to his sobriety. "Um…sure," she finally answered. "Do you have the address?"

Siobhán nodded. "Joe Wayne wrote it down for me." She turned toward Joey. "Two?"

Emmy watched her brother nod as he bent forward slightly, and the question *Is he going to kiss her?* ran through Emmy's head. But he caught himself and straightened. "See ya."

Siobhán gave a girlish wave and headed toward the parking lot on the other side of the building while Joey got into the passenger seat of Emmy's car.

"Joey—" Emmy started as she pulled out onto the street.

"You don't have to say nothing, sis. I know what I'm doing."

"But—"

"My whole adult life, I been using my God-given talent to pick up women, and I got to learn to relate to them in a different way than just taking care of my needs."

Joey used the phrase "relate to" in a sentence? In a way that made sense?

She lowered her sunglasses and squinted at

him. "Who in the cornbread hell are you, and what have you done with my brother?"

Before he could answer, her cell phone rang. She pushed the button on her steering wheel to answer the call. "Hello?"

"Hey, Emmy. It's Sol."

Her lower belly clenched in a delicious way at the sound of his voice. "Hi."

"I'd like to pick you up at seven tonight, if we're still on."

She felt like shouting that she'd never been so still on, but that would require an explanation to Joey, who, at that moment, decided to make himself known.

"Hey, Sol." He shouted toward the car's speaker much louder than necessary. Emmy visualized Sol jerking the phone away from his ear. "Two meetings in two days. I'm batting a thousand."

"Good for you, Joe." Sincere congratulations warmed his tone. "You can do this. I believe in you."

"I believe in myself."

"That's what it takes. So, Emmy…seven?"

"I'll be ready." *Soooo ready.*

"Don't wear good clothes. Shorts. Flip-flops. None of those outrageous heels you're so fond of."

"Now you have me wondering. Whatcha got planned, sugar?"

"It's a surprise. See you then."

When he hung up, she took a couple of deep breaths through her nose. She had to keep her mouth closed for a few seconds lest the swarm of butterflies Sol released inside her all escape.

"Sol's learning to relate to people in a different way, too. It's part of that pennant we made yesterday. He's flying it for you."

She had no idea what her brother was talking about, but she ruffled his hair and laughed. "Whew! Thank God you're back!"

IF HE'D WORKED as hard to impress Emmy the first time around as he had today, they might be married now, Sol thought as he climbed in his truck to pick her up. His breath stilled. He hadn't been wanting marriage or anything remotely linked to commitment back then. Was that truly where his mind was headed now?

"You're rushing things, fella." He shook his head, clearing away the serious attitude. Tonight was all about fun—something the two of them hadn't had nearly enough of lately. So why were his hands trembling?

He hadn't been this nervous his very first time with a woman—well, technically, a girl, since they were both seventeen. He knew nothing about a woman's needs back then or about firing too quickly. But now, eight years without a woman had him worried about his ability to hold back at the all-important time. That was something he hadn't practiced, and tonight he would be called on to bat. How would he look to her naked? Should he take his prosthesis off? Would it be clumsy and get in the way?

He should've thought this through better. Should've given himself more time to prepare.

Too late now.

He turned into her driveway, pulling his truck all the way to the end.

Emmy met him at the back door. "Hi, sugar."

Her smile and kiss calmed him down and stirred him up at the same time, and he realized that was the effect she had on him. "Hello, gorgeous." Her hair was pulled back in a ponytail, she wore only a little makeup and she'd taken his advice, wearing a T-shirt and cutoffs. But they clung to her curves like sap on a maple, and damn if he wasn't already battling to control the effects the sight had on him.

She must've read his mind or the look on his face or felt his heart when it kicked into that unsteady rhythm, because she brushed her fingers through the side of his hair, her eyebrows drawn in worry. "Slow and relaxed tonight, right?" she whispered.

"I hope so."

She tilted her head toward the front of the

house. "Would it help to just hightail it into my bedroom and get this first time over with real quick?"

When she tiptoed her fingers down his chest, he realized she was serious. "Hell no. Getting it over real quick isn't the problem. *Not* getting it over real quick is the problem."

He watched the worry dissolve from her face as the precise problem he was describing dawned on her. "My grandma always threw the first waffle away because she'd say the iron was too hot. And then all the rest of them would be perfect."

The outlandish comparison made him laugh even while it made sense. His muscles loosened, and the anxiety seeped away.

"Should I bring syrup?" she asked.

That tore a groan from him, and he blinked to get the image out of his head before it took hold. "Maybe next time."

"What about my purse?"

He let go of her to step back, squinting one eye. "You stalling, woman?"

"Let's go." She practically pulled him out the door and down the steps toward the garage. "I just need to tell Joey and Bentley I'm leaving."

Her quick pace helped him relax even more because it told him two things—that she was anxious to be with him, and her mind was definitely not on his bum leg.

JOE WAYNE GRINNED as he heard the truck pull away. "They may think they're fooling me, Patsy." He ran a loving hand across the chrome fuel tank he had lying across the plastic shoe box. "But I recanize that glimmer I seen in both their eyes. 'Bout time, I'd say."

He looked around at all the parts of his motorcycle spread out on the tarp. He hadn't had the courage to give her the burial he'd planned, but putting her back to rights would cost a fortune. He'd been pricing stuff on the internet. The new gas tank alone cost seven hundred dollars. He'd drained and dried and wiped and used a blow drier on every tiny piece, but his gut still told him if he didn't do more, she was just going to rust away bit by bit right in front of his eyes.

And that was more than he'd be able to bear... sober.

He stood up to stretch his legs as a wave of need flared in his belly. His hands shook. He stepped out into the backyard for a few breaths of fresh air. That seemed to help, though it didn't actually curb the craving. Only distracted it for a minute.

"I can get through the next minute without a drink." He started making a lap around the pool. One became two and two became ten, and he finally felt like he was in semicontrol again.

He went back into the garage and squatted,

picking up the bottle he'd been using. "I-so-pro-pyl alcohol." Good thing it was the poison kind. He'd heard stories of guys getting so desperate for a drink they'd actually drunk the damn stuff and died. He'd never understood that need until now.

He set the bottle down and stood. If Emmy-Lou had some oil in here somewhere, he could at least lube some of Patsy's parts to keep them from getting brittle.

He began rummaging around in the cabinets. One was full of hair products—definitely Em-myLou's. But the next one, from the looks of it, still had stuff from the previous owner like spray paints and glue and glitter he couldn't imagine EmmyLou ever using.

He stood on tiptoe to check out the top shelf and pulled down a sack, pretty sure it didn't have any oil or anything he could use, but he was just being nosy. It was full of clear Christmas ball ornaments.

As he reached to replace the bag, his eyes caught on the red-and-white gingham ribbon in the corner. A few steps back gave him a better view, but it caused his head to reel. He couldn't get to the stepladder fast enough. It brought him eye level with the item on the top shelf. There in the back corner sat a jar of EmmyLou's home-made apple pie moonshine.

He pulled it out, handling it as carefully as he would a baby, but gripping it tighter because his hands were shaking so bad. The tag said, *To Maggie from EmmyLou. Don't open until next Christmas. Like you and me, it gets better with age.*

Evidently Maggie had put it away to follow the instructions and had forgotten it.

Joe Wayne eased down the ladder, cradling the magic jar to his chest. When he held it up, the sunlight from the open door caught in the liquid, turning it to the color of honey and showing the cinnamon stick. His mouth watered, clogging his throat with want.

Just a taste.

His hand gripped the top and loosened it, but he didn't take it off, knowing the smell would be more than he could take.

One minute at a time, he'd said to Chevron just this afternoon.

"For me, sometimes it was seconds," she'd said.

He tore his eyes away from the jar to look at Patsy. A good, long and hard look. And there was Bentley, asleep with a metal piece pinned in his leg that might leave him with a limp. The sweet dog, who'd run so free and playfully, might be getting old before his time.

Like me.

Because of the alcohol.

He tightened the lid. He really should just pour it out, but somehow it seemed more honorable to keep it up there. Keeping the temptation in his face, a reminder of what it did to his life—like a pennant waving, only better.

At least, that's what one part of his brain told him.

The other part that told him to put it back for safekeeping, he tried really hard to ignore.

CHAPTER TWENTY

WHEN SOL TURNED off the main road onto a gravel lane on his property, Emmy undid her seat belt and slid over to the middle of the bench seat, pressing right up against him. He had worn shorts, which had surprised and delighted her, and she lightly scraped her fingernails across the skin on the inside of his knee and up the thigh to the hem.

He chuckled. "I feel sixteen again."

"If we were sixteen, I'd already be out of these clothes." She continued with her admission despite his groan. "Gravel crunching under the tires affects me like the ringing bell did for Pavlov's dogs, except I don't salivate—if you get what I'm saying." She nibbled his earlobe, giggling softly at his shudder, which made him shudder harder.

"You're driving me insane." He leaned toward his door, getting his ear out of her range...*unless* she crawled on top of him, which had actually crossed her mind. "I mean, those short shorts were almost the end of me." He laid his arm across her lap, smoothing his hand down her calf. "If you don't behave, I'll have to pull over right here, and then the surprise I've worked on all day will be ruined."

"You've worked all day on a surprise?" That took her mind off her craving for the time being as she tried to guess what he was up to. This was the lane she'd taken to his beach the night Bentley found his prosthesis. "Are we going swimming?"

"Nope. Well, we could later, if you want. But that's not the surprise."

Sure enough, he passed the dirt path leading to the beach. A cornfield to her right, woods to her left. "Where're we going?"

"Tonight, let's just say I want to take you to places you've never been." His grin was turning her insides out.

She rested her head on his shoulder and sighed. "Now you're driving *me* insane."

Past the cornfield, he made a right turn onto another dirt path. Another field to the left, which had been mowed for hay, and then another beyond it that hadn't been mowed yet.

She held her breath in anticipation as he slowed the truck.

And then, they were there. She shrieked in surprise and delight and grabbed his neck for a tight hug.

Before her was a section of field that had been freshly mowed—that day, likely. The mowed area was about the size of her pool and garden area at home. In the center, a tarp had been spread out with a large green tablecloth, held down at the corners by oil-filled ceramic torches, which were lit, their flames doing a welcome dance.

Sol opened the door and climbed out, then held out his hand to her.

The sight before her stunned the speech right out of her.

A large bouquet of flowers from his garden lay across the middle of the tablecloth, separating two place settings of real china with cloth napkins and silverware. A wineglass and a champagne flute lay next to each plate. Two coolers—a large and a small—sat off to the side with an old-fashioned wicker picnic basket.

He took her hand but gestured with his other in a sweeping motion. "Tonight seemed like the night for a picnic."

"Good Lord have mercy, Sol." The effort he'd put into this left her breathless. "I never expected anything like this. You've even timed it perfectly with the sun behind the trees enough to give it shade."

"I tried to think of everything, but there's one thing I can't control." He reached into the side compartment of the truck door and brought out a bottle of insect repellent. "I did get the gentle, good-smelling kind, though." He coated her with spray and rubbed it in, maybe taking a little extra time on her upper thigh.

"I never knew how erotic bug spray could be," she said.

"We may have to do a more thorough job later."

The mention of later brought a smile to her lips. "This is amazing." She squeezed his hand, and the look in his eyes set fire to her heart.

"Glad you like it. Now." He closed the door and pointed to the ground beside one of the place settings. "Your seat for the evening, m'lady. I'll be your server."

While she got comfortable, which wasn't too difficult—he must've put several layers of padding beneath the tarp—Sol opened the small cooler and took out a bottle of white wine, which he uncorked. He poured them each a glass. The large cooler produced a small platter of olives and cheeses, and a crusty baguette came out of the picnic basket.

Watching him move with hardly a limp, she wondered if he'd chosen the spot because it was so level. He handed her the platter before he tried to sit on the ground, which proved to be difficult as he landed hard with an "*oof.*" But once he was down, he seemed fine.

They toasted the night and each other and dove into the appetizers—at least, she hoped they were appetizers—and as they ate, she told him about Siobhán.

His reaction was the same hers had been at first. "I don't know." He stretched out on his side and propped up on an elbow as he munched. "Do you think that's a good choice for him? Dating someone who's going through the program, too?"

"That's just it. I don't know if they're dating or not. He truly did seem to be giving her a guitar lesson this afternoon."

"Yeah? Wait him out another couple of days." He popped an olive into his mouth and chewed slowly. "Of course, if she's been sober for that long, she knows what she's doing. She might be good for him."

"That's what I thought, too." She liked how Sol made her feel better about Joey.

She'd barely swallowed the last bite of cheese before he asked, "Ready for the main course?"

It was fun seeing him so excited, though whether it was to eat or to get finished with the eating part she couldn't tell.

"This won't be pretty," he warned her before he got up. Sure enough, he wobbled some, but it could've been worse.

He brought another dish from the large cooler and handed it to her—an aluminum pan covered in foil. The delicious smell gave it away, but she had to peek. Just as she'd guessed—fried chicken. But not just any fried chicken. "Oh man. Patti's chicken? I could eat this whole pan by myself."

"You'd better consider sharing," he suggested. "Especially if you want any of this other stuff." He handed her two more containers, which she didn't even have to open to know what they held. Patti's ambrosia fruit salad was a staple along with her fried chicken picnic carryout, and the third would be her marinated broccoli and cauliflower with raisins and bacon.

"Is there pie in there, too?"

Sol grinned as he dropped into a seated position again. "That's a surprise."

"No." She stopped dishing out the food long enough to point at him with the serving spoon. "Patti's dessert isn't something you can spring on a woman, sugar. If there's gonna be pie, I have to pace myself."

"There will be pie, then. Maybe blueberry, or maybe rhubarb, or *maybe* Hershey Bar pie with toasted coconut crust."

"Aiee! Stop it!" Emmy covered her ears. "I'm going into happiness overload, and if I'm not careful, my heart might just pop out of my chest. And where would the poor thing go then? Lord knows my bra can't hold any more."

Sol raised his wineglass to her. "I'll drink to your happiness overload." The twinkle in his eyes remained, but the smile on his lips softened into a look tender and sweet. "And if your heart decides to run away, I hope I'm the one to catch it."

She raised her glass to him in return.

WITH THE FOOD cleaned up and put away, it was time for the next surprise Sol had planned. He opened the champagne and poured them each a glass, but he held back on a toast and pulled the paper out of his pocket instead.

"What's that?" Emmy's face still glowed with the same smile she'd had all night, and his heart filled his chest cavity, knowing he was the cause of that smile.

"This is my copy of the bill I gave you when I got home from Gulf Shores."

And then the smile vanished. "Oh."

"What you've done for me...what you've brought to my life...has repaid this debt many times over, EmmyLou Creighton Fuller." He touched a corner of the paper to the nearest torch and let it go up in flames. A hand flew to Emmy's mouth, but he could see that the smile had returned. He ground the small pile of ashes under his foot, and a second later, she was in his arms.

"That bill, obnoxious as it was, actually jumpstarted the two of us." She smoothed her free hand down his back. "None of this would've happened if you hadn't given it to me."

"Are you glad all this happened?" It was important to hear her say she was before they took this relationship to the next phase, so her long pause threw him a curve. His breath stilled as he waited for her answer.

"I'm happy for every second with you." She touched her glass to his. "Here's to lots more."

Her answer made his head so light he thought it might float away on one of the champagne bubbles.

They sipped and exchanged champagne-flavored kisses, the expensive liquid tasting even better on Emmy's tongue than it did from the glass.

He tuned his phone to the portable speaker he'd brought, bringing up the playlist of slow songs he'd carefully picked. "I'm not much of a dancer anymore, but if you'd like, we could try."

She set their glasses down and then snuggled against him, and he rested his cheek on top of her head. As they swayed back and forth, shuffling their feet only a little, their hands began a natural exploration. Soon his fingers found their way under the back of her T-shirt. She made a mewling sound of encouragement as he reached the enclosure of her bra. A little pressure between his thumbs and finger and the bra fell open in the back, making him thankful that technology hadn't changed that much in eight years.

Emmy pulled her hands away from him long enough to rid herself of the undergarment. Her taut nipples pressing through the fabric of her tee and her heavy breasts swaying with every movement were the stuff of teenage fantasy.

He stroked her back as she fingered the hem of his T-shirt. "Take this off," she said. He did, and she stepped back slightly and gave him an appreciative look. Her palms ran along the planes of his stomach. When she moved them up to his chest, she drew her thumbs lightly across his nipples, causing the majority of his blood to surge southward.

He reached for her, but she shook her head. "Just give me a minute." The backs of her fingers stroked his stomach up and down. "You're a gorgeous hunk of manhood, Sol Beecher."

He fought for control as the muscles in his stomach quivered beneath her touch. He took deep breaths, releasing them with a hiss through his teeth as she kissed his nipples and nipped them softly.

After what seemed like an eternity, she moved her hands away from him and lifted them into the air. "Now take off my top."

In one movement, he'd swept it over her head and thrown it…somewhere. And even though his hands were shaking with the effort to not pull her to him, he had to pause a moment and appreciate the sight. He reached up and loosed the ponytail holder, letting her hair spill onto her shoulders, across her breasts and down her back. He'd never seen anything so beautiful as Emmy, bare-breasted, with her hair down and her tiny waist accentuated by the curve of her hips in those denim shorts bathed in moonlight.

His heart stalled for a moment and then kicked into a heavy beat as she pressed her breasts against him.

"Sol?" Her voice was quiet and edged with concern. "Are you stalling?" She raised her head to look him in the eyes. "Because I'm ready when you are."

"Then it's time for the next surprise." He couldn't hold back the chuckle at the worried look that pinched her face as he led her to the truck.

SOL WAS TAKING her back to the truck? Had he lost his freaking mind?

They were adults, not teenagers. It really *had* been too long if he thought the backseat of a pickup was the best place for an intimate rendezvous.

"Hey, I have an idea." She pointed to where they'd eaten. "Why don't we go to the picnic spot, sugar? You put several layers of padding under that tablecloth, didn't you? It sure felt soft. I'll bet it would be pretty comfortable."

Sol ignored her suggestions and pulled her forward again, still wearing that Cheshire cat grin. Toward the *bed* of the truck.

Lord have mercy, this was going downhill faster than a greased sled on an icy slope. She couldn't even imagine how sore her back was going to be tomorrow after rolling around on that ribbed steel.

He lowered the tailgate and threw her a wink.

Great. That tarp he had spread out over the truck bed would keep them clean, but it wouldn't pass for any kind of padding. The backseat suddenly didn't seem like such a bad option.

"It might be kind of nice in the backseat." She used her most seductive tone. "I haven't done it there in years."

Not since she'd traded boys in for real men.

Sol shrugged. "Maybe next time." He gave the tarp a jerk and sent it to the ground.

A bedroom appeared in the back of the truck— or at least the bed part of it. And not a small one. A queen-size, filling the width of the truck bed, and two feet thick. Fully made up with white sheets and pillows with pillow cases. The top sheet had even been turned back on one corner like in fancy hotels.

"Holy moly, bless my stars and garters. How'd you ever come up with such an idea?"

He swiveled her around to look at him. "I can't tell by your tone. Are you pleasantly astonished, or have I screwed up?"

"Oh, sugar!" She did a happy jig and threw her arms around his neck. "The hometown hero just knocked it out of the ballpark!"

His relieved laugh sent warm breath down her neck and back, heating her outside and in, priming her with its simple honesty.

"It's one of those inflatable guest beds," he explained. "I was hoping you and I might need something other than my cot if we're ever at my house."

He'd gone to all this trouble for her? Emmy's heart did a happy jig of its own. "It's perfect. And beautiful."

With his hands on her waist, he lifted her onto the tailgate, but before she crawled onto the mattress, she gave in to the impulse being drawn out of her by the music and the stars. She stood up, swaying her body to the slow, erotic rhythm, and lazily unzipped her shorts, pushing them down the length of her legs until she could step out of them, leaving only the tiny yellow lace thong in place. She met Sol's eyes and held them, along with his rapt attention, and he crossed his arms and moved back enough to enjoy the full-length show, the heat from his gaze burning up the distance between them.

She raised her arms over her head, the slow, seductive movement of her hips turning her around. She danced. Just for him. Her hands lifted her hair away from her neck, then let it drop as her hands moved lower. Hooking the lace with her thumbs, she inched it down, until it, too, was left behind.

As the song ended, she dropped to her knees and climbed onto the bed. Rolling onto her back with her knees slightly bent, she eased up onto her elbows and let her head fall back as the last note played.

She'd never felt more sensuous.

Or more ready.

WATCHING EMMY'S DANCE contracted every muscle in Sol's body except one, which swelled to its full length and girth. He could only look, because touching her would most assuredly blow his gasket.

She came to a stop in the most seductive pose ever witnessed, meant for only him. His breathing came in spurts, out of control, and he gripped the lowered gate of the truck. When had he moved? He didn't remember. His body had reacted instinctively to Emmy's seductive call.

She lay back, her hands caressing the places

he so wanted to touch, and still he stood at the tailgate, mesmerized by her, terrified of his own body's treacherous lack of control.

"Sol?" Her sultry voice floated around his ear. "Are you coming, sugar? 'Cause if you're not, I'm gonna have to go on without you."

Her comment slapped him back to reality. "No, don't go on without me. I'm coming."

"I hope you mean you're getting your ass into the truck and not using that term in the sexual sense."

"Yes." He hopped onto the tailgate and toed out of his shoes. His hands were in a frenzy now, undoing his shorts. "I'm getting undressed. Give me a minute."

She let out a long sensuous groan. "Don't know if I can last another minute. Mmm."

"Condoms are in one of the pillowcases," he barked as he slid out of his shorts and boxers, letting them drop to the ground.

And there was his prosthesis. He'd forgotten it completely in his hurry.

"Should I take this off or leave it on?"

He felt the mattress shift and looked over his shoulder. Emmy leaned up on her elbows again, eyes wide with bewilderment. Or was that aggravation?

"Seriously? You wait until now to worry about your leg?" She lay back down. "Three hours of foreplay, and I'm about three strokes away from the most intense orgasm of my life." She raised her voice a notch. "I don't care! Just get up here and let me have my encore performance. We'll worry about the leg next time around."

Sol wasn't aware his prosthesis could move so quickly. He launched himself onto the mattress and crawled backward until his head was on the pillow. Emmy had a condom ready and took no time getting it into place. And then she was astride him, her body absorbing his with its delicious heat.

His hands were on her waist as she began rocking, and he realized all that worrying and fretting he'd been doing about not lasting long enough to bring her pleasure had been wasted time.

Maybe the last eight years had been wasted time.

Her back arched, her head dropped back and the air around them filled with her sounds of ecstasy.

With no thought, his body responded, allowing release to eight years of pent-up frustration, need and passion.

He plunged into darkness, and then the night exploded around him into tens of thousands of stars.

And EmmyLou Creighton Fuller.

CHAPTER TWENTY-ONE

THE DRIVEWAY ALARM told Joe Wayne that Chevron was pulling out. Five seconds later, it sounded again, telling him EmmyLou was home. His own alarm sounded in his head, telling him he was about to get a lecture from his sister.

He hurried to clean up the mess he and Chevron had made fixing breakfast, but EmmyLou waltzed in just as he set the jelly back in the fridge.

"You been taking care of the lady's needs, have you, brother of mine?"

He propped his elbow on the top of the door. "Everybody's got needs, sister dear. Seems to me Sol's been taking care of a whole bunch of yours lately, too."

She grinned. "Two shay."

Whatever that meant. "I invited Chevron to the pool party. Hope that's okay?"

"Sure. I'm glad she's coming. I think she's good for you."

"Yeah. She knows all the twelve steps by heart and spouts 'em all the time. It's kinda like being at a never-ending AA meeting. 'Course, she's been adding a few steps all her own, which I ain't having no trouble at all following."

EmmyLou stuck her fingers in her ears. "TMI, Joey."

He pictured the letters in his mind, but they didn't make a word. Leastways nothing English. "You hungry?" he asked. "I'll fix you some breakfast."

"Sol already did that." Her face broke into a grin again. "But thanks. I'll have a cup of coffee, though. Where's Bentley?"

"On your bed." Joe set about fixing her a cup while she went in the other room to check on the dog. By the time she got back, he had them both a steaming cup.

She tilted her head toward the back door. "Want to sit on the back porch? It's a beautiful morning."

"Sure." He let her lead the way, following her to the small metal table and chairs. They were girly chairs and not very comfortable to a guy's ass, but he could stand it long enough for a cup of coffee.

"Sol said he'd be expecting you around nine. If you're ready by eight-thirty, I'll drop you off."

"You'd like that, wouldn't you?" He poked her in the ribs, which used to get him a slap. These days she tolerated it better. "Getting to see Sol again so soon?" She didn't answer, but he saw the grin behind the cup. "Well, sorry to disappoint, but I'd rather walk on this pretty day."

"The fence looks good. He said you work fast and you do a real good job."

It meant a lot to him that Sol was bragging on his work. But it didn't hold a candle to the applause that came when he finished performing a song he'd written. God Almighty, he missed singing.

EmmyLou patted his hand. "What's the matter, sugar? You look like you used to when Knox ate the last cookie. You feeling bad?"

"Hell, no. I never felt better in my life, physical." He held his right hand up. "Gospel truth." He dropped it back to the table and took a sip of coffee. EmmyLou sat quiet. Listening. So he went on. "But what's the point of my body feeling good if my attitude's shitty? Life ain't fun anymore. I miss singing and playing the guitar and being in crowds. I miss the applause. I miss seeing the women with stars in their eyes when I'm the star they come to hear." He shook his head and took another sip. "I guess I miss the feeling the liquor gave me. How it smoothed the edges."

"Life has edges." Emmy had his hand in both of hers now. "There's good and there's bad. The liquor didn't smooth your life. It just made you bleary enough that you didn't feel the sharp, painful places. But if you never feel the pain, you can't fully appreciate the good. Once you've been sober for a while—and liquor's not such a temptation— maybe you'll be able to play the bars again, if that's what you want to do. You'll just have to turn down the free beer and ask for a ginger ale instead."

He thought about the jar of moonshine in the garage—and not for the first time this hour. "It's always going to be a temptation, sis. Don't fool yourself into believing no other way." He pulled his hand free and waved it toward her. "But don't you be worrying about me. I'll find my place in the world—my purpose. And if it don't involve music…" He shook his head. Couldn't bear to let his thoughts go there.

EmmyLou finished her coffee and stood. "I got to get ready for work. Since you're going to be at Sol's all day, I'll take Bentley with me so I can get him to exercise that leg. Oh, and Sol said he'd take you to a meeting this evening."

Joe Wayne shook his head. "He don't have to do that. I'll go with Chevron."

EmmyLou walked over and put her arms around his neck from behind. "I'm so proud of you, Joey. You're sober and you're working hard." She kissed the side of his head. "We're going to have the pool party Saturday—liquor-free. You'll see there's life after alcohol. Even sober crowds can be fun."

"Is Sol going to be there? How'll he keep his fake leg a secret in swim trunks?"

"He's thinking about it. But if he comes, he definitely won't swim with everybody around."

Joe Wayne could hear the disappointment in her voice. He'd work on Sol today and convince him to come. "What's the big deal about his leg, anyway?" He dropped his head back to look at his sister. "Why don't he just show people it's fake and get it over with?"

She sighed and shrugged like she agreed. "He doesn't want people feeling sorry for him. Making a deal out of it."

"Don't not talking about it make a bigger deal out of it? Like that old man who lived next door to Grandma—Mr. Crowder? Remember that wart on his nose? Grandma always told us not to say nothing about it, and damn if the whole time I was around him I didn't always think about it. If, just once, I coulda said, 'Hey, Mr. Crowder, you got a wart on your nose,' I coulda forgot it. If, just once, Sol would let people say, 'Hey, Sol, you got a fake leg,' then they'd forget it and go on about their never mind."

"There's a purpose for your life, Joey. Talking Sol into revealing his leg."

She laughed as she walked back into the house,

but sure enough, that might have been something he *could* help his friend with.

Hell, that song was already written. He'd even tried it out that once at the Break-'Em-Up. He sang softly, "And he ain't gonna wallow, he ain't gonna beg. But Sol lost his heart when he lost that damn leg."

Yep, if Sol ever came clean, he just might have a hit on his hands.

"I'll drink to that." He saluted the sun with his cup and gulped down the rest of his coffee.

"Ain't you hot in them pants, Sol?" Joe stepped out of the pool and shook himself like a dog before grabbing the towel. "Why don't you put on a swimsuit and get in?"

"I'm fine, Joe," Sol lied as he smoothed the tablecloth over the table he'd set up. He *was* hot. He'd become fond of the pants Emmy had bought him, usually wearing them as shorts around his house or hers. But with everybody coming around tonight, he felt more secure in his jeans. He'd forgotten how hot they could be when the mercury rose to almost one hundred.

It might've been a mistake to attend the pool party, but it seemed to mean a lot to Emmy. And he was having a hard time saying no to that woman about anything these days. Was the picnic really only a week ago? He felt like they'd been together for years.

And he felt years younger, too. Maybe had even lost a few pounds, if sperm weighed very much.

"What's putting that shit-eatin' grin on your face?" Joe Wayne popped him with the wet towel.

"I'm thinking where I'm going to shove that towel the next time you do that."

Emmy came out, toting a watermelon she'd carved into a basket and filled with watermelon balls. "I was just thinking—"

"Uh-oh." Sol exchanged a look with Joe.

"Nothing too difficult," Emmy assured them as she set the melon on the table. "But Tess is bringing Cher and Bandit, so I told Bree to bring her dog Peanut because I think playtime with his mama and his siblings will be good for Bentley. But they're going to need a place to romp." Sol was only halfway listening. Even in that one-piece swimsuit, Emmy had his thoughts running ahead to when he could get her out of it.

"There's a roll of chicken wire in the garage," she went on, not even realizing what a stir she was causing within him just by *being*. "Why don't we open the garage doors and stretch it across, and I'll turn on that big fan in the corner. We can put Bentley's pool in there, too, and fill it with cool water. It'll be a perfect doggie playhouse."

The melon ball Sol popped into his mouth exploded into juicy sweetness—like Emmy did when he kissed her. He really wanted to kiss her right then, but he settled for a quick brush of his lips across hers. "Good idea."

She flashed him a triumphant smile. "Hammer and nails are in the toolbox on the bottom shelf." She hustled back inside, and his eyes followed until she was out of sight.

Joe snorted. "You got it bad, dude."

"No, I've got it good, my man," Sol corrected him.

Per Emmy's wish, they headed to the garage. Emmy's car took up one side of the space and Joe's motorcycle the other. While Sol moved the car, Joe pushed Patsy out of the way. Sol couldn't remember ever seeing a more pitiful look on a guy's face regarding an inanimate object. But it wasn't just around Patsy. Gone was the funny, happy-go-lucky clown he'd met in Gulf Shores. Day by day, he saw his friend sinking deeper into despair.

They found everything where Emmy said it would be, and they set to work screening off the large doorways.

"Joe." Sol had held back saying anything, but maybe now was the time. "You've done a great job with my fence, and you've saved me a lot of time. I'm thinking I'd like to give you a bonus."

"I don't need no bonus, Sol." Joe nailed the screen wire to the wood facing of the doorway. "You're paying me enough. Hell, I shouldn't even be 'cepting any money from you with all you done for me."

"Well, I'm thinking I might get Patsy repaired." A few of the nails slipped from Joe's hand, and while he knelt to pick them up, Sol continued. "You're going to need to find a job, which means you'll need to have transportation. Think of it as an investment in your future."

Joe stood, the tears in his eyes glistening in the afternoon sunshine. "I don't deserve that kinda investment."

"Yeah, you do." Sol didn't want this to become some heavy, dramatic scene. He started walking backward, unrolling the screen wire. "But I understand your need to earn her back, so how about this? We'll take her to the shop in Benton tomorrow. And when you reach two months of sobriety, we'll pick her up. I've talked to Perk— the mechanic. He says he can get her done in a month."

"That'd…" Joe cleared his throat and wiped his hand down his face. "That'd be like getting a chunk of my life back."

"Getting your life back after you've been knocked way off course is important. So, what do you say? It'll give you an extra incentive to stay sober. You mentioned how at the meetings, they encourage you to set attainable goals."

A huge grin broke onto his friend's face, and Sol couldn't tell if the water streaming down his cheeks was tears or sweat. "To get Patsy back, I'd fence this whole end of the state of Kentucky."

"Let's just concentrate on getting this one done right now." Sol pointed to where the next group of nails needed to go.

EMMY PROPPED HER feet on the table and leaned against Sol, finally getting a chance to relax after playing hostess all evening. Sol's barbe-cued ribs and her brisket had dwindled fast with only enough left for a light lunch tomorrow if she combined it with the dab of slaw she'd tucked away in the refrigerator.

A breeze picked up around sundown, turning the insufferable heat to balmy and comfortably warm, and perfect for sitting around and talking like they were doing now. No one seemed in a hurry to get home. Not even Sol.

She rested her hand on his good leg, trying not to be disappointed that he hadn't revealed his secret as she'd hoped. He hadn't swum or even worn shorts, choosing to fool himself into think-ing it was pride and not shame that kept him in those jeans.

But everything had a season. Someday Sol

would come into his. And someday soon—if the joy she felt when she was with him was any indication—these feelings he stirred in her would open into the full bloom of love. She only needed to be patient.

Joey had fit in easily with her friends, and she wasn't surprised. His easy, likable manner endeared him to everyone, but no one more than Sol. Watching the two of them was almost like seeing Joey and Dustin together. Her oldest brother had always watched out for Joey like she had. Listening to him share his struggle for sobriety tonight with unadulterated honesty made Emmy's heart ache for him *and* burst with pride. He was working hard at the twelve-step program, taking it to heart and making it his own.

"The value of the farmland has greatly declined. And with no factories and no large businesses, we simply don't have enough tax income to keep up with our revenue needs." The frustration in Mark Dublin's voice was reflected in the faces of his friends, but especially those who'd attended Taylor's Grove Elementary. The school's remodeled kitchen was costing double what the board had budgeted.

"You could have another fund-raiser," Emmy suggested. "Raffle the beach house again. I haven't checked with Mama, and it's usually booked up until sometime in October, but we could hawk it as a preholiday getaway."

Audrey's smile held a hint of sadness. "That was a great grand prize, but I think it's too soon to try it again. Next spring we'll take you up on it. We need some kind of benefit that would draw people like the beach house did."

"We could get Kale to sing," Sol quipped, bringing a wave of laughter from the group. Kale's lack of singing ability was legendary around Taylor's Grove.

Emmy laughed especially hard, delighted to hear Sol loosening up. The turtle finally stuck his neck out of his shell.

Her laughter caught in her throat when her eyes met Siobhán's, though. Something in the young woman's wide-eyed, innocent excitement sent apprehension trickling down Emmy's spine.

"What about having Joe Wayne and EmmyLou give a concert? A lot of people would be interested in a reunion of The Fullers, wouldn't they?"

Emmy looked to her brother for reassurance that she hadn't just heard what it sounded like and met the same look of sheepish apology he'd given her when confronted about Bentley.

The night swirled around her. Did the group grow deathly silent or was the blood pounding in Emmy's ears drowning out all other noise? Sol's arm dropped from the back of the love seat to rest around her shoulders—trying to keep her from running away, screaming?

She watched everyone's eyes search the others, questioning.

"What did you say?" Kale was the one who finally asked for clarification.

"Oh, EmmyLou and I used to sing together." Joey made a good effort at passing it off with a dismissive laugh. "But that was when we was kids."

"You were The Fullers?" Bree's eyes ping-ponged between Emmy and Joey. "The *actual* Fullers?"

Emmy's breath made her lungs quiver. In fact, everything was quivering except Sol's solid hand, which gripped her shoulder and pulled her closer.

"EmmyLou and Joe Wayne Fuller. Of course!" Kale slapped his leg. "I'd never made the connection, but now that I know, I can't believe I didn't figure it out. Wow!"

Audrey's chin buckled. "But y'all go by Creighton."

"Just EmmyLou does," Joey explained. "That's her middle name. She started using it when she left the business."

"I've heard you sing so many times, Emmy, when you're just puttering around. And I thought you were good, but I never realized..." Bree's affectionate smile was meant to be supportive, but Emmy had read the writing on the wall and where this was all leading—disaster.

She summoned enough courage to speak, though her voice vibrated. "I don't sing professionally anymore. Nerves get the best of me."

"But you could maybe do it just this one time, couldn't you?" Siobhán wasn't going to let the subject die. "Just think what it would mean to the community, the children y'all care so much about like Tess and Isaiah." She nodded to the lounge chairs that held the sleeping children. "Giving back is such a vital part of Joe Wayne's recovery."

"It's not that I don't want to." Emmy needed them all to understand. "I just can't. Physically. It makes me too nervous. I get stage fright like you can't imagine. That's why I gave it up and hid for all these years. Changed my name. My hair. For a while, even the color of my eyes."

"What a shame, Emmy." Audrey, who sat next to her, patted her hand. "It must be really frustrating to have that kind of talent and not be able to share it."

Emmy shrugged, wishing the part of the subject involving her would die a quick death. "Joey has a great solo voice. Makes his living that way."

Joey shook his head. "Like I was telling y'all earlier, I'm all honky-tonks and bars."

The group fell silent, the moment's enthusiasm squelched by harsh reality.

And then Siobhán spoke up again, a Chihuahua refusing to give up her bone. "Well, maybe y'all can think about it."

Joey's eyes met Emmy's, and her heart sank at the flash of hope she read in his look. "Yeah," he answered. "We can think about it, at least."

"I KNOW YOU think I shouldn't have told her." Joe Wayne was tired of listening to his sister's lecture. Ever since the visitors had gone—including Sol, who said he thought The Fullers needed time alone to talk tonight—Emmy had been on his ass, preaching his funeral about sharing her true identity with Siobhán. "But you told Sol. How's me telling her any different?"

EmmyLou closed her mouth long enough for a long blink. "It just is."

"No, it ain't. Chevron means just as much to me as Sol does to you." Okay, that was probably a lie, which was something he wasn't supposed to do according to his twelve-step program. He took a deep breath. "No, that ain't so. I ain't in love with her yet. But I may be someday. And I've lied so much to women in the past that I was just trying to be up-front with her from the very start and let her know all about my life."

Emmy threw a punch to the air. "You could have left out *my* part!" She stomped off into the kitchen.

He turned to go up to his room and then thought better. This boil had been festering for years, and it was time to pop it. "That don't even make sense, EmmyLou." He followed her into the other room. "How's I supposed to tell her about being one of The Fullers without bringing you up? Hellfire! There ain't no *Fuller*. It was The *Fullers*." He drug out the *S* sound, slamming his fist against his other palm. "And by the way, in case you weren't paying no attention out there, them people in your backyard didn't want me. They wanted *us*. What kind of draw would I be by myself? 'Buy your tickets here, folks.'" He used his announcer voice. "'Come hear *half* of The Fullers. Sorry, but it's not the *best* half. This is the used up, alcoholic, has-been half. But wc know how you're itching to part with your money to catch the show he's performing for all the honky-tonk bars between here and Gulf Shores.'"

"Stop it, Joey!" Emmy leaned against the island and threw her hands up to cover her ears. "You're making me feel bad."

He pulled her hands away and held them firm. "You *should* feel bad. You left me dangling out there with nothing. Walked away and left me just when my career was starting to take off. I've been a nothing ever since." He dropped her hands and stepped back, hating how his voice and hands were shaking. Hating the hurt he'd brought to her eyes. Hating the tears. Hating that he was craving a drink to numb the god-awful feelings.

Emmy's chin quivered, her silence shouting at him.

"I'm sorry, sis. I shouldn't have said that." He ran his hand through his hair and squeezed his eyes closed. "It's just that…when they brought it up about the benefit concert—" he opened his eyes but raised them to the ceiling to avoid the hurt he'd brought to hers "—my heart started kicking in my chest like a mule with a hornet on his ass. I thought, maybe just this once, I'd catch a break."

"Oh, Joey." Emmy's sniffles threw a wrench in his gut.

He pulled her into a hug. "Don't cry. Please."

"I never meant to hurt you, Joey." She shook her head against his chest. "I was just so scared every time I went onstage. Scared of disappointing everybody."

"Scared of disappointing Mama."

She didn't answer.

He hugged her tighter. "You don't have to be afraid anymore, you know? Like that Senility Prayer people's always quoting—you gotta learn to accept the things you can't change and change the things you can. It's good solid advice for everybody."

"You've grown up into a good man, Joey."

"Love you, too." He kissed the top of her head and felt her pull in a long, deep breath.

"And because I love you, I'm willing to give it a try." She pushed away from him and held up one finger. "I will do this one last concert with you to send you off on your new path, but then I'm done forever. We will be even-steven. Agreed?"

That damn mule kicked in his chest so hard, he let out a yell that could be heard from Taylor's Grove to Nashville. "Hell yeah!" He picked up his sister by the waist and twirled her around until he was dizzy. It was almost like a shot of good whiskey.

"I'll call Audrey in the morning and see if we can get the ball rolling," she said.

A reunion concert and the promise of getting Patsy back? This sober lifestyle might be bearable, after all.

CHAPTER TWENTY-TWO

"JUST A MINUTE, SUGAR." Emmy pressed the phone against her breast and stuck her head out of her bedroom door. "Joey, the reporter's coming up the driveway. Will you let him in?"

"'Kay."

The answer came from the kitchen as she lifted the phone back to her ear. "I guess I have to get off now. I wish you'd come hold my hand through this. I'm like that proverbial cat on the hot tin roof."

"You'll do great," Sol assured her. "Call me when it's over, and we'll go grab a bite somewhere."

"I don't think I'll be hungry, so you go ahead and eat something. The way my stomach's rolling, I may never be hungry again. But I'm pretty sure I'll need some of your magic therapy that gets rid of my anxiety."

Sol's chuckle brought a comforting warmth to her belly that calmed her. "Considering all the *therapy* you're demanding for your nerves, I'm going to need a prosthesis for another body part if this concert isn't over soon."

"Two more days, sugar. Then your body part— my favorite one, by the way—can go back to whatever schedule it wants, as long as it doesn't have a hankering for another eight-year vacation."

Another chuckle, but this one definitely didn't calm her. *Aiee!* And there was the doorbell.

"See you later, gorgeous. Call me when you're done."

Emmy tossed her phone on the bed and went to check herself out in the mirror one last time. Should she have pulled her hair back on one side? Would her royal blue top have been a better choice? *Lord have mercy!* She was coming apart at the seams. She reached for the bottle of pills on her bathroom counter, the beta-blockers the doctor had prescribed. They calmed her physically but did nothing to relieve the emotional distress. She'd used the pills twice during rehearsals without Joey being aware, and both times he'd complained that she was "off"—just didn't seem into the music.

She put the bottle back on the counter.

In the next room, she heard Joey open the door and let the reporter in, heard them start chatting and move into the sitting room. A wave of nausea rolled through her. She plopped in the chair by the bed to let it pass.

Oh dear Lord, what was she doing? Why was she putting herself through this again? She had such a good life—a quiet life with a solid business and a wonderful boyfriend. There was no doubt in her mind that she'd found in Sol whatever she'd been searching for all those years and that he was the one she could spend her life with.

But her forever couldn't begin until she'd fulfilled this detestable obligation to Joey and the town of Taylor's Grove.

Two more days and she could go back to being EmmyLou Creighton.

She pressed her fingertips together lightly and took some deep breaths, but her hands still trembled. "Just do it." She pushed out of the chair and went to face the reporter.

"They've moved us to the high school auditorium and doubled the number of tickets 'cause demand was so high," she heard Joey saying.

The reporter stood when she walked in the room. He was a guy about her age with a receding hairline and a paunch around his middle. "EmmyLou Fuller." A huge smile broke out on his face as soon as he saw her. He stuck out his hand and they shook. "Flip Phillips. I've been wanting to meet you for years, and I've finally tracked you down." His wording slithered up her spine as he looked her over. "The years have been good to you. You look fabulous as ever."

"Thanks." She sat in the chair nearest Joey.

"You're from the Nashville paper, right?" The excitement in Joey's voice couldn't be missed.

Flip pushed his glasses back up to the bridge of his nose. "Yeah, *The Spin*. We're a weekly that mainly runs where-they-are-now stories. Feel-good human interest stuff. We're based in Nashville, but we have circulation all over the country."

Joey flashed her a smile, which she tried to reciprocate, but her lips felt tight, like they wouldn't stretch wide enough.

Flip immediately went to work, asking all sorts of questions about what happened when they broke up all those years ago, what the *real* story was behind Emmy's breakdown, how it affected their relationship, and on and on until Emmy's head spun.

Joey seemed to eat it up, joking and laughing and sharing things she wished he hadn't about his personal life and his recent sobriety. "I just got my Patsy back two weeks ago, and let me tell you, no binge I ever been on felt as good as when me and her's racing against the wind."

Flip's fingers tapped quickly on his small keyboard, not missing a word. He turned to Emmy, squinting hard, and she got the feeling he was trying to see through her. "And what about you, EmmyLou? I know I was madly in love with you, as were a million other teenage boys. How's your love life been? Ever been married?"

"No." She shook her head, forced a smile.

"Do I still have a chance, or are you in a serious relationship?"

"Um…" She shouldn't have hesitated. It made him peer harder. "It may be serious…still too new to know for sure." Even she could hear the lie in her tone.

"Your eyes say it's serious. Somebody from around here?" he pressed, and she felt the noose tightening around her throat.

Please leave Sol out of this. She so didn't want their relationship plastered across the page for curious eyes to explore. And she had no doubt that Sol would abhor the idea.

"Well…from the area." She kept it vague, tried to make it sound like he could be from anywhere in a hundred-mile radius.

"You're sure being mysterious." Flip's smile reminded her of a shark in some animated movie she'd seen. "I like mysteries. They make me want to dig." The comment came across as a veiled threat.

"Oh no. No mystery." She tried for a light giggle, but it came out as a cackle, causing Joey's eyes to narrow. "Nothing newsworthy."

The smirk Flip gave her said he wasn't convinced, but he let it drop. "I'd like to get some pictures. I saw a pool area out back that would make a great background." He stood without even waiting for a reply.

They cut through the house on their way to the backyard, and nothing got by the reporter. He commented and made notes on everything.

During the photo shoot, it occurred to Emmy that Flip hadn't pulled his car to the back but had parked it around front like most first-time visitors.

So how did he know about the pool unless he'd snooped around before he rang the bell?

After years of peace, she was back in a place where she had to watch everything she said or did. Nothing in her life was private. Not her business. Not her property. Not her love life.

Her heart pounded, and she broke out in a cold sweat.

She'd done many things in her life that she regretted, but instincts told her this concert would be one of the highlights.

"I'LL SEE YOU tomorrow night. After the show." Chevron stood on tiptoe and gave Joe Wayne another long kiss that made him want to stay with her tonight. But he and EmmyLou had a full day scheduled tomorrow with special appearances at some local businesses and even an interview at the TV station. He needed to be up and ready to go early. Staying with Chevron would definitely keep him up and ready to go, just not in the right way.

"I'll look for you in the audience and sing directly to you, sunshine."

He started to walk away, but she grabbed his arm and turned him around. "You can do this, Joe Wayne. Living it without the alcohol is something you'll never regret."

"I know. I'm good."

Her pleased grin followed him out into the darkness, but his died before he got astraddle Patsy. He'd had a hankering for a drink all week. The first few days he'd gotten Patsy back, he'd felt like a kid again without a care in the world. But this past week, the jitters had him all over the place.

Twice he'd gotten the moonshine out of the cupboard in the garage, and twice he'd put it back unopened. But tomorrow night was the biggest night of his career. It would either label him as a has-been or launch him a second time.

His head kept telling him he needed more rocket fuel for that launch, but his heart kept whispering *no*. Only long rides on Patsy calmed him enough that he could find sleep.

He pulled out of Chevron's drive, thinking to

take the long way home, but decided against it. Instead he headed home for a nice, relaxing swim and then a good night's sleep.

It didn't seem unusual that the car behind him made the same turns to get out of Benton or even through Draffenville. But when he made the turn off the main highway toward Taylor's Grove and the car did the same, he knew he was being followed.

Some fan wanting to find out where he lived? One of Chevron's ex-boyfriends?

He didn't care who it was. They weren't following him all the way to EmmyLou's.

At the next stop sign, he put Patsy's kickstand down, climbed off, and headed back to the car to confront whoever was invading his privacy.

As he approached, the window rolled down.

"Hey, Joe Wayne." That reporter, Flip Phillips, gave him a big ol' possum grin. "How you doing, man?"

"I reckon I'm doing fine. Want to tell me why in the hell you're following me?"

"Oh." The possum reached over and pulled up his little computer. "You kept talking about your motorcycle—Patsy?—the other day, so I decided it would be cool to get some shots of you on it." He brought up some pictures he'd taken the past few minutes—Joe Wayne throwing his leg across Patsy, revving her up, pulling out of Chevron's drive.

Joe Wayne leaned against the window edge for a better look. Cool shots. One with him stopped right here at the stop sign, getting off Patsy with the moonlight all around. "Them's damn beautiful," he had to admit. "Some of the best pictures I ever seen of me and my best girl."

"Yeah, well, that's what I do. You headed home to bed?"

Joe Wayne pushed away from the car. "Yeah. Maybe a swim first. EmmyLou's idea. She said it'd make us sleep better."

Flip's head jerked toward him real quick. "EmmyLou's going to be swimming? Man, what I'd give for a shot of her in a bikini."

No way would EmmyLou approve of that. "Sorry, dude. This one's a private party."

"Will her boyfriend be there? The mysterious Sol Beecher?"

"How'd you get his name?" These guys had a way of finding out everything.

"I went to the salon and talked to some of the stylists. Took a few pictures of the place as part of the story. Shame EmmyLou's been off this week. It would've been great to have a picture of her working on somebody's hair. Anyway, the people around Taylor's Grove tell me Sol was injured during his time in service. Could you get him to talk to me about it? It'd be a great addition. Former country music star hooks up with the local war hero." He swiped his hand across the air like he was writing it on the sky.

"You'd best leave Sol out of it," Joe Wayne warned. "He'd hate any publicity. He don't want nobody calling him hero, either."

"Oh, really?"

Joe Wayne was familiar with that tone. It was the one that usually led to a bar fight. Well, this wasn't a bar, he wasn't all liquored up and he wasn't getting in a brawl.

He walked away without saying another word…well, except "asshole."

But he muttered that one under his breath after he got far enough away not to be heard.

"I COULD DO this every night for the rest of my life." Sol kissed Emmy's temple. She shuddered softly and let out a contented sigh.

"It is nice." She tilted her head back and kissed his neck, which sent a pleasant sensation rumbling through him. "Too bad I have to close the pool this week."

Sitting on the steps in the shallow end, immersed to their chests in the still-warm water, made it hard to believe September was here. Frosts wouldn't be a threat for another month or so, but soon the air would become too brisk to swim.

"I wasn't necessarily talking about the pool." He shifted so he could look her in the eye as he made the admission. "Holding you is the something I could do every night for the rest of my life. I love you, Emmy."

He waited for her reaction.

She gave a little smile and brushed her hand through the side of his hair, then down his cheek. Her eyes held his, but they started to glisten in the moonlight as tears welled up in them. "I love you, too, sugar."

Her reaction was sweet, and his heart beat a happy rhythm that she reciprocated, but he'd expected...*more*. "You took one of those beta-blockers, didn't you?"

She nodded, her bottom lip protruding sullenly. "I had to. I've been so nervous, I actually threw up twice, but I hadn't really eaten, so there was nothing to throw up. I'm afraid if I can't keep something in my stomach, I'll get up there tomorrow night and pass out."

"You're going to do fine. You and Joe are wonderf—" Headlights coming up the drive caused him to lose his train of thought. He was in a swimsuit and his prosthesis and long pants were several feet away. He slipped off the step into the water, immersing himself completely as Joe roared to a stop on Patsy.

It would take his heart several minutes to return to a steady beat.

"Hey, y'all!" Joe waved and ran for the back porch. "Gimme a minute and I'll join you."

Emmy shook her head. "Joey's a born musician. His timing's always been perfect."

Sol swam over to her, taking his seat back beside and giving her a kiss that would have to last for a while since being too affectionate in front of an audience wasn't his thing. "We'll continue this discussion tomorrow night when you've realized your amazing success."

There might be time for one more long kiss to seal that promise…

Just as he moved in to claim it, Joe came bursting out the back door, running like a three-year-old and giving a rebel yell. He did a cannonball into the pool and drenched them and Bentley several feet away.

The man was wild with nervous energy, and more than once, Sol almost wished Joe could take a drink to calm down—or have one himself to filter out the noise.

The fourth cannonball had Sol calling it quits. He backed his way up the steps in the shallow end and across on his butt to the chair by the table where his crutch and prosthesis lay. He sat and toweled off, waiting to get a little drier before he donned the artificial limb.

Joe Wayne's mouth was moving a mile a minute, talking about everything they had to do tomorrow, while Emmy swam in uncharacteristic silence.

Sol hoped he never had to see her like this again, and he understood now why she'd chosen to leave all this behind.

It really wasn't her.

Just as he grabbed his prosthesis to put it on, Bentley sat up and let out a low, ominous growl. His run wasn't quite as fast as it used to be—a fact Emmy had used to make all kinds of comparison jokes about Sol and the dog—but he took off toward the side yard, barking and growling. Sol glimpsed a shadow of movement.

Faster than Sol had ever seen Joe move, his friend was out of the pool and running across the yard. A dark figure was chugging out in front of him—a man, and he was losing ground fast.

Sol hustled to equip himself to be able to move. "Get in the house, Emmy, and call 911," he ordered, but she ignored him, already loping toward her brother and dog.

By the time Sol reached the scene, Joe had tackled the guy and hauled him to his feet.

"No need to call the sheriff, sugar. It's that

sniveling reporter." Sol had never heard so much disgust in Emmy's voice. "Flip Phillips."

Joe Wayne held the guy's tablet, flipping his finger across the screen. "He's got pictures. Look."

Sol did look, and wished he hadn't. Close-ups of Emmy's voluptuous curves, including one where her swimsuit bottom had crawled up, exposing a cheek. Joe Wayne in the middle of a cannonball with a wild grin on his face that made him look slightly deranged.

These had a deliberately malicious feel to them.

"Oh, God." Sol broke out in a sweat. The reporter had caught him crab-walking backward across the patio, the stump of his leg glowing white in the moonlight. The wounded and crippled creature from the lagoon, crawling for safety.

He grabbed the tablet from Joe and slammed it against his good thigh, breaking it in half.

"You'll pay for that!" The obnoxious reporter actually sputtered the words.

"That so?" Sol bent down into his face. "We'll see what Sheriff Blaine has to say about trespassing on private property first."

The pudge hiked his pants and pushed his glasses up on his nose, hands fisted and an expression on his face that would've been the end of them all if looks could kill. "We'll see who gets the last laugh, *hero*. I already hit Send, so they're in my computer at the office. And furthermore—" he flashed them all something that Sol figured was supposed to be an evil smile "—they'll all be in print Sunday. Be sure and pick up a copy of *The Spin*."

Joe pulled back his fist, but Sol saw the punch coming. What The Fullers didn't need was an arrest for assault the night before their concert. Trying to block the blow with his arm diverted it to his stomach. He doubled over, fighting for breath and balance, but the force knocked him on his ass.

Emmy screamed, Joe cussed, Bentley barked, and the reporter took the opportunity to hightail it out of there, but not before his screech of laughter landed in Sol's ears.

Sol sat gasping, trying to get air into the areas where the punch had forced it out, when reality came on with a second, even harder blow.

His picture—the one that showed him at his weakest—would be made public Sunday for all the world to see.

The Fullers had done it again.

"You okay, sugar?" Emmy had her hand under one arm and Joe had the other, lifting him to a standing position.

Sol jerked free as soon as he had his balance, shame and humiliation rolling through him on a tidal wave of anger. "Leave me alone, Emmy." He caught his breath and repeated it just in case she hadn't understood. "Just leave me alone."

He stalked back to his truck and drove home.

CHAPTER TWENTY-THREE

"You SHOULD QUIT using that powder makeup. You're getting to the age where adding any extra texture to your skin is a mistake. It gets into the creases, shows every wrinkle."

"I'll make a note of that, Mama." Emmy kept her voice flat, not giving any hint of the time bomb ticking inside her. This surprise breakfast idea was a horrible one, but Joey had accepted the offer from Mama and Daddy without her knowledge, and then wolfed down his food and took off to help unload sound equipment. She used her fork to push a piece of cantaloupe around on her plate. Was Sol as miserable as she was this morning?

"I think you look pretty as a spring morning, Buttercup."

"Thanks, Daddy." EmmyLou gave him a smile she didn't feel.

"Oh, stop lying," Mama snapped. "She looks awful and you know it." She shook a finger in Emmy's direction. "That shade of green is not in your palette, and those swollen, red eyes—

you obviously slept way too long last night. You should limit yourself to eight hours. Anything over that is unnecessary and self-indulgent."

Emmy bit her tongue. She could explain that she'd hardly slept at all last night—that she'd lain awake, worried about how she and Sol had left things—but what good would it do?

Her hand shook as she reached for the glass of orange juice.

"Will your boyfriend be at the concert tonight?" Mama didn't notice the juice sloshing from the glass or Emmy setting it back down. "I'm looking forward to seeing him, though I must admit that I don't have my expectations set too high. Forty and still single?"

Heat flashed through Emmy. "I don't think he'll be there." Then she was chilled.

"It's just as well." Mama gave that laugh, which wasn't a laugh at all. "When it comes to you and men, I learned a long time ago not to get attached."

Conversations about *her* shortcomings were something Emmy largely ignored. But talking about Sol today, when her misery level had skyrocketed out of sight, when her nerves were frayed and her emotions exposed and raw, advanced the counter on the time bomb instantly to zero.

She rose slowly from her chair...and exploded.

"Do you ever consider that you might not be the center of the universe, Mama? Have you ever thought that somebody besides you might have feelings or—Heaven help us—opinions?" She slapped her napkin onto her seat.

"Don't you dare raise your voice to me, young lady."

The demanding tone urged Emmy to speak louder. "I'm not a young lady. You take every opportunity to remind me of that. I haven't been a young lady for a long time. I'm a woman—"

"Who's acting like a child. Show some respect." Her mom was on her feet now, chin lifted imperiously.

Emmy mirrored the body language. "Respect is something that's earned...and it goes both ways."

"You talk too much, EmmyLou." Her mother gave another disapproving sniff. "You always have."

"And yet you've never listened."

Emmy turned away and headed for her car.

"Where are you going?" The question was intoned as a demand that Emmy chose not to answer.

She'd unlocked the floodgate now, and her emotions were pouring through unchecked. Might as well take full advantage of the situation and get them all out at once.

She roared out of her driveway, and in three minutes was walking toward Sol, who was out by the road, working on his fence.

He looked at her quizzically. Opened his mouth.

She didn't give him a chance to speak. "Don't talk. Just listen. I've shared things with you in a way I've never done with anybody else. Told you my deepest, darkest secrets. Bared my soul. You know all my insecurities. You've seen me at my worst, with no makeup of any kind to hide the flaws."

"Emmy."

"I'm not done. If you can't accept me the way I am, that's your choice. But know that somewhere out there I'm going to find somebody who loves *me* for who I am." She tapped her chest and then threw the finger his direction. "But that's never going to be you, Sol Beecher, and you know why?" She didn't wait for an answer. "Because you can't accept yourself for who *you* are. That's got to come first."

"I love you."

"No!" Had she actually shrieked that word? "You aren't allowed to love me. Not until you can quit living in hiding. Come clean about your leg. Love yourself so you can love me and love what we are together." Lord, she was coming apart at the seams, unraveling thread by thread.

No, not in front of this man. "Until then—" she lowered her voice to an icy whisper "—stay the hell away from me."

She left him standing mutely, his face void of expression.

His heart was apparently made of the same steel as his leg.

Joe Wayne's body shook like an earthquake had hit.

If the day was any indication of how the night was going to turn out, he and EmmyLou were destined to be the Casey Joneses of the country music world.

Shitfire! He hated hearing her cry.

She'd prowled around downstairs all night long and he'd even gone down to check on her once. She was sniffling and blubbering about Sol, and how she'd ruined his life. He'd thought the surprise at breakfast would make her feel better, but nothing seemed to help.

And then, all day long, during the guest appearances and interviews, she'd been nearly silent, letting him do all the talking—which he really didn't mind. It just pained him to see her like this.

Three hours till showtime. They needed to get final sound checks done.

He picked up the Stetson EmmyLou had insisted on and stopped in front of the mirror for a quick assessment. The black Western shirt already had sweat marks under the arms, and the damn bolo tie was gonna choke off all his air.

He threw the hat against the wall and jerked the tie loose until he could get it off. With one pull, the snaps down the front of his shirt popped open. He shimmied out of it and wadded it into a ball before throwing it to the ground. The T-shirt came off next, and he was panting hard and sweating harder.

A drink was the only thing that would fix this.

He flopped onto the bed, staring up at the ceiling, swallowing hard to get rid of the damn lump in his throat. But the more he tried, the bigger it grew.

Just one drink. Just enough to take the edge off and get him through this night.

He sat up on the edge of the bed and leaned forward to rest his elbows on his knees, pressing his fingertips together. He was supposed to do it lightly, according to EmmyLou—"Pressure causes pressure," she'd always told him—but right then his fingers were insisting they needed to do push-ups against each other.

If he couldn't get his fingers to relax, he'd never be able to pluck the right string.

He pushed off the bed and went into the bathroom to dry off and add another layer of deodorant to his underarms. Then he got another white T-shirt out of the drawer and put it on but didn't tuck it in. He caught a glimpse in the mirror. Better. More Joe Wayne Fuller.

His heartbeat slowed a mite, but the need for that drink was hanging on like a baby possum to its mama.

Just go to the garage and grab a shot of moonshine, and let that be the end of it.

He hit the stairs at a near-run but paused by EmmyLou's door. "Sis, we need to leave soon."

"I'm about ready."

At least it didn't sound like she was crying anymore.

"I'm gonna go put Patsy in the garage. I'll meet you at the car."

"Okay."

He stopped in the kitchen and grabbed a tin of mints from the drawer. A couple of them would cover the scent on his breath.

He raised the garage door and walked Patsy in, then hurried to let the door down and get the stepladder. The jar of moonshine was right where he'd left it at the back of the cupboard. He eased it out real careful, not wanting to slosh it on him, and unscrewed the lid.

He had it to his lips when the side door opened.

"Joey? Oh, Joey. No."

He saw EmmyLou's horrified expression. "I need a drink, EmmyLou." He needed to make her understand. "It'll take the edge off…and I got a big ol' sharp edge cutting me right in two."

"Joey." She walked over to stand beside him, raising her voice. "You *don't* need it."

The top of the ladder provided a safe surface to rest the moonshine on until his feet were on the ground. Then he picked the jar up again. "One shot's all I need. I promise."

She grabbed for it, but he was too quick. He held it up out of her reach.

"Joey." Her eyes were squinting real tight. "Think what you're doing. More than two months' sobriety. Gone with one sip."

Two months that had given him back Patsy, all fixed and running like she was new. Sol's generosity twisted in his gut.

"Give it to me now! You don't need it!" EmmyLou yelled real loud this time, and it loosed the devil in him.

"Hell yes, I need it!" He could taste the shame on his tongue. "I need it just like you need those damn pills."

Her eyes went wide, but her lips nearly disappeared as she pressed them together hard. They just stood there staring at each other like two cats in a standoff.

Her neck rippled when she swallowed. "You're right." She didn't yell this time. She whispered, and her voice sounded little and tired. She reached into the pocket of her dress and pulled out the brown bottle. "I was waiting to take one when we got there." She held the bottle out to him. "But I won't if you won't. Trade?"

His hand was cold as he wiped it down his face. "I never faced a crowd without a drink, sis." The confession poured out of his soul. "Even when I was fifteen, I was sneaking Daddy's vodka before concerts." The fear that had rankled his spirit for nigh on to half his life came to the surface. "It's not the singing in bars that scares me. It's the singing without the liquor. What if I ain't no good without the sauce?"

A tear careened down EmmyLou's cheek as she patted his chest. "I've heard you without the sauce for the last two months, sugar. You're good. You're damn good."

He took a deep breath and blew it out. "Well, if I ain't, Sol says I got a knack for fence building."

Damnation! He shouldn't have mentioned Sol's name, 'cause now she was crying again.

He tightened the lid and swapped the jar in his hand for the pill bottle in hers. "Let's go back to your bathroom. While you're redoing your makeup, I'll flush this stuff down the toilet."

He took her cold and clammy hand and ushered her back inside.

EMMYLOU'S HANDS WERE chunks of ice, she couldn't contain the tremors making loops through her system, and the pounding in her temples didn't keep the rhythm to any of the songs they had lined up.

Above all, her heart was broken.

If Sol had only called, everything would've been better.

But he didn't, and as the announcer made a big deal out of the concert and the curtain pulled back, she prayed he wasn't in that front row seat he'd bought the reserved ticket for.

He wasn't.

Mama and Daddy were there, though, which surprised her. Then again, Mama was sure to be getting some attention from the event. The thought didn't bother her enough to dwell on it. She'd promised herself—and Joey—she'd never put herself through this again.

The applause cued the automatic smile as she barely focused over the tops of the heads of the six hundred patrons, reminding herself they stood for six thousand dollars for Taylor's Grove Elementary.

Joey's fingers flew into the melody and her shaky ones picked up the harmony, and then their voices blended, words coming without much thought.

Just as they'd practiced, she finished with a quick "Thanks, y'all, for making us feel so welcomed. We're glad to be here." The lie hung in her chest like dead weight. But Joey had his say—something that made everybody laugh— and then they fell into sync with one of their old hits, and the audience applauded its approval, and she survived another one.

The third song was her first solo—a new one Joey had written for her. Its beautiful, lilting melody was perfect for her voice, and she was supposed to introduce it, but she went blank on what she'd planned to say, so she just dove in. The words wobbled out of her throat, with not enough air behind to lift them. The muscles in her throat convulsed in fear. She stopped and cleared her throat. "Sorry. I'm a little nervous," she apologized and started over. This time, she got the first line out, and then the screen in the front of her brain went blank. All the words erased. Her hands started to quiver, fingers jerking the strings haphazardly. Above the roar in her ears, the song dissolved into a mass of nonsensical notes.

She stopped again, and the quiet gasp from the audience sucked every bit of air from her lungs. As she sat there, panting, she watched her mom get out of her seat and leave the auditorium.

She didn't care. That didn't matter. What did matter was how she'd laid into Sol about not accepting who he really was, yet here she was, the biggest fake of all. "I can't do this," she said at last, and the audience stilled. Looking down the front row, she made eye contact with Siobhán, Bree and Kale, Audrey and Mark. Tess. Her dad, who smiled—she smiled back. She wasn't sure when it happened, but Joey had reached over and taken her hand.

His touch was as warm as his look. "It's okay, sis."

It *was* okay. Her heart nodded.

"A very wise man once told me—" she smiled at Joey "—that you have to accept the things you can't change." She turned her smile to the audience—a real one this time. "I can't change who I am. Fact is, I don't *want* to change who I am. I'm a hairstylist—a good one—and a good businesswoman. It makes me happy. It's what I want to be. Not this." She motioned to the guitar hanging on her shoulder. "Never this." She looked directly at Tess. "Tess, and all the rest of you kids out there, follow your own dreams, not somebody else's. Find your passion. And when you find it, go after it with everything you got."

She slid off her stool and gave Joey a kiss on the cheek, then turned back to the audience. "You're not going to attend the reunion tour of The Fullers tonight, but you are going to attend the launch tour for a new solo artist, Joe Wayne Fuller."

The audience responded with a more enthusiastic applause than she'd expected. Still, there were some disgruntled faces in the crowd.

"Now, I know that you paid for The Fullers, so if you want your money back, I'll see that you get a refund."

With a regular wave—none of that pageant whoop-de-do—she walked off stage...and straight into something warm and solid.

EMMY'S HEAD JERKED up at him to see what she'd run into. "Sol!" Her eyes widened when he grasped her arms. "I didn't think you were here."

"I was afraid I'd make you nervous if I sat out front." He lifted the guitar from around her neck and laid it on a chair. "You were wonderful out there."

She snorted. "I was a mess, but it's over."

"How about us? Are we over?" His breath stilled, but his heart pounded as he waited for her reply. "I'm sorry. I didn't mean what I said last night. I don't ever want you to leave me alone. You're my passion, the dream I'll always follow."

"I…" She stopped, then shook her head.

Oh God. She was going to repeat what she'd said to him this morning—insist he get the hell away from her.

She said, "I don't ever want us to be over."

Their eyes locked, and the love he saw reflected back at him was all the confirmation he needed to know she was the one he'd waited for. Their joyous laughter rang through the wings of the backstage area. She was in his arms and he picked her up, not daring to swing her around, though his heart was swinging far out into space.

"I love you." He set her back on her feet and took her face in his hands. "I love you." He kissed her. "I love you."

She squealed and threw her arms around his neck in a tight hug. "I guess loving you is one of those things I have to accept, because it's never going to change."

"Um…sis. EmmyLou…" Joey's voice surrounded them, drawing both of their attention to the stage. He pointed to his chest and then to her. "Your, uh, microphone is still hot."

"Oh my Lord!" Emmy shrieked, and the audience burst into laughter.

This woman he loved enjoyed nothing better

than telling a good tale, and Sol decided right then to give her one she could tell for the rest of her life.

He grabbed her hand and pulled her onstage. There in front of six hundred witnesses, he went down on one knee. Or he tried to. The damn pants didn't give enough. He reached down and gave each pant leg a jerk, ripping apart the Velcro, and letting the bottom half of the trouser legs fall to the floor.

A gasp passed through the crowd at the sight of his prosthesis, followed by a titter.

He shrugged and leaned forward to speak into the mic attached to the neckline of Emmy's dress. "We all have to accept the things we can't change." He dropped to his good knee, and the crowd roared its approval, so he waited until they'd quieted before reaching into his pocket with one hand and taking Emmy's hand with the other. He held up the ring and looked her in the eye, willing her to see the love pouring from his heart. "EmmyLou Creighton Fuller, I love you and want to spend the rest of my life in your arms. Will you do me the honor of becoming my wife?"

"Yes," she answered quietly, slipping the ring onto her finger. But then she threw her hand into the air and pumped it toward the ceiling, screaming, "Yes. Yes. Yes. Yes!"

She grabbed him under the arm and helped him to his feet as the audience rose to theirs in a standing ovation. After a hug and a kiss that was long enough to draw some catcalls, they scurried off stage, seeking a little privacy where they could have another, more intimate embrace.

As he leisurely explored Emmy's sumptuous mouth—something he'd never grow tired of—he heard Joe Wayne saying, "Man, am I glad Sol finally let his secret out. You see, I been sitting on this song I wrote. I been wanting to see what y'all think about it." Soft notes blended into a lovely melody, and Joe Wayne's deep baritone sang out.

"Now, here is the tale of Sol Beecher, a man who fought for his country in Afghanistan…"

Sol broke the kiss abruptly. "What the hell…?" He blew out a disgusted sigh.

Emmy used her finger to turn his face toward her and grinned up at him. "You're never gonna change him, sugar. Might as well accept that."

Sol returned her grin and shook his head in surrender.

Then he returned to his favorite pastime.

Loving EmmyLou.

* * * * *

LARGER-PRINT BOOKS!
GET 2 FREE LARGER-PRINT NOVELS PLUS
2 FREE GIFTS!

HARLEQUIN®

Romance

From the Heart, For the Heart

LARGER-PRINT BOOKS!

LARGER-PRINT BOOKS!
GET 2 FREE LARGER-PRINT NOVELS PLUS
2 FREE GIFTS!

HARLEQUIN®

INTRIGUE
BREATHTAKING ROMANTIC SUSPENSE

YES! Please send me 2 FREE LARGER-PRINT Harlequin® Intrigue novels and my
2 FREE gifts (gifts are worth about $10). After receiving them, if I don't wish to receive
any more books, I can return the shipping statement marked "cancel." If I don't cancel,
I will receive 6 brand-new novels every month and be billed just $5.49 per book in the
U.S. or $6.24 per book in Canada. That's a saving of at least 11% off the cover price! It's
quite a bargain! Shipping and handling is just 50¢ per book in the U.S. and 75¢ per book
in Canada.* I understand that accepting the 2 free books and gifts places me under no
obligation to buy anything. I can always return a shipment and cancel at any time. Even if
I never buy another book, the two free books and gifts are mine to keep forever.

199/399 HDN GHWN

Name	(PLEASE PRINT)

Address	Apt. #

City	State/Prov.	Zip/Postal Code

Signature (if under 18, a parent or guardian must sign)

Mail to the **Reader Service**:
IN U.S.A.: P.O. Box 1867, Buffalo, NY 14240-1867
IN CANADA: P.O. Box 609, Fort Erie, Ontario L2A 5X3

**Are you a subscriber to Harlequin® Intrigue books
and want to receive the larger-print edition?
Call 1-800-873-8635 today or visit www.ReaderService.com.**

* Terms and prices subject to change without notice. Prices do not include applicable
taxes. Sales tax applicable in N.Y. Canadian residents will be charged applicable taxes.
Offer not valid in Quebec. This offer is limited to one order per household. Not valid for
current subscribers to Harlequin Intrigue Larger-Print books. All orders subject to credit
approval. Credit or debit balances in a customer's account(s) may be offset by any other
outstanding balance owed by or to the customer. Please allow 4 to 6 weeks for delivery.
Offer available while quantities last.

Your Privacy—The Reader Service is committed to protecting your privacy. Our
Privacy Policy is available online at www.ReaderService.com or upon request from
the Reader Service.

We make a portion of our mailing list available to reputable third parties that offer products
we believe may interest you. If you prefer that we not exchange your name with third
parties, or if you wish to clarify or modify your communication preferences, please visit
us at www.ReaderService.com/consumerchoice or write to us at Reader Service
Preference Service, P.O. Box 9062, Buffalo, NY 14240-9062. Include your complete
name and address.

HILP15

WESTERN PROMISES

YES! Please send me **The Western Promises Collection** in Larger Print. This collection begins with 3 FREE books and 2 FREE gifts (gifts valued at approx. $14.00 retail) in the first shipment, along with the other first 4 books from the collection! If I do not cancel, I will receive 8 monthly shipments until I have the entire 51-book Western Promises collection. I will receive 2 or 3 FREE books in each shipment and I will pay just $4.99 US/ $5.89 CDN for each of the other four books in each shipment, plus $2.99 for shipping and handling per shipment. *If I decide to keep the entire collection, I'll have paid for only 32 books, because 19 books are FREE! I understand that accepting the 3 free books and gifts places me under no obligation to buy anything. I can always return a shipment and cancel at any time. My free books and gifts are mine to keep no matter what I decide.

272 HCN 3070 472 HCN 3070

Name	(PLEASE PRINT)	
Address		Apt. #
City	State/Prov.	Zip/Postal Code

Signature (if under 18, a parent or guardian must sign)

Mail to the **Reader Service:**
IN U.S.A.: P.O. Box 1867, Buffalo, NY 14240-1867
IN CANADA: P.O. Box 609, Fort Erie, Ontario L2A 5X3

* Terms and prices subject to change without notice. Prices do not include applicable taxes. Sales tax applicable in N.Y. Canadian residents will be charged applicable taxes. This offer is limited to one order per household. All orders subject to approval. Credit or debit balances in a customer's account(s) may be offset by any other outstanding balance owed by or to the customer. Please allow 4 to 6 weeks for delivery. Offer available while quantities last. Offer not available to Quebec residents.

WPBPA16R